THE
F FACTOR

ALSO BY DIANE GONZALES BETRAND

Alicia's Treasure

Close to the Heart

*The Empanadas that Abuela Made /
Las empanadas que hacía la abuela*

El dilema de Trino

Family, Familia

The Last Doll / La última muñeca

Lessons of the Game

El momento de Trino

Ricardo's Race / La carrera de Ricardo

The Ruiz Street Kids / Los muchachos de la calle Ruiz

Sip, Slurp, Soup, Soup / Caldo, caldo, caldo

Sweet Fifteeen

Trino's Choice

Trino's Time

Uncle Chente's Picnic / El picnic de Tío Chente

Upside Down & Backwards / De cabeza y al revés

We Are Cousins / Somos primos

THE F FACTOR

Diane Gonzales Bertrand

PIÑATA
BOOKS

PIÑATA BOOKS
ARTE PÚBLICO PRESS
HOUSTON, TEXAS

The F Factor is made possible through grants from the City of Houston through the Houston Arts Alliance and by the Exemplar Program, a program of Americans for the Arts in collaboration with the LarsonAllen Public Services Group, funded by the Ford Foundation.

Piñata Books are full of surprises!

Arte Público Press
University of Houston
452 Cullen Performance Hall
Houston, Texas 77204-2004

Cover design by Mora Des!gn

Bertrand, Diane Gonzales
    The F Factor / by Diane Gonzales Bertrand.
        p.   cm.
    Summary: Javier Ávila, a smart but clumsy sophomore at St. Peter's High School, thinks it is a mistake when he is placed in the new course, Media Broadcasting, but over the course of the year, he discovers self-confidence, the value of extracurricular activities, and a talent for broadcast journalism.
    ISBN 978-1-55885-598-4 (alk. paper)
        [1. Television broadcasting—Fiction. 2. Self-confidence—Fiction. 3. Stereotypes (Social psychology)—Fiction. 4. Catholic schools—Fiction. 5. Schools—Fiction. 6. Hispanic Americans—Fiction. 7. Family life—Texas—Fiction. 8. Texas—Fiction.] I. Title.
PZ7.B46357Faf 2010
[Fic]—dc22   2010000645

∞ The paper used in this publication meets the requirements of the American National Standard for Information Sciences—Permanence of Paper for Printed Library Materials, ANSI Z39.48-1984.

Printed in the United States of America
April 2010–May 2010
Versa Press Inc., East Peoria, IL
12 11 10 9 8 7 6 5 4 3 2 1

For

Suzanne and Nick

and

to my students

past, present, and future

PROLOGUE

Flashing lights roamed the neighborhood like red ghosts. Emergency vehicles blocked the street. Thick drizzle made for a messy rescue. The crackle of radios, men yelling orders, and the quick appearance of neighbors staring from their porches and standing in their front yards made Javier Ávila think he was watching a movie. But when the emergency technicians placed a mask over his friend's face, Javier knew he wasn't looking at a screen with carefully edited images for dramatic effect. This crisis was in-your-face reality.

"Why don't you open your eyes? Can't you hear all the noise?" Javier whispered. He stood a few feet away, living the surreal experience of watching an EMT pressing his fingers against pulse points, his friend lying in the wet grass, unresponsive.

Someone tugged Javier's arm. A young policewoman tried to pull him toward the ambulance. He jerked his arm out of her grip. "No," he told her. "I want to stay—" He started coughing and gasping for air. His raw throat, the throbbing in his head; he bent over, gripping his hands on his knees, hoping he wouldn't pass out again.

The woman took advantage of his weak moment and pulled Javier firmly across the yard. Too miserable to fight her, he stumbled toward the ambulance. He looked over his shoulder one last time. Two men were lifting his friend onto a stretcher.

A thin black man wearing an EMT uniform helped Javier climb into the ambulance and gently placed him on a side bench. In moments, Javier was wearing a plastic mask over his mouth and was told, "Breathe easy. Relax." The technician went on to check his pulse and blood pressure.

Javier saw the old woman sitting across from him, her face streaked with black, her dirty nightgown ragged at the hem. Someone had wrapped her in a blanket and given her slippers that looked way too big for her feet. When she saw him looking, her brown eyes filled with tears. Tears trickled down her weathered dark face. She made the sign of the cross over herself and prayed, "*El Señor es mi luz y mi salvación.*"

Witnessing this act of faith made Javier's breathing easier. He leaned his head back and closed his eyes. *God, please help my friend.*

CHAPTER ONE

Javier's itchy feet always warned him when something was going to change. He never called himself psychic, but he could trust the itch for what it was: an annoying reminder that he had little control of his own life.

That humid August day of tenth grade orientation at St. Peter's High School, his itchy feet practically forced him up on tiptoes when he stood in the library before the Dean of Students, Mr. Roy Quintanilla. Javier pressed his heels into the carpeted floor and tried not to look surprised by the sudden irritation. He was a sophomore, back for another year in a familiar all-boys environment. Upperclassmen swore sophomores were nobodies; sophomore year was so dull that even the teachers got bored.

Why would Javier's itch start *now* when orientation day was almost over?

Mr. Q. glanced up and handed Javier a half page with columns and words in computer print. "Ávila, here's your schedule."

Javier looked down, scanning the paper quickly. The first-period class looked unfamiliar. "Uh, Mr. Quintanilla?"

"Yes? What!" He crossed through Javier's name on the list in front of him.

Javier hesitated. Any extra contact with the big man was scary. Roy Quintanilla had been a basketball superstar when he was a student at the school twenty years earlier. Now Mr. Q. owned the reputation of being visible and invisible at the same time, and those who crossed the man either changed their ways or filled out transfer forms.

Javier's voice squeaked slightly when he said, "Media Broadcasting. I have it first period. Sir, I didn't choose this class."

"New elective. You're one of the lucky ones. Now move along, Ávila," Mr. Quintanilla answered with a wave of his hand. The line of sophomores behind Javier grumbled, coughed, and shifted around him. They all wanted to get through the line and go home.

Javier's itchy feet prickled inside his black dress shoes as he moved to a side table to pick up the sophomore supply list. He felt a rap of pencils on his shoulder and turned to see his friend Andy Cardona grinning at him. Andy always heard a beat in his head. He drummed on anything and anyone around him.

"Hey, did you get that new elective first period?" Javier asked.

"Get real! It's always band first period for us." Andy glanced from his schedule to Javier's. "We got English, History, Chemistry, and Algebra together. That's good!"

Ignacio Gómez wandered up to where they stood. The guy was a one-man sweat machine. Since they were all in ties and long-sleeved shirts, the sweat poured down his chunky brown face in rolling drops that he wiped away with his thick fingers and swiped across his dark pants. "Andy, let's go over to the band hall and see if Mr. Henley's there. I need to talk to him."

Javier decided to follow his friends out when someone grabbed his arm. "Javier Ávila, here you are! I want to talk to you."

He turned back and saw the school counselor. Brother Calvin wore his usual uniform of a white shirt and thin black tie with black slacks. Behind his back, the boys called him "Brother Calavera" because he looked like a skeleton. His long face and light blue-gray eyes seemed to disappear in his pale white skin.

"Gotta go!" Andy and Ignacio said together and quickly hustled out of the library.

Cowards! Javier thought as his friends left him alone with the skeletal counselor. He tried to sound relaxed, even though every conversation with the man left Javier feeling irritated. "Do you need something, Brother?"

Brother Calvin released Javier's arm. "Come with me, Javier. There's someone who needs to meet you."

If only the words had come from anyone else but a middle-aged teacher! In an all-boys school, everybody wanted "someone" to be the good-looking sister or pretty friend of a girlfriend. In this case, a new student probably needed a tour or something.

Reluctantly, Javier followed Brother Calvin out of the library and into the hallway of the main school building.

Paper banners decorated the walls above the lockers with colorful proclamations: "Go Guardians! All the way to state! Guardian football players are winners!"

Regardless of the school spirit around them, walking in the empty halls left Javier feeling uneasy. He started a conversation just to break the silence. "So, Brother, what's the mystery? Who are you taking me to meet?"

Brother Calvin pointed the way out the side door. "Saint Peter's got approved for a grant last spring that comes with a brand new program."

Javier stepped on an uncomfortable itch under the soles of his feet. "And this involves me because?"

"Because I told everybody you'd be good for the job."

"What job?" Javier pushed away the urge to stop and scratch. "Brother Calvin, I don't have time for anything else on my schedule this year."

He just replied, "Follow me, Javier."

A wide portable building now sat where an empty lot used to be. The guys called it "Q's Graveyard." Students who got into trouble would spend their Saturdays cutting the lot with a push mower.

There was little grass left around the building, a one-story structure the color of faded bricks. Just below the roof ran a series of six narrow windows, each one no bigger than a shoebox. There were two doors, both wider than regular doors, and both had wooden access ramps in an L-shape. They met up with brand new sidewalks that reached from the new building to the school cafeteria.

The building looked similar to the portables where the computer classes were taught. Javier asked, "Is this a new computer lab?"

The old man didn't answer.

Javier followed Brother Calvin up the four long steps between the ramps that gave the building a front porch with railings. Brother reached the wide door and opened it. "Step inside, Javier."

Javier shivered from the unexpected cold air against his sweaty skin. He walked inside the door and looked around. Unlike other classrooms, this one had short tables with chairs in three neat rows to replace the typical school desks. The tabletops look shiny and unmarked. Four computers were set into individual cubicles near the teacher's desk.

"Mr. Seneca? It's Brother Calvin, and I've brought along Javier Ávila," he called out. Then he gestured for Javier to walk further into the room.

Two large black cabinets faced each other along the side rear walls. One of the black doors was open. Slowly, a motorized wheelchair backed out and the door swung closed. The man in the chair shifted the stick on the right and moved forward until the door was closed and the keys in the lock were turned and taken out. Thick brown fingers on his left hand formed a tight fist over the keys while his right hand worked the stick shift. His chair backed up, then swiveled around. Quickly, he moved forward.

He sat tall in his chair and looked directly at Javier as he rode up. His dark eyes were set deep in his brown face. His long nose and high forehead made Javier wonder if he was from an Indian tribe. His black hair was streaked with gray, and he wore it cut close around his head. Once the chair stopped, he extended his right hand. "Good morning, Javier. I'm Winston Seneca." His handshake gripped hard around Javier's fingers. They shook twice before he released Javier's hand. "Brother Calvin said I can count on you to help me out."

Javier stared at Brother Calvin. Now he knew! The counselor was going to make him help the teacher in a wheelchair—probably like an aide or something. And Brother knew Javier couldn't refuse without looking like a selfish loser.

"I'll leave the two of you to talk. Good luck!" Brother Calvin slapped Javier's back with a firm hand.

Surprised, Javier flopped forward. Mr. Seneca's hands jerked up.

He was going to fall on a man in a wheelchair! Javier swallowed his breath, fighting against his own clumsy self. He twisted away, his *flaming* itchy feet tripping over one wheel of the chair.

"'Ss—scuse me," came stuttering out as Javier tried to stand up straight. He stumbled sideways from Mr. Seneca's chair.

He couldn't believe how bad it looked! This teacher barely knew him and would tell everybody, "Oh, yeah, I know Javier. He's supposed to be my aide, but I have to help *him* walk on two legs."

"You should be more careful, Javier," Brother Calvin muttered before he walked out with rapid steps.

"Your face is red," Mr. Seneca spoke, as if Javier wouldn't feel the obvious.

He resisted the urge to rub his cheeks. They felt plenty hot, but he didn't want to bring any more attention to them. Instead, he gave a half-shrug and stared up at the ceiling like he had never seen electricity at work.

"Javier—just so you know—you wouldn't have hurt me. Do you think you're the first person to trip over me? There are worse klutzes than you, trust me."

Javier could have laughed, but he didn't. His arms and legs felt like somebody had strapped him up with duct tape. He tried not to stare at the teacher's thick legs and firm black shoes, but he had never been so close to a disabled person in his life.

Mr. Seneca casually said, "I'm usually on crutches, but my favorite pair cracked at the cuffs, and my back-ups somehow lost a screw. When I set up a new classroom, though, I get more done on my wheels. I'll give you and your *compadres* the gory details on Monday." He clapped his hands together. "So, Javier, have you ever had the desire to be on TV?"

Javier took a step back, remembering the day his dad had entered Javier's name in a grocery store contest to sing a baloney commercial tune. Javier was only six. He ate so much free baloney that he vomited on the camera man. "Umm, no, Mr. Seneca."

"Not a spotlight-grabbing guy, huh?" Mr. Seneca replied as he shifted the wheelchair and turned it toward one line of tables and chairs. He pulled out a chair and twirled it on two legs in Javier's direction. "Here, Javier. Let's talk."

Javier pulled the chair closer and sat down. He thought, *This man doesn't seem to need any help from me, that's for sure.*

Even though they should have been at eye level, Mr. Seneca still appeared taller as he steered his wheelchair closer and then sat back comfortably. "We now have the equipment to televise morning announcements here at St. Peter's."

"Nobody ever listens to announcements, Mr. Seneca."

"Don't you think it's time to change that?" He stared hard at Javier. "Our first broadcast goes into every class-room on Wednesday morning."

Javier clutched both sides of the chair. A terrible itch slithered up and down his legs. "You don't mean me, right? Talk on TV and . . . me?"

The door to the building opened suddenly. Javier turned to look at the woman who stepped inside. She wore dark slacks and a red blouse and carried an armful of newspapers. "Sorry to interrupt, Win, but I have the front sections from the last two weeks like you wanted.

I'll just leave them on your desk." She turned away before Javier could see her face well.

Mr. Seneca looked over and said, "Could you stay a minute, Frances? I have a couple questions you might be able to answer." In the next breath, he said, "Okay, Javier, we're done. I'll see you first period on Monday. Good-bye." He suddenly reversed the wheelchair and started moving toward the teacher's desk at a brisk speed.

Javier stood up. He left without looking at Mr. Seneca or the woman; he just walked out of the building.

The August heat rapidly melted Javier from the inside out. His thoughts still smoldered like burning coals. Why didn't anybody *ask* him if he wanted a new elective? Why would anybody *choose* to look stupid in front of the whole school every morning?

The trip around the building left him soaked and thirsty. The gel in his hair mixed into his sweat. As it ran down his face, his skin felt sticky and stiff. He wanted to remove his tie, unbutton his blue, long-sleeved shirt, and push his feet out of his dress shoes. He never understood why students had to get so dressed up for orientation.

Javier's grumpy mood matched his body's misery as he joined other students in front of the main building. He felt stupid, still waiting for a ride home. He counted the days until his September fifth birthday, his permanent driver's license, and the promise of his uncle's old truck to drive to school.

About a dozen students were scattered over the cement steps leading up to the tall steeple above the front doors of the school. Luckily, the building was positioned so that the steps were shaded at this time of day.

He found a step near Pat Berlanga and sat down. They had been in a couple of freshmen classes together. Pat often napped in class, so they didn't talk much. He was a big guy with nut-brown skin and a short, spiked haircut. He stood tall and husky like a football player, but Pat didn't play any sports. Javier had heard the talk about Berlanga's hot-looking sister, but he had never seen her.

"Hey, Pat," Javier said, easing his back against the stone steps. "How's it going?"

"Huh?" Pat said, shaking his head slightly. He blinked at Javier like he was trying to focus. "Whad'ya ask me?"

Javier smiled. "I've never seen anybody who can sleep like you do."

Pat shrugged. "I can sleep anywhere. Always been that way." He turned toward the street that ran in front of the school. "There's my sister. It's about time!" he growled and stood up.

Javier saw a sleek sports vehicle pull up to the curb. The windows were tinted, so he couldn't see the driver.

"See ya," Pat said and yawned widely.

That's when Javier saw his dad's work truck not far behind the Berlangas' vehicle. Despite the earlier energy drain from the hot day, Javier jumped up and caught up with Pat. Javier couldn't wait to get out of his tie and go home.

"Hey, did you get that new elective on your schedule?" Javier asked, walking down the last two steps with Pat.

"Yeah . . . media something. Doesn't matter. School is school," Pat replied. He reached for the handle of the black vehicle and opened the door.

The car's air-conditioning felt like a cool breeze across Javier's face. He stepped a bit closer to Pat and said, "I'm in that media class too. I'll—" His words stopped when he saw the pretty driver inside the car—a girl who belonged on a tropical island sunbathing in a bikini, not driving Pat Berlanga home from school in Texas.

She removed her sunglasses before she turned toward her brother. Her light brown eyes shifted to Javier. "Hello! Do you need a ride?"

When she smiled at him, Javier forgot about itchy feet, new teachers, and an elective he didn't ask for. He saw her bare brown legs, white shorts, and yellow tank top. He admired her small, straight teeth, twinkling eyes, and wavy brown hair that spread over her tanned shoulders like a cape.

"Javier doesn't need a ride," Pat said. His tone was abrupt, his words sharp. He moved his body, using his wide back and shoulders to block Javier's view.

"My name is Feliz," she called out loudly. "Hello!"

"I'm sure he knows your name. Everybody does," Pat grumbled before he slid into the front seat. "Just leave Javier alone." And with that, he grabbed the inside handle and pulled the car door toward him.

For the second time that morning, Javier stumbled over his own feet. This time he tripped over the curb before Pat smashed his head in the car door.

Javier toppled back with several wobbly steps before he found his balance. He heard cackles of laughter from the other guys on the steps behind him, but Javier didn't turn around. Surely they all knew it was Berlanga's sister in the car, and Javier had just joined every other guy in her St. Peter's fan club.

Get real, Jack. How does a klutz like you even stand a chance with someone like Feliz Berlanga? Still, it was great to imagine getting to know Feliz better, to call her on the phone and maybe get a chance to . . . His fantasies were rudely interrupted by a loud honk from his father's truck. The noise made him jump, and he nearly fell off the curb.

Javier caught the grin on his father's face as he parked the green Ávila and Sons Construction truck right in front of him. Javier braced himself for some kind of joke. His father noticed everything and loved to tease others about their faults or mistakes.

Javier slid into the bench seat and just said, "Hey, Dad."

"Can't walk on two feet anymore, Son?"

"I just lost my balance, that's all," Javier said, pulling his tie loose and unbuttoning his shirt.

"And what was so interesting inside that black car that it knocked you off your feet?" his father asked, driving his truck away from the school. "Was the driver somebody's good-looking sister?"

"Something like that," Javier answered, slouching down in the seat.

"Only a beautiful woman makes a man lose control of his feet that fast. Ask your mother! She can make me trip just by asking me to take out the garbage!" He laughed so easily that Javier had to smile too.

He looked at his father and noticed again their physical resemblance. Even though his dad's hair was gray, it still favored Javier's wavy brown hair. They had the same thick eyebrows and the same straight nose. They were the same height now, almost 5'9".

But while his father could effortlessly make and take a joke, Javier never had such an easygoing personality. He wondered, *Is self-confidence something that grows on a person like facial hair, or is it something you have to dig out of yourself like a splinter?*

Javier leaned forward and unlaced his dress shoes. Whoever said nothing happened during sophomore year didn't own a pair of itchy feet.

With his fingers gently searching for a bump on his throbbing forehead, Javier walked into the kitchen. He went straight for the ice bags his mom always kept in the refrigerator. He didn't comment to his older brothers or to his father. They sat at the kitchen table drinking coffee after their Saturday breakfast of pancakes and *chorizo con huevo* that his mom had cooked before she left to run errands.

"What happened, Javito?" his big brother Eric asked, but he was already chuckling. He leaned back in the chair. "Don't tell me my scven-year-old scored a goal against your head again?"

Javier yanked one of the canvas ice bags from the freezer section. He wantcd to make a joke, but truthfully, it was *always* Javier who needed ice bags, Band-aids, or had the stitches to show for his clumsiness. Even his little nephews and nieces were sure-footed, natural athletes like their fathers.

"Face it, Eric, your son kicks like a wild man," Leo remarked. He was the oldest Ávila brother, and like Eric, he worked with their father and uncles in the construction business. They were both tall, muscular men with round faces. They wore their black hair cropped short like the days when they had served together in the Marines.

"Hey, what happened this morning is nothing new, right, Javito?" Eric grinned. "It's a good thing my baby brother has all the brains in the family."

"He won't have any brains left if Trey doesn't stop aiming for Javier's head," their father joked as he stood up to get another cup of coffee. As he passed his youngest son, he squeezed his arm. "Javier, are you okay?"

"I'll survive." Javier wore the humiliation like an old jacket. *Why can't I be like the rest of this family?* he asked himself for the zillionth time. He sat down at the kitchen table, and then pressed the ice bag against his head. "Ouch!" he groaned.

"Everybody knows Javito can't hit, run, or throw," Eric continued. "He spends more time on the sidelines or holding a bag of ice. But . . . " He turned to Javier. " . . . if there's a school project my kids need help on, my super smart little brother would be my go-to guy. You've got the best book smarts in the family."

Javier said nothing. All his life, his family excused his clumsiness by over-exaggerating his academic skills. In fifth grade, he started to bring home *all* his textbooks every day, read ahead, and study hard so he would always get As. He wanted to prove he could be more than the "book smart" guy they all expected. In elementary school, it was easier to be top student because he loved to read and liked to build science projects. In middle school, his classmates cared more about "who liked who" than learning new algebra equations. But when high school started, Javier's insecurities began to nag at him from all directions.

First, the St. Peter's High School acceptance letter arrived in the mail, stating Javier had earned a partial scholarship because of his entrance test scores. Everyone thought it was so great, but Javier knew he wasn't a student who had earned a *full* scholarship.

"The Guardians have one of the best football teams in the city," Eric had told him then. "It's too bad you can't throw or hit. I'd go to your games if you played ball!"

Second, the letter arrived inviting Javier to attend a preparatory science program for freshmen and sophomore students at St. Mary's University. His big brother Leo had told the family, "Our baby brother's so lucky! When we were in high school, Eric and I worked our butts off in the hot sun building houses with Dad. Javito's got it way too easy!"

Now, Javier adjusted the ice bag and sighed. Those summer programs at St. Mary's University were never easy, in spite of what Leo thought! That summer before high school he met others who were genuinely "smart." They had plans to be engineers, do medical research, or become surgeons. They were competitive and confident —not like Javier. At fourteen, he didn't have his life mapped out like those prep kids. He always wondered if something was wrong with him.

And then Ignacio, Andy, and all the guys from their elementary school had immediately spread the word around St. Peter's campus that Javier Ávila was "the smartest guy ever." He felt so much pressure to keep up his reputation that he did nothing else but study his freshmen year. Ignacio and Andy constantly gave him a hard time for not going to the football games to see them perform. Brother Calvin had called Javier to his office once a month to discuss joining a club or working for Student Council. "There's more to life than studying twenty-four-seven, Javier," Brother Calvin would say.

Javier had politely said, "Yes, Sir," but never did what the counselor wanted.

The summer before sophomore year, Javier had to deal with students at prep camp again. They came up with quicker answers, better results, and higher test grades than he did. He also took driver's education classes at night with Ignacio and Andy. All summer, the pressure to keep up and look smart filled up every waking moment.

The ice bag did little to relieve the headache Javier had felt since he first saw his school schedule. Even if his nephew Trey hadn't kicked the ball off the back porch without warning anybody, Javier might have still needed an ice bag that morning. He left his father and his brothers discussing the upcoming Dallas Cowboys pre-season game, and went to inspect the damage in the bathroom mirror.

Javier hated the row of bright lights his father had installed so his mom could easily put on her makeup. The yellow globes only magnified the red blotch that spread over his forehead. One eyebrow looked higher than the other. He noticed the scar under his eye and the brown fuzz above his lip. Pimples dotted his chin. The only thing missing was a frantic movement in his eyes, but that would reappear as soon as school started on Monday.

Wasn't it enough that he was a sophomore taking junior classes like Algebra II and Chemistry? And what about those four honors classes also on his schedule? And now he had to be on school TV too?

He stared hard at his own reflection. When the guys at school looked at the classroom monitors, would they realize they were watching the face of a fraud?

CHAPTER TWO

"Feliz Berlanga?" Ignacio slammed his metal locker shut and stared at Javier. His brown eyes were wide open under his raised black eyebrows. "You talked to Feliz Berlanga? What did she say?"

Javier half-smiled at his friends. "She offered to give me a ride home."

"And you said yes, right?" Andy poked his drumsticks into Javier's shoulder. "Tell me you said yes, Jack." He jabbed Javier again, a little harder.

"Hey!" Javier stepped back and rubbed his shoulder. "Stop it with the sticks, man. And, no, I didn't say 'yes' because Pat jumped between us and said 'no'. Besides, my dad was in the truck right behind her car ready to pick me up."

"Ugh!" Ignacio groaned and slapped his sweaty forehead. "You blew it, Jack! Shot down before you ever got the launch sequence."

"Hey, I didn't get shot down. Circumstances weren't good, that's all."

"Circumstances? Yeah, right," Ignacio said. He shook his head. "You can be so pathetic, Javier."

Javier couldn't argue because the first morning bell clanged in the hallway. As if a stink bomb were dropped in a crowd, everybody rushed around and pushed along to get to his assigned homeroom where attendance was taken and announcements were made.

Javier headed out to the new portable building on Q's Graveyard. A handful of guys stood in front just staring at it. "What's up?"

Kenny García, one of the taller sophomores who had made the varsity basketball team as a freshman, untwisted his lips long enough to reply, "When did they build this?"

"Over the summer, I guess. Didn't you notice it when we came for orientation?" Javier acted matter-of-fact, but he also wondered if he should tell him the teacher inside was in a wheelchair or if he should let Kenny and the others find out that little surprise on their own?

"Get to homeroom, gentlemen," barked Q's voice. It came out of nowhere, but no one stopped to see where the Dean of Students stood.

They quickly climbed up the steps and went inside the portable building.

Kenny muttered "What the—?" under his breath and stopped where he stood. Javier nudged him from behind, and the athlete stumbled forward.

Mr. Seneca wasn't in his wheelchair this time. He stood by a television cart near the teacher's desk. His forearms were balanced inside the metal cuffs of his two-piece steel crutches. His silver crutches looked heavy but they'd have to be made like that to hold up a man over six feet tall.

Javier realized the guys inside the classroom were dead quiet. There wasn't any of the usual before-class talking and kidding around. Six guys had filled the back chairs. Only Pat Berlanga sat behind the third table by the whiteboards, not much closer than the others.

Javier was about to follow Kenny and the others to the middle of the room when Mr. Seneca spoke up. "Javier, you and your crew need to fill the chairs up front. And you dawdlers in the back, I need you to move up too! There are only eleven students in this homeroom. Besides, I like you guys close by, where I can whack you if you fall asleep. This crutch only reaches the length of my arm, you know."

Would Mr. Seneca really "whack" a student? None of them were stupid enough to find out on the first day of school. Every guy shuffled forward without comment.

Javier seated himself at the second table, not wanting to look like a teacher's pet. It was bad enough the new teacher already knew his name.

The bell rang again, and like robots, everybody stood up even before the school Principal, Brother Lendell, said, "Good morning, students. Welcome back to a new school year. Please stand for the morning prayer and our Pledge of Allegiance."

Javier followed along then sat back down as Brother Lendell spoke a couple of minutes about working hard in academics and showing the Guardian spirit both on and off the athletic field. Then Vice-Principal Domínguez, droned on about rules and regulations everyone had already heard at orientation.

After Mr. Domínguez said, "Have a good day," Mr. Seneca quickly took attendance.

Just as Landry Zúñiga replied, "Here," the bell to end homeroom period sounded, but no one left for their first-period class because they were already in it.

Javier glanced around. It was weird that his home-room and his first-period class was a mixture of sopho-mores, juniors, and seniors. Usually homerooms were alpha order by grade level.

"Good morning, gentlemen. I'm Mr. Seneca." His deep voice broke the awkward silence after the bell rang. "You! Sitting there across from Javier, what's your name?"

"Uh—Pat—Patricio—uh, Sir." Pat straightened up in his chair, and blinked rapidly as he stumbled over his words.

Mr. Seneca gave Pat a stern look and said, "Uh-Pat-Patricio-uh, Sir, please tell me one thing you heard on today's announcements."

Pat's fingers rubbed through his thick hair. He looked around at the rest of the students. His face turned dark-er as he said, "Uh, Sir, I don't . . . can't think . . . sorry!"

Mr. Seneca shook his head. "A remarkable answer. Are you always so articulate?"

Pat's dark eyes grew wider. "Huh?"

The teacher nodded. "That's what I thought. How about you, tall boy?" He used his chin to point in Kenny's direction. "What do you remember from this morning's announcements?"

Kenny slouched across the row from Javier. He half-sat on the chair, stretching his long legs in front of him. He gave a slow smile, like he knew the perfect answer. "I remember the Pledge of Allegiance."

The other guys chuckled. Javier hid his grin under his hand.

Mr. Seneca didn't smile. He shifted his weight on the crutches, glanced down at his footing, then looked back at Kenny. "I'm going to make you Number One Pledge Man, tall boy. When you have to stand in front of a

camera, with everyone in the school watching just waiting for you to mess up and make just one little mistake
so they can tease you about it all day long, will you still
be laughing?"

Dead silence ensued. Kenny slowly straightened up
in his seat.

"Does anyone sitting in this room know why this new
elective was put on your schedules?" Mr. Seneca asked in
a voice that bellowed with such an unfriendly tone that
no one wanted to answer.

Javier wondered what had happened to that nicer guy
in a wheelchair he had met the previous Thursday. He
kept his eyes forward, staring at some invisible spot
behind Mr. Seneca, praying the teacher wouldn't call on
him.

"Javier! You want to tell your *compadres* about this
class, or shall I?"

"You can." Javier's voice squeaked like his seventh
grade hormones had returned. He cleared his throat and
tried to sound like a sophomore. "Mr. Seneca, you can
explain it better than I can."

"Good answer." He walked forward slowly. Each step
carried a creak of metal and a *thud* from his solid black
shoes. His hips rolled to adjust his balance in an awkward
waddle as he moved to the center of the room.

Javier tried to push the image of Frankenstein's monster out of his head. He couldn't imagine what it was like
to have legs that didn't work. It pained him just to look at
Mr. Seneca, so he stared at the wheels on the TV cart
instead.

The teacher's voice commanded Javier to listen to
him though. "Gentlemen, this class is called Media
Broadcasting. In two days, we are going to start doing

announcements on the new monitors. The system is called Guardian TV. Every morning, a pair of you will become the St. Peter's version of anchormen, and the rest of you will run cameras, write scripts, and do all the grunt work to put on a program during homeroom period that better be good—real good, gentlemen."

The sophomores Javier knew started to look at each other, and from the looks on their faces, he bet they were all thinking, *Transfer.* All weekend, he had been thinking about schedule changes too. Maybe he could learn to play drums and be in band first period. If his parents saw him doing some intricate pattern at half-time, wouldn't they be impressed?

Javier glanced around. He bet none of them *asked* for this elective, but for some reason, they got stuck in it. All the guys had the wide-eyed look of experimental monkeys.

At that moment, Ram Fierro came into the classroom. He wasn't a tall guy, but he made the most of his size and speed when he played football. His athletic success had made him popular, but so did his friendly reputation with the cheerleaders. "I'm sorry I'm late, Mr. Seneca, Sir." He walked comfortably up to the teacher and extended his tardy slip. "I'm Ramiro Fierro, Sir. Everyone calls me Ram."

Mr. Seneca balanced his weight on one crutch and took the tardy slip. "You won't be late to my class on a regular basis, will you?"

"Today was weird. It won't happen again. I know this is a very important class, Mr. Seneca, Sir."

"Suck up!" somebody behind Javier half-coughed.

Ram frowned right at Javier, who lifted his hands palm-up in front of his chest as if to say, "Hey, it wasn't me!"

After Ram took a spot in an empty chair, Mr. Seneca pulled out a sheet of paper and called out names again. As each guy raised a hand and said "That's me, Sir," he asked each boy what afterschool activities he participated in. Ram, two other seniors, and the three juniors were on the football team. Kenny played basketball but didn't need to report to regular practice until next month. Steve and Landry were sophomores like Javier and Pat who didn't do sports or play in the school band.

After Mr. Seneca told everyone about writing and presenting announcements, he took them to the back of the room and described the two video cameras, extra monitors, and the two laptop computers for the transmission from the media classroom to the new system. He issued everybody a thin book about writing for broadcast news. He explained his policy on handling the equipment and emphasized the monetary value of each piece. "You horse around with something and it breaks, gentlemen, you *will* buy the school a new one." He gave out homework assignments just before the bell rang: "Start watching the news anchors every night and write out three fifteen-second announcements. That's due tomorrow."

Javier picked up his binder and slipped the media textbook inside it. He glanced up as Pat picked up his book and spiral and thought again about Feliz. He wondered how to bring up the girl without sounding stupid.

Pat didn't even look Javier's way. He just moved toward the door, following the other guys out. Javier picked up the pace to walk with him and was glad when Pat gave him a questioning look and started conversation.

"How do I know if something is fifteen seconds long?" Pat asked Javier as they walked out of the building.

"Stopwatch, stupid," Kenny said loudly. "Maybe if you stayed in sports, Porky, you'd know what fifteen seconds means."

Javier watched as Pat turned away and practically ran down the steps. He felt sorry for Pat, who was heading for more classes with Kenny García. At least Javier could get away from Kenny's attitude and see his friends in English. This was one advantage to the honors courses he took. The prep courses for advanced placement filtered out the guys like Kenny who didn't care about anything at school except for the sports program.

As Javier entered the main building, he pulled his schedule out and read an unfamiliar teacher's name: "F. Maloney." He pushed his way through the crowded hall near his second-period in Room Six. The woman he had seen yesterday in Mr. Seneca's room was talking to Mrs. Elliott, the geometry teacher whose husband coached the soccer team. Every guy who passed them acted like a rubbernecker gawking at a highway accident. Any woman caused the guys to stop and stare. It was just the nature of the beast since girls weren't the norm at St. Peter's. But this new teacher looked younger than the other women, so the traffic jam was thicker than usual.

Javier saw Mr. Quintanilla moving against the current of students like a big ocean liner. He growled at students to tuck in their shirts, keep moving, stop talking in halls, and kept repeating, "Get to class! NOW!"

A sudden itch on the bottoms of his feet caught Javier's attention about the same time he realized the new lady teacher was walking toward the same room where he intended to go. She had to be Maloney; she would be his English teacher.

Javier saw Mr. Q within eyeshot. He knew the Dean was a stickler for old-fashioned rules, so Javier stopped right at the door to let the lady teacher enter first.

Immediately, he felt half a dozen hits in the back from the guys behind him who weren't ready to stop so suddenly. He dug his heels into floor, using his body to push back against the tide. Like a punching bag, he was slugged with elbows, shoulders, and books.

The Maloney woman moved right past without even a "thank you" or nod in his direction. She stood just inside the door and gestured at the boys. "Take a seat, gentlemen. We have a lot to cover this morning."

As usual, no seats were left but the front desks, so Javier didn't have much choice but to take one. He sat down to stare at the whiteboard in front of the room, *Ms. Maloney* was printed in swirling letters with a black marker.

The second-period bell rang. Ms. Maloney walked over and closed the door firmly. As she came to the center of the room to speak, Javier saw Ignacio's sweaty face peeking through the diamond-shaped window on the door. The brass knob turned, and the wooden door opened.

Ms. Maloney half-turned toward the sound. "You are late to my class, Sir. Get a tardy slip from the front office."

"But, Miss—" Ignacio took a couple of steps inside the room. "The band hall—"

"Don't challenge me. I told you—" She didn't have to say anymore.

A large tanned hand had come through the door, grabbed Ignacio by the back collar of his uniform shirt, and yanked him back into the hall. It had to be Mr. Q. The door closed with a firm *thud,* and the new English teacher turned back as if nothing out of the ordinary had happened.

Her brown eyes scanned the room. Her lips straightened into a serious line. "If you are sitting in this class, you are preparing for the advanced placement courses as juniors and seniors. I take that preparation very seriously."

Javier studied her face, wondering how old she was. The teacher's thick hair was like a black triangle framing her head. She wore a silver cross on a woven necklace. The blue dress she wore had no sleeves, and her arms were thin but not skinny. The dress stopped just above her knees, and he thought her legs were shaped well for a woman.

"I was born here in San Antonio and grew up not far from this school. I attended college in Nevada and received my advanced degrees in Austin. I've taught many levels of English, gentlemen, but I prefer the pre-AP classes. To me, the foundation is the key element in creating a solid structure." She moved back to the desk and picked up a paper on her desk. "I'm going to take attendance now."

She had gotten to the "P" names when Ignacio, Andy, and two other band members came in with tardy slips. After they handed them to her, she said, "See me after class, gentlemen."

She spent the next forty-five minutes going over lists of rules for classroom conduct, handing out a class syllabus and reading through it word for word. She also gave her first writing assignment: "Tell me who your friends are, so that I will know who you are."

After the bell rang, Javier waited outside the classroom for Ignacio and Andy to finish their talk with Ms. Maloney so they could all walk to history class together.

Ignacio wiped a hand over his sweaty forehead when he saw Javier. "I don't think I've got a butt left. I've been chewed out today by so many people. Started with my dad in the car, Mr. Henley, Mr. Q., and now this freaky English teacher."

"That woman's something else," Andy said, as they all picked up the pace and walked outside to Mr. Seneca's building. "Didn't anyone explain to the new teacher about the band guys? Last year, teachers usually gave us a break about tardy slips."

Javier squinted into the sunshine of the outdoors. "What did Mr. Q. say about it?"

"He said we needed to get our sorry selves to class on time or we'd be in detention after three tardies. He was no help at all. We got to talk to Mr. Henley," Ignacio said, hustling up the steps beside them.

Walking inside Mr. Seneca's room, once again Javier was surprised by the silence, despite the fact that at least twenty guys sat at the desks. The teacher on metal crutches in the front of the classroom intimidated everybody. Javier wondered if word got around that the guys didn't act up because of it, would all the teachers want a pair of crutches to maintain control?

Ignacio led the way to three empty seats in the middle row. As the last one, Javier got the desk in the front with Andy and Ignacio sitting behind him.

Mr. Seneca nodded at Javier with a hint of a smile on his face. It disappeared as quickly as it showed. The bell rang, and Mr. Seneca slowly moved a few steps until his position was directly in front of Javier.

"Javier," he said quietly, "wheel that teacher's chair over here so I can sit down later."

Ignoring a kissing sound behind him, Javier stood up and walked over to the teacher's desk. The black leather chair looked comfortable with padded arms and a cushioned seat. It rolled easily on thick rubber wheels. Javier pulled it back from the desk and then effortlessly wheeled it toward the teacher. "Here?" he asked, leaving the chair within arms' reach for Mr. Seneca.

"Good, thanks."

After Javier sat down, the teacher stepped closer to the first row and said, "I am Mr. Seneca, and this is World History class. When I was your age, I thought history was dull and boring, but I had a teacher in college that made me realize that I *am* history. You are history, gentlemen, and if we don't pay attention to history, we are going to blow ourselves right off the planet." He paused to glare at Pat Berlanga, who had squeezed himself behind the second table in the second row. His chin rested on his hand. It was Pat's favorite position for napping. "Mr. Berlanga, do you think I sound melodramatic?"

Pat lowered his hand and glanced around like he wasn't certain where he was.

"Mr. Berlanga, do you know what 'melodramatic' means?"

Pat shrugged. "Uh, not really . . . uh, Sir."

Mr. Seneca shook his head. His eyes turned up to the ceiling. "Give me patience down here."

Everyone chuckled a little. Javier felt relief when Mr. Seneca's serious mask relaxed through the mouth. "Mr. Berlanga, you have me for two classes. Make a note to increase your vocabulary this year."

Pat nodded and shifted his bottom around like he had a rash.

Javier glanced down at his desk. He wondered if either one of them could meet Mr. Seneca's expectations. He hadn't been afraid to get up for show-and-tell in elementary school. He wasn't afraid to answer in class, and with group projects, he didn't mind when the other guys asked him to step up and speak first. But could he pull it all together when there was a camera rolling? How did he get so *lucky* to get the new elective?

At the same time, Javier wondered what it might be like to be part of a "school first"—to be one of the first guys to work the new equipment and get on school TV. Of course, that could also make him the first guy to mess up in front of the whole school too. *What did Mr. Seneca tell Kenny? Everyone in the school watching, just waiting for you to mess up, make just one little mistake so they can tease you about it all day long.* Javier's head filled up and replayed various mess-ups in weird daydreams.

"And what's your opinion, Mr. Ávila?"

Javier gripped the sides of the table. Mr. Seneca stood directly in front of him. Javier realized he had no idea what the teacher had been saying for the past few minutes.

Javier stared at Mr. Seneca as an imaginary drum roll sounded. Slowly, he said, "I'm not sure, Sir. It's one of those things with no easy answer."

Mr. Seneca stared down Javier, who tried not to flinch. He knew the teacher was trying to decide if Javier spoke honestly or was trying to save his butt because he wasn't paying attention. He grunted at Javier. As Mr. Seneca moved his crutches and walked away, Javier felt like he had just escaped a firing squad.

"What about the rest of you? Do you think nations are destined to repeat the same mistakes without a serious study of history?"

As a few guys raised their hands and made comments, Javier regretted his earlier response. He would have enjoyed answering that question. As a rule, he liked history classes. From then on, he made a better effort to pay attention.

Mr. Seneca spoke at length about his world travels as the son of military officers. After college, he had enlisted in the Marines and had served in Japan, Africa, and the Middle East.

He made the class laugh with a couple of stories about American stereotypes in foreign countries, when like a sudden cloud covering the sun, his facial expression darkened. His mouth turned down slightly. "Some of you are probably thinking I am on crutches because of a military accident, right?" A few guys nodded, but Mr. Seneca shook his head. "I'm on crutches because I made a stupid mistake, boys. I got distracted and crashed my truck about three years ago." His crutches tapped the floor in a quick series of *thuds*. "Can't blame this mistake on somebody else, and when the buck stops right inside your back pocket, you learn pretty fast that life means nothing unless you pay attention."

Javier resisted the urge to move in his chair. He didn't want others to see the discomfort he felt hearing the teacher's tragic story.

Mr. Seneca drew a breath before he continued. "Want to know the most important lesson I learned? Some of the best things happen when circumstances are at their worst. Spending all those months in a rehab hospital, I learned how to repair computers and went online to get

my master's degree in history. I also learned to play basketball in a wheelchair. What new things have you
learned the past three years, huh?"

He looked over the entire room. "After what I've been
through, I won't take excuses from you, especially since
every one of you has two moving legs and a working
brain. You try something in this class, and I'll know it. I
may not be able to run after you, but I can assign enough
history research that will keep you in the library seven
nights a week."

Mr. Seneca stood right beside the chair. With a hint of
exhaustion crossing his features, he gave a grunt and
maneuvered his body and his crutches to sit down. Javier
felt like somebody should jump up and help, but Mr.
Seneca knew exactly how to balance himself and use his
arms to sink into the chair. He leaned the crutches on the
TV cart behind him.

No one said a word.

Javier just watched him, uncertain and embarrassed.
He assumed Mr. Seneca would waste time telling more
stories, but the man had the energy to distribute textbooks, explain the first unit of study, and give out the first
three reading assignments. He also described the first
research project that was due in three weeks.

Javier felt exhausted by the end of third-period but
knew he couldn't complain without sounding lame—
what a terrible word choice with Mr. Seneca's disability!
He wondered how he could be around this teacher twice
in one day and not say something totally insulting. The
word, *transfer*, echoed in his head again. *How hard can it
be to keep a drumbeat? I'd be with my friends. I could
have some fun.*

As the bell rang to end history class, Javier turned around in his chair, ready to ask Andy if there were any beginners in the drumline.

That's when Mr. Seneca called out a command that easily rose above the noise. "Javier Ávila, Patricio Berlanga, I want to talk to you. Right now. Up here, up front."

CHAPTER THREE

Javier's friends quickly said, "Gotta go!" Ignacio and Andy slipped around the desks and hustled out of the room like a fire drill had started.

At least Javier wasn't totally alone. To help him feel a bit less nervous as they approached Mr. Seneca in the front of the room, Javier focused his gaze on Pat.

"I made an executive decision," the teacher said. He gestured from one boy to the other. "You two will be the first newscast team on Guardian TV Wednesday morning."

Oh, crap! Javier thought, but to his teacher he said, "Okay." He didn't move, as if he was already on camera and caught in a spotlight he didn't want or need.

Pat swayed back and forth on his feet. "Why can't the seniors go first?"

"I don't teach seniors, but you two I see twice a day, and neither one of you has to run to football practice after school. You two are good to go."

"Javier is the smart guy," Pat replied. "I'm not good at this stuff."

Mr. Seneca frowned. "How do you *know* you're not good at this stuff? Have you even tried? Well, have you?" When Pat said nothing, he repeated louder, "Have you?"

Pat looked like he had swallowed a wasp. He just shook his head again.

Mr. Seneca sighed and settled back into his leather chair. "Gentlemen, this isn't national TV. It's a closed-circuit broadcast for school announcements. We'll meet after school today and go over the fundamentals."

"Uh, I don't think I can stay." Pat started to say more, but Mr. Seneca interrupted him quickly.

"Let me guess! You have a dentist appointment after school? You need to pick up your little sister at daycare? You have to catch the *only* city bus that leaves you at your house so you don't have to take the later one on a different route and walk four miles in the barrio? Or maybe you need to get to a job that begins exactly at three-thirty, and if you're late, your boss will hire his brother-in-law's *primo* in your place?"

Javier stared down at his tingling feet. Mr. Seneca's sarcastic tone made him feel guilty, and he hadn't even given an excuse.

"Never mind!" Mr. Seneca straightened up and slowly inched his body forward. "We will just start practicing tomorrow during class and finish up after school. Mr. Berlanga, with a day's notice, can you stay after school tomorrow until five o'clock?"

"Yes, Sir," Pat answered, but his shoulders sagged like he was getting sent to detention.

"I'll be here, too, Mr. Seneca." Javier hated how he sounded. He even imagined kiss-up sounds inside his head.

By this time, the next period of students had filed into the room, at first noisy, then abruptly silent, no doubt when they saw the wheelchair against the back wall.

"You two can leave now," Mr. Seneca said and reached for the crutches.

Once he and Javier had gotten outside, Pat complained, "Man, I can't do this stuff. Javier, help me get out of this job."

He didn't like the idea much either, but to argue with a teacher like Mr. Seneca seemed pointless. With a shrug, he told Pat, "I think you're stuck."

Pat lowered his head. "Mr. Seneca has it in for me, I know it. You just watch. I'm going to look like an idiot, and everyone will make fun of me." He picked up the pace of his steps. "Man, that's all a dumb guy needs. I got it bad enough because of my sister, and now *this*."

"Your sister?" Javier walked faster, matching Pat's stride. "What does your sister have to do with anything?"

"Come on, Javier, you've seen her. You've heard the guys talk. I get it all the time. She's a ten, and I'm a zero. They step all over me to get to her." Pat's voice sounded frustrated and tired. "Why don't people leave me alone?" He opened the door to the main building. That's when the tardy bell clanged loudly around them.

Both Pat and Javier cussed as they looked at each other.

Pat's eyebrows lifted above his brown eyes. "If we tell Mr. Q. it was Mr. Seneca who needed to talk to us, will that save our butts? The guy's a cripple. Maybe we can use the pity factor to help us."

Javier took a step back. Bad luck maybe, but to blame Mr. Seneca felt wrong. He replied, "You say what you want, Pat."

"You talk to Mr. Q., Javier. You're the smart guy, not me."

"Stop saying that, Pat. If you just—" Javier didn't finish the sentence because there was Mr. Quintanilla coming inside the door right behind them.

The Dean of Students used his height to his advantage as he stared down at them. "Why are you two standing in the hall? Didn't you hear the tardy bell?"

"We heard it, Sir. We were just on our way to get a tardy slip," Javier said, keeping his voice steady. He prayed his reputation as a "smart guy" could keep him off a detention list. "We lost track of time discussing the new broadcast system."

Pat stood there, his brown face dotted with perspiration. He gave off a blank look like he had no clue they were both late for class.

Javier looked back at the school disciplinarian. He had seen enough guys get into trouble to know what to say. "I'm sorry, Mr. Quintanilla. Pat and I used very poor judgment. It won't happen again."

Mr. Q. gave another glare before he pulled two slips of paper from his pocket and handed one to each boy. "Get to class, gentlemen."

Javier took the slip and turned away from Pat. He walked rapidly to his next class and had no idea what classroom Pat walked into. Frankly, he didn't care.

Two classes later, he still felt edgy. By the time he joined Ignacio and Andy standing in the lunch line, he really needed to unload. He described the first-period elective and what had happened after World History class.

"Can you believe Mr. Seneca paired me up with Pat Berlanga?" He put his lunch tray on the table in front of him and sat down across from his friends.

"Too bad he didn't choose *Feliz* Berlanga instead," Andy replied. He tapped his plastic spoon against his water bottle. "Maybe you can get a video of Feliz to show on TV. One look at her, and it wouldn't matter if you mess up or not."

Javier sighed at Andy's stupid idea. He started eating the hot dog and chips from his tray and kept thinking about Pat. He had called himself a "zero," and then he said nothing when Mr. Q. showed up. What kind of news team would they make if nobody had a backbone?

Ignacio wolfed down his own hot dog before he added his comments. "The best thing is that Pat is related to Feliz. Use this chance to go to his house so you can—you know—practice. Who knows what could happen?"

Nobody got it! In two days, Javier would be on TV with a guy who would prefer to nap rather than talk, and this whole TV program was brand new. Javier and Pat would be the first ones to do it. What if the whole thing was a disaster—a very public, in-front-of-the-whole-school, disaster?

He looked from Andy to Ignacio and tried to explain things another way. "Okay, so what would happen if Mr. Henley suddenly said that for Friday night's football game, he wanted to change the half-time show? That in four days he wanted the band marching an all-new routine. How would you feel?"

Ignacio wiped his hands down the sides of his sweaty face. "He wouldn't do that. It took us half the summer to get the freshmen to march without tripping."

"That's beside the point. Ignacio, how would you *feel*?" Javier stared hard into his friend's dark eyes. "How would you feel about his decision? How would you feel about learning an important program in three days?

You're going to go out on the field in front of everybody and do something brand new."

"He wouldn't do that to us, Javier," Andy answered. "It doesn't happen that way in marching band." His spoon tapped rapidly on Javier's tray. "What's your point, man?"

Javier slapped down the annoying spoon. "I have *two* days before I go on TV and make school announcements. That's my point." He lifted his hand and pointed from Andy to Ignacio. "You guys get a whole summer to learn a new band routine."

"Would you relax, man?" Ignacio shook his head. "You got your underwear in a knot over a few announcements. Get over it! How hard can it be to say . . . " His voice deepened like a newscaster. "'Any student who doesn't turn in his handbook form to Mr. Domínguez by Friday will start serving detention on Monday' or something like . . ." His voice pitch changed again. " . . . 'Will the student who stole Brother Calavera's IQ tests from the filing cabinet please collect them from the urinals in the main building'."

Andy smiled, and so did Javier. His friends often made him laugh. They also swore he took things way too seriously. And he wondered, *Is this one of those times?*

"Look, Javier." Ignacio's grin changed into a more serious expression. "You'll be good at this. I've seen you up in front of the class. You don't sweat like me or start shaking pencils or drumming spoons like Andy does. I know you can be Mr. Cool. And as for Berlanga, don't sweat it. Do your job, and if he comes off like a lump of *masa*, it's not your fault."

Javier nodded. Ignacio was right. It wasn't up to Javier to change Pat. "Okay. I'll just take care of my job and leave Pat to worry about Pat."

Ignacio nudged Andy and grinned at Javier. "But if you get inside the Berlanga house, let Feliz know I'm available, okay, Jack?"

"Yeah, right! You can just stand in line behind me," Javier replied. Then he yanked the spoon out of Andy's hand before he could start tapping it again.

After school, Javier stood in front of his locker, wondering why his stupid lock wouldn't open. He had done the combination three times. Had Ignacio or Andy switched locks as a joke? Luckily he knew their combinations too, and it was Andy's numbers that finally worked. They must have done the switch while he was busy helping Mrs. Alejandro take down lab equipment from the shelves after chemistry class. By the time Javier had made it to his locker, few boys were left in the halls, and his practical joker friends were long gone to band practice.

He not only got his lock back, but also switched up Ignacio and Andy's locks. He had a spare lock from last year's gym class and switched that to his locker instead.

He had just picked up his heavy backpack when he saw two of the guys talking and pointing at something behind Javier. He turned just as he heard a female voice.

"Hello. Have you seen my brother anywhere?"

Even though she was dressed in a white uniform blouse with a navy blue tie and a uniform blue-gray plaid skirt, Feliz Berlanga had model qualities. She moved gracefully as she walked toward him. Even the silly white socks didn't detract from the tanned, shapely legs. She was one of the prettiest girls he had ever met.

"You're one of Pat's friends, right? I think I saw you with him," she said and then offered an apologetic smile. "Sorry, I'm terrible with names."

"I'm Javier Ávila." He cleared the squeak out of his voice. "We met last week."

She breathed a laugh and pointed at him playfully. "Oh, yes! I just forgot. Any chance you've seen Pat today?"

"We have morning classes together, but I haven't seen him this afternoon."

Feliz looked from side to side. "I know I'm not supposed to wander around the school alone. I don't want to get into trouble, you know?"

Javier nodded. "Yeah, I know."

Her light brown eyes sparkled with touches of gold. "But you're one of his friends, right? Could you look for him? My car's near the baseball field."

What else could he do? He smiled at Feliz. "I'll try and find him."

"Great! I owe you one!" She stood up on her toes and gave him a finger wave. "See you later!"

As she turned away, he could only fantasize about what a girl like Feliz might "owe" him. He walked in another direction, searching through empty classrooms. Could Pat have fallen asleep and no one bothered to wake him up? He walked into two of the bathrooms, and finally went toward the administration wing. Maybe Pat got into trouble and was sitting up there.

As Javier reached the main hall, Pat walked out of Brother Calvin's office. The guy's brown face drooped from eyelids to lips. He saw Javier and shook his head. "I tried to get into a different elective. Brother Calvin won't let me switch. Sorry, man, you're stuck with me."

Javier wanted a different partner, sure, but he didn't want Pat to feel like a total loser. "We're stuck with each other, Pat. I don't know anything about broadcasting either. At least you had the guts to ask Brother Calvin to change your schedule. I just let things happen and go along. I hate dealing with the man unless I have to."

Pat nodded. "Me too." His eyes widened as if he had just remembered something. "Oh, man, I bet my sister's waiting for me. I didn't expect Ol' Calavera to start lecturing me about college after I asked for a schedule change."

"I saw Feliz. She said the car's by the baseball field."

"You talked to my sister?" He gave Javier a pointed stare. "Just stay away from her. She doesn't need guys like you sniffing around her."

Javier stepped back, hurt and insulted by Pat's quick judgment. "I'm not some horny dog, Pat. I was trying to help keep your sister out of trouble. Feliz broke the rules by coming inside the building, so I said I would look for you . . . and just for the record, I have two sisters myself."

"So where do they go to school?"

"They both work in Lubbock. They're older than me, but they're just as pretty as your sister."

"Then you know how it is, Javier." Pat's glare diminished but not much. "Guys just want to be your friend so they can meet your sister. I never knew any guy who wanted something different."

What could he say? Javier *was* interested in Feliz. "Uh, well, you'd better go find your sister, Pat. She might come back inside and get into big trouble with Mr. Q."

Pat looked at Javier for a long moment. "Okay." He turned away, took a few steps, and looked back at Javier. "Where do you live anyway?"

"Across from Woodlawn Lake. Why?"

Pat's face brightened up. "Yeah? My *abuelita* lives near there."

Javier felt a sudden itch under the toes of both feet.

"I live with my grandmother during the week," Pat said. "You need a ride home?"

Javier's fingers wrapped tight around the strap of his backpack. He thought of his itchy feet, his algebra home-work, and his weekend job to wash the work trucks for his father—anything to keep a goofy grin from spreading across his face. He even tried to sound bored when he said, "Thanks, Pat. Anything is better than the school bus."

Pat gave a sly smile. "You might change your mind later. Come on." He motioned to Javier, and the two of them walked out of the front door of the school.

The August heat slammed down on them, so aside from "Man, it's a living hell out here," Pat and Javier didn't say much as they trudged around the buildings toward the large parking lot behind the school. By the time they got close to the classy black sports vehicle, Javier felt like he was Ignacio's sweaty twin.

The car hummed in its space, engine purring and windows rolled up. As soon as Pat opened the front pas-senger door and Javier opened the door behind it, the air-conditioning rushed into their faces.

"Where have you been? Some of us have a life, you know!" Feliz's angry voice raised high above the noise of the air conditioner.

"Sorry. Hey! Javier lives near Welita's house. He needs a ride home," Pat said as he climbed inside the car.

Javier tried to see Feliz's expression, but she turned away and said, "Whatever! Let's just go!"

Javier didn't want to make Feliz angrier, so he quickly tossed his backpack on the floor, then pulled himself into the vehicle. He had never seen the luxury of ash-gray leather seats, a monitor for each person in the backseat to watch his own movie, and cup holders on the doors and between the backseats.

Wearing narrow, dark sunglasses, Feliz raised her head and looked into the rearview mirror. "I get off on Woodlawn to go to my grandmother's house. Where do I have to take you?"

Have you already forgotten you owe me? Javier thought, and just said, "I live on the corner of Woodlawn and Lake streets."

Feliz adjusted her sunglasses. "Close the door, Pat. I need to get home."

Pat cranked up the music. The harsh guitars of heavy metal thundered inside the car. Javier felt invisible and stupid, not worthy enough for a girl like Feliz to remember.

He clicked his seatbelt into place just as Feliz shifted the vehicle into reverse. The mighty vehicle rolled back, back, back then stopped with a jerky lurch. She stomped on the brakes, propelling Javier forward. The seatbelt slapped him back, scraping across his throat. The car jerked back, backwards right into a *thump-gump*. Rolling forward, lurch, rolling backward, *th—thump*, up, up, back . . . *thump-crunch!*

Javier didn't look out to see what she had hit, twice now. He just stared down at his fingers, squeezing tight around his knees. He seemed to be sweating again, despite the full blast of the backseat air vents. The car rolled forward again, then lurched into reverse, but this third time, Feliz managed to avoid whatever she had hit before. Javier started to breathe normally again.

As the big vehicle finally backed out of the space between an older truck with a bumpy fender and a mini-van with a scratched door, Javier could only hope the worst was over. Shifting forward, Feliz sped the car through the parking lot toward the exit gate. The car jerked to a sudden stop as she hit the brakes. The seatbelt cut across his throat a second time. The rise and fall on the asphalt speed bumps rolled and jerked, *ja-bump, ja-bump, zoom, stomp, ja-bump, ja-bump* . . . to the last *zoom, jerk, jerk, ja-bump, ja-bump* just before she stomped on the gas at the front gate and drove into the street with a loud car horn blaring behind them at her too-wide left turn.

Javier gripped the side door, feeling a little comfort in the fact that the vehicle he rode in was heavier than the cars around them. In case of an accident, he could —would—should be protected, right?

She drove up the freeway entrance and sped up even faster as she passed freight trucks, small cars, long cars, and even a park ranger's car without slowing down. Javier looked around the front seat and realized Pat had fallen asleep. *How did he do that?*

Feliz wove between cars, never once using a blinker as she changed lanes to pass up vehicle after vehicle. She drove right past the Woodlawn Street exit like she was heading for the mall instead.

"Feliz!" He didn't mean to yell, but the music was loud enough that even his tone-deaf uncles could have sung along.

"What?" she shrieked. "What's wrong?"

"Didn't you miss the exit?" He hated to yell, but it was hopeless to speak naturally in the speeding, music-throbbing car.

Feliz screamed curses that Javier had never heard a girl use. She swerved the black car toward the right lane, three sets of horns honking around them.

Javier's shoulder hit the door with enough force to scare him. Even Pat woke up and yelled, "What the heck are you doing, Feliz?"

She pulled off at the next exit and raced the car toward the signal light on the access road like she was trying to beat a world record. Javier looked toward the front window and saw the signal turning yellow. Was she going to try to beat the light? No one needed to get home that bad, right?

In the split second the light turned red, Feliz pressed on the gas and raced forward. The tires squealed as she battled the steering wheel to make the turn under the bridge. Javier stared at the two lanes of cars speeding in the other direction toward them. He repeated the pro-fanity he had heard from Feliz. Who'd hear him over the noise anyway?

Somehow she made the turn. She drove the car out of the way of the oncoming traffic and sped down the road like nothing dangerous had just happened.

Javier's heart was shoved up inside his head, thump-ing faster than the speed of sound. He couldn't breathe, couldn't find his saliva or his eardrums. His back pressed into the leather seat that should have comforted and relaxed him, but in this moment, he would have given *anything* to feel the stiff bench seat of the school bus instead.

As they neared the Woodlawn Lake neighborhoods, Feliz finally slowed down. Someone in the front seat had turned down the music, and Feliz asked in a nice voice, "What house am I looking for?"

Javier wasn't prepared for the Driving Demon to rematerialize as Friendly Feliz, so it took him a moment to speak in a normal voice. "Down the road—that stone house on the corner."

"Oh, I've seen this house," Feliz said as she slowed the car in front of the white gate. "I always thought the flowers were pretty."

"Thanks," Javier said. If he hadn't been so relieved to be still alive and breathing, he might have told her it was built by his great-grandfather and that his father and brothers had renovated it just before Javier was born. He might have told her she should stop by some time and see how "pretty" his mother decorated inside. But all he said to both Feliz and Pat was, "Thanks for the ride."

Javier dragged his backpack as he stepped out of the car. He closed the door with a loud *thud*, and quickly jumped up on the sidewalk in case the Driving Demon tried to run over his feet.

The tires spun out in the loose dirt by the curb before the black car sped off.

No "goodbye," or "see you later"? not even a moment to hear, "You're welcome"? Hmm, Javier thought.

Even though he stood in front of his own home, Javier still felt like a hitchhiker abandoned by random strangers on the highway. He tossed his backpack strap over one shoulder and sighed.

His mother was home early from her job as a bank loan officer. When she was all dressed up for work with her hair colored a light brown, she didn't look at all like a woman of fifty-four. She had stayed thin, always seemed to have a lot of energy, and knew how to carry on a conversation with anyone: just ask questions.

When Javier came into the kitchen looking for a cold drink, she stood at the kitchen counter slicing up avocados. After a quick hello, she started questioning him like he was under state investigation. "Did you get a top locker? Did you buy a lunch card? How do you like the new teachers? Any changes in the dress code I should know about? Are there any fundraisers coming up? Can I see your schedule?"

Javier caught a break from the interrogation when his father yelled through the back door, "The fajitas are ready. Javier!"

He immediately grabbed two potholders off the tile kitchen counter and walked out to the patio. When he came back inside, he saw his mom reading his class schedule. "What's Media Broadcasting class?" she asked.

He didn't answer until the cast iron *comal* of sizzling chicken fajitas, bell peppers, and onions that his father had cooked on the patio grill was set down on the stove. "It's a new elective, Mom. Now there's equipment at the school to do the morning announcements on TV."

"That should be fun," she said. She put down the schedule on the table and wandered toward the refrigerator. "Will you have to dress differently?"

"What do you mean?" Javier tossed the pot holders by the sink. "Why would I dress differently?"

"The people on TV wear suits and ties, don't they?" She pulled a package of flour tortillas from inside the refrigerator. "If you're going to study broadcasting, won't you need to dress like a news anchor?"

"I hope not." Javier twisted his lips into a crooked line. It was bad enough for the guys to watch him on TV. Who wanted the added spotlight of wearing different clothes from everyone else too? He liked that school uniforms let a guy disappear into the crowd. He didn't want to stand out like a big zit on someone's nose.

His father came inside and said, "Nivia, your daughter called me today—you know, Selena the screamer."

She gestured at her husband with the package. "You always say 'your daughter' when Selena acts up. Doesn't she get that screaming thing from your side of the family?"

"Ávilas are not screamers." His dad washed his hands in the sink. "Isn't that right, Javier?"

Javier shrugged. "Yeah well, Vivian and Selena are exceptions to the rule." Maybe his big sisters were hot-tempered, but he had always admired their popularity and the way they never backed down from an argument.

There were qualities in *all* his older siblings that he wished had been passed down to him. *Maybe the gene pool gets too shallow after a twelve-year gap*, he thought.

Suddenly he heard a *fwrapp* sound and saw the package of flour tortillas beside his bare feet.

"You were supposed to catch them!" His mom was laughing. "Heat those up, please. So, Javito, what else happened on your first day of school?"

Her question made him feel like he was still in first grade. Javier scooped up the plastic bag and walked toward the microwave. He wanted to say, "I'm supposed to go on school TV with the guy who sleeps in class. And his hot-looking sister almost got me killed today driving us home."

Instead, he told her, "Not much to tell you, Mom, it was fine."

CHAPTER FOUR

"**F**ind a good reason why you *can't* do announcements, Ávila."

Javier turned from his locker to face Dylan Romo,
one of the senior football players. The tall guy owned
shoulders the width of three lockers. He glared down like
Javier had tried to steal a girlfriend.

"I heard Seneca chose you sophomores to be on TV
tomorrow. That's not the way we do things at Saint Pete's.
Us seniors go first, got it?"

Javier's mouth went dry, but he forced himself to
speak. He had faced his share of bullies, and knew he had
to think fast. "We didn't ask for the job, Dylan. Seneca—
uh, Mr. Seneca—chose guys who could practice after
school. All the seniors—well, and the juniors too—have
football practice."

"Seniors do things first. That's how it is at this school.
You tell him, Ávila."

Javier frowned and almost said, "Tell him yourself,"
but Ram Fierro and Omar Narsico, the other seniors in
the broadcasting class, had suddenly materialized behind
Dylan. Without Javier's friends behind him, it would be
pointless to argue—and worse if he made a senior angry.

In a slow, steady voice, Javier said, "I'll talk to Mr. Seneca."

"Do that." Dylan pushed Javier aside and swaggered down the hall as if he owned it. Ram and Omar laughed together as they followed behind him. As they passed other athletes at their lockers, they slapped high-fives and made rude remarks. Most guys just backed against the walls and let them pass.

"What's it like to have that kind of power?" asked a rather sad voice on the other side of the locker door.

Javier stepped out and saw Pat Berlanga opening his combination lock a few doors down. Pat didn't look up. Perhaps he asked the question but didn't expect an answer—not that Javier had one to offer. "Did you hear what Dylan told me?"

Pat shrugged. "He's right. Seniors always do things first." He jerked off the lock and hooked it on his shirt pocket. "Just let them talk on TV if that's what they want."

Javier walked closer to where Pat stood unloading his backpack and grabbing books he'd need from the locker. "Mr. Seneca told you and me to do the job."

"Yeah, well, Welita and I watched the TV news last night. Smooth and cool, those guys. No kidding, Javier. You and I would look more like Bugs and Daffy."

Javier shook his head. "Not if we practice together. I watched the news last night too. I saw what the anchors did. Why can't we be like them?"

"Get serious." His words dripped with sarcasm.

"I am serious." A sudden anger made Javier's face feel tight and stiff. "You're the one who isn't serious. Nobody said talking on TV would be easy, but that doesn't mean you and I can't do it well . . . or first. Don't you think we deserve our share of the power?"

Pat turned to face Javier. For the first time, Pat looked wide awake, his dark eyes shining with interest. "What about Dylan and the other seniors?"

"I don't know." The itchy sting inside Javier's shoes pulled him back to the reality of being a sophomore. "This is the first time I've ever had seniors in a class. We sophomores need to stick together. That's all I know for sure, especially in a class where everything is new to both of us."

Pat scratched his head. "Well, then, can I see your homework? There's still time if I need to write my practice announcements over."

Javier's shoulders relaxed. He could always rely on schoolwork to give him focus, help him think better. Maybe if he concentrated on the assignments, he would find a way around the senior blockheads in the class. "Let's go over to Mr. Seneca's room early. We can talk about our homework there."

"Maybe we could read what we wrote out loud to each other."

"Good idea." Javier turned to shut his locker door and quickly snapped the lock.

"Is that a new lock?" Andy grinned widely as he walked up. "Javier, can you give me the combination in case I need to borrow something?"

"Yesterday I stood here twenty minutes trying to get the stupid lock open, thanks to you." Javier only pretended to be mad. The lock switch he had made yesterday would be sweet revenge, especially if it led to tardy slips and a face-off with Mr. Q. "My combination is off limits to you . . . forever!"

Andy laughed off Javier's words and rapidly thumped Pat on the shoulder. "Hey, Berlanga, how's your hot-looking sister? Did she ask about me?" He turned his back on Pat and said to Javier, "I wrote a great essay for English class. How you, me, and Ignacio are great friends, been friends since kindergarten. How we like the same movies, put the same stuff on our hot dogs, stuff like that."

"Third grade crap," Pat said, just loud enough for them to hear. He slammed his locker door and hung his lock into place. "You think Maloney wants to read that?"

Andy spun around. "If you ain't talking about your sister, keep it to yourself!"

When Pat's upper lip lifted in a snarl, Javier jumped quickly between them. He couldn't believe how quickly Pat changed moods. He made eye contact with his best friend and spoke forcefully. "Andy, lay off." He used his shoulder to move Pat aside. "Come on, Pat. We need to go over our homework before class." He called back, "See you in second period, Andy!" then yanked on Pat's shirt sleeve until the guy followed.

"Andy was just kidding around," Javier said as they walked toward the side doors. "He's pretty harmless."

"Andy's just like the rest of them, talking about my sister. Like she'd pay attention to a band geek," Pat replied, a rumbling of anger between his words.

"She probably likes the Dylan and Ram types, huh?"

Pat glowered at Javier. "What's it to you?"

"I'm making conversation, Pat. Untie the knot in your underwear, okay?" Javier had made his own scowl. "And stop acting so defensive about your sister. If Feliz is anything like *my* sisters, she doesn't need you acting like her guard dog."

Pat inhaled and exhaled slowly as they walked outside into the humid, sticky morning. "I hate this weather. I should have written an announcement declaring school cancelled until October fifteenth."

"Wish I had thought of that." Javier sighed, feeling the sweat rise under his collar. "The announcements I wrote sound so lame—ugh! I need to stop using that word! Could I act more stupid around Mr. Seneca?"

Pat stopped and grabbed Javier's arm. "Wait! There's our answer."

"What?"

"We sit back and wait for those seniors to act stupid, say the wrong thing. It'll happen, trust me. Dylan, Ram and the others think with their shoulder pads." Pat's eyebrows wrinkled together. "I played football last year. Got hurt in the first scrimmage, and I was done." He lowered his eyes to the sidewalk. "All that stuff about teamwork they shove down your throats? It means nothing when you get hurt." He snapped his fingers. "Like that, you're outside the circle, labeled a quitter for life."

The bitterness in Pat's voice kept Javier silent. Some upperclassmen were jerks, true, but Javier figured it was just because they were on top of the food chain. The athletes in his classes usually treated Javier okay.

"You've got the rep for being a brain," Pat said like he had read Javier's thoughts. "They're not going to mess with you because they might need help with their homework someday. I'm just the guy who sleeps in class." He suddenly raised his head as if he realized he had just spilled his guts and regretted doing so. He walked faster and called out, "So how did you figure if your announcements lasts fifteen seconds?"

Javier raised his wrist and flashed him the black band and chrome digital face. "I used my watch. It has a stop-watch feature."

"Woo hoo. Fancy. Does it chop meat and make margaritas too?"

He laughed and said, "I'm still reading the instruction book. I'll let you know."

They were both chuckling as they walked up the stairs to the portable building where Mr. Seneca's classes were held. As soon as they walked inside, they heard their teacher's commanding voice from the back of the classroom. "Javier! Pat! I need you two to set up the desk area."

Any thoughts that Javier kept about going over homework were immediately replaced by following Mr. Seneca's orders. Pat and Javier lifted the last row of tables and moved them in front of one side wall with the whiteboards. They created a line of tables and put chairs behind them into what Mr. Seneca referred to again as "the desk area."

Meanwhile, the other sophomores, Landry and Steve, untangled cords. Kenny followed Mr. Seneca's sharp directions about camera set-up in front of the tables.

Just as the warning bell rang, the three juniors came through the door.

"Do I need to remind all of you to arrive at seven-thirty? There's too much to do if we want to roll the cameras at first bell," Mr. Seneca announced loudly.

"I can't get here any earlier," the tallest one said. He nudged the boy beside him and said, "I take my little sisters to St. Vincent's before I come here."

The one beside him grinned. "Yeah, me too."

The third one chuckled beside them. "Me too—too."

"Fine!" Mr. Seneca's face looked brick red and sweaty from the exertion of using crutches to walk around and direct the sophomores. "If you guys can't get here early to help with set-up, then you three are in charge of strike. Before first period ends, you three take all this down. You move the tables back and store equipment in its right place. Better be quick and efficient or you'll be late to your second-period class."

Their grins melted into serious frowns and hard stares at their teacher.

Javier could only wonder what Mr. Seneca might have planned for the seniors if they showed up after the tardy bell. However, Dylan, Ram, and Omar wandered in just seconds later.

"Take your seats, gentlemen. Let's pay attention to announcements this time."

Mr. Seneca slowly moved between the tables. His crutches and his legs followed their own creaking cadence to move him forward.

Javier glanced at Pat, who used his chin to point at the opposite direction from where the seniors sat. Pat sat down, and Javier sat in front of him. Just before the homeroom bell rang, Javier caught a scowl from Dylan. He ignored it and just pulled his homework paper from the small class textbook on his desk.

They all stood up for the morning prayers and Pledge, then sat back down as Mr. Domínguez began the announcements. Javier had never noticed what a monotone voice the vice-principal owned. Each word sounded dull and lifeless. *No wonder students tuned him out. He was boring like a rock.*

While watching the news the night before, Javier had noticed the way the anchors talked to their TV audience as if they sat across the table listening. They used graphics, video clips, and even good-natured jokes to help keep the viewers interested.

The idea of delivering the announcements on school TV was slowly emerging from a frantic fear to a curious challenge for him; like the first time Javier saw an algebra equation—only this time the X variable involved Pat Berlanga. He didn't hear any snoring behind him, so maybe Pat was still awake.

As soon as Mr. Domínguez said his dull ending, "Have a good day," Mr. Seneca immediately asked, "Anybody notice the tone of today's announcements?"

No one responded, probably because Kenny's answer yesterday had made Mr. Seneca mad. He must have guessed the reason for the silence, because he added, "Our job here is analysis, gentlemen. What did you notice about the way the announcements were presented to you?"

Javier raised his hand and waited for a nod from his teacher. "There's no difference in his voice. Whether it's 'Pick up PE uniforms' or 'The cafeteria is serving tacos,' everything sounds the same."

Mr. Seneca's lip lifted with a slight smile. "Good. Anyone else?"

"I just have a question." Kenny had half-raised and lowered his hand limply. "Does this mean Brother Lendell will be on TV too? He always does the morning prayer."

Mr. Seneca adjusted his weight on his crutches. "Let's talk about what we want on Guardian TV. This is a brand new program for our school. Do you want Brother Lendell in here every morning, or should we all share a role in finding and reading a prayer to start the day in a traditional fashion?"

"I volunteer Ram to find prayers," Omar said. "His mom's a Guadalupana. They pray in his house all the time."

"Dylan can do announcements. He knows better than anybody what goes on in this school," Ram said. "Even Mr. Quintanilla asks Dylan Romo for news."

"Kenny'd be good at saluting," Dylan said and ignored the profanity Kenny mouthed in his direction. "Kenny should always lead the Pledge."

Mr. Seneca lowered his head and stared at them. "Do you think this is a show on the comedy network? I don't attach my name to anything that isn't professional in quality, and if Guardian TV becomes a school joke, it'll be worse than the football team losing every game this season."

"Hey! Don't say that. You'll jinx us!" Dylan growled his words. "Nobody talks about us losing, especially not some new teacher."

Mr. Seneca took one step forward. His pit-bull expression didn't change. "You're right, Dylan. I *am* a new teacher. I'm a new teacher who has an attitude about teamwork that doesn't involve passing a ball or wearing a cup." He looked over the class. "Our first broadcast is tomorrow morning, gentlemen, and we have a lot of work to do."

Dylan suddenly raised one long, muscular arm. "Mr. Seneca, Sir, Javier Ávila and I were talking before class. Javier has something important to tell you."

Everyone turned toward Javier. Mr. Seneca raised an eyebrow as he stared purposefully in his direction.

Slowly, Javier straightened up in his chair. He saw Dylan's sneaky grin, Kenny's smirk, and the trio of juniors sizing him up. Mr. Seneca was a man who hated contradiction, and if the seniors made him mad, Javier couldn't help but wonder if the fallout would crack across his head too.

Just as he was about to say something totally vague, Pat's fist pressed firmly between Javier's shoulders. He didn't turn around, but he did remember what Pat had said about the football players. He looked up at Mr. Seneca and said, "Pat and I can stay after school and practice. Why not let the seniors work on presenting the announcements during class time? We should all be prepared to do announcements just in case someone is late or sick."

"Or dead," someone murmured.

Javier kept his eyes focused on Mr. Seneca. It felt like everyone was dumping more and more rocks on top of an already heavy load. How to please a teacher, satisfy egomaniacs, and work with a sleepy sophomore weighed him way down.

"Actually you've given me a good idea, Javier," Mr. Seneca said, his voice sounding relaxed for the first time that morning. "Why don't we try everyone out? I have a couple of things we need to do during this short homeroom period, but as I take roll and let you pass out a few forms to the others, we can take care of business and get started at first period."

Javier started to stand up but felt a heavy hand on his shoulder, pushing him back down. Pat had stood up. He was already walking toward the front of the room. "I'll pass out the forms, Mr. Seneca. It'll help keep me awake."

Some of the guys snickered, but Javier felt relieved that Pat volunteered. The last thing Javier needed was for one of the football players to *accidentally* trip him.

As first period began, Mr. Seneca directed all the students to turn their chairs so that they faced the desk area. He explained that the students doing announcements would read as if they were behind the desk of a real news station. The camera would film in front, and two other students would feed graphics from the computers across the room. Other students would be assigned technical positions to check sound, keep time, and write copy. "We will keep it very simple this week, but we'll have more options this semester if you guys use some creativity and plan well."

Mr. Seneca sat down in his wheelchair located in front of one of the rear black cabinets. He settled in comfortably before he said, "Let's see what kind of novice broadcasters I have. Let's try it. Omar, Dylan, you too. What kind of newsteam will you two make?"

"The best kind," Dylan said and smiled widely when all the class chuckled. Even Mr. Seneca gave an uncharacteristic grin as the two boys took their places in the chairs behind the desk area.

Omar held up his notebook paper and read slowly. "The following students should report to Mr. Quintanilla's office . . . Javier Ávila, Pat Berlanga, Kenny García, Dylan Romo, and Ram Fierro."

"That's really boring!" Mr. Seneca had folded his arms across his chest.

Omar shrugged. "It's announcements. It's always boring, but I got something else." His eyes searched over the paper, and then he said, "Uh, the seniors will have a bake sale on Friday. Our moms cooked good stuff to eat. If you're not there, you're square." He grinned as he looked up from the paper. "Good rhyme, huh?"

"Not really. Read it again, and this time try to sound like you actually want students to come to the bake sale."

Omar frowned then read, "Uh . . . the seniors will, uh . . . have a bake sale . . . "

"No 'uh' sounds! Just the words on the paper."

"Uh—no—uh—sorry, okay—okay—uh—ugh! The seniors—uh—"

"Stop, stop, stop!" Mr. Seneca waved his hands. "Forget it." He sighed. "Dylan, let's hear your announcements."

Dylan had been laughing silently during his teammate's performance. When Mr. Seneca called on him, his face still looked amused, but he read out, "The Quad dance . . . happens Saturday night . . . eight to twelve . . . five dollars . . . to get in."

"I didn't say write a telegram. Is that the best you could do?"

Dylan flipped over the page. "No problem. You want to hear the next one?" He looked down and read quickly, "TheGuardiansplaytheAngelsatseventhirtyatcathedral fieldFridayDylanRomoatdefensiveendOmarNarsico attightendwithRamFierroplayingquarterback."

"Wait! Stop. You didn't even write complete sentences!" Mr. Seneca told him. "Again, Dylan, slow, steady, and with some enthusiasm."

Dylan squared his shoulders and said in a strained voice, "The school football team has its next game—"

"Which team?" Mr. Seneca's voice snapped like a whip.

"What?"

"Which team? Varsity? JV? Freshmen? Be specific."

"I meant the varsity." Dylan's dark eyes glowed. "Who cares when the freshmen are playing?" The paper in his hands shook. "Okay, fine! The varsity squad will play the Angels—"

"From what school? What sport?"

"Okay. The varsity—Guardian football team plays the Saint Gabriel Angels on Friday night at Cathedral field. Tickets cost five dollars."

"You sound so mad, Dylan. Do the students want to watch an angry football player doing announcements?"

Dylan tossed the paper up in the air. "Mr. Seneca, just let the sophomores do this job first. They got the extra time to practice it like you want it. I'll just watch 'em and then I can have my chance on TV when football season is over, okay?"

Javier rolled his lips inside his mouth to keep a smile off his face. He didn't dare look at Pat Berlanga for fear they would both jump up and high-five.

But happiness at this small victory fizzled out quickly as Javier watched the juniors roast under the harsh spotlight of Mr. Seneca's criticisms. They also begged for the sophomores to go first. That's when Kenny García volunteered to work the camera. "My dad has a digital camera and I used it all summer," he said. Landry and Steve wanted to work the computers and stay behind the scenes.

That left Javier and Pat as the first broadcast team on Guardian TV Wednesday morning and probably for the next week. Javier only wished a vote of confidence had gotten him the job, not the fact that nobody else wanted to do it. He saw Pat staring at the desk area. Was Pat picturing their practice session, or was he sleeping with his eyes open? How would they make the first broadcast exceed everyone's expectations, particularly Mr. Seneca's?

As they gathered up their books after the bell rang to end class, Javier said to Pat, "Do you think we can get it all together by tomorrow morning?"

"Who knows?" Pat zipped up his backpack. He yawned and blinked his sleepy eyes. "But no matter what happens, you and me, we'll just roll with the flow."

"Yeah," Javier muttered, "roll with the flow."

CHAPTER FIVE

"First-period is *so* annoying," Javier told Andy and Ignacio as they pushed through the side doors and walked toward the portable building for third-period class. "And it's not just during class. Now I have to stay after school to practice."

"Welcome to our world," Ignacio said, tugging on the front of his white shirt to pull it away from his sweating body. "You've gotten spoiled by going home at four o'clock every day. If we make it out of here by seven, we're lucky."

Andy had a pencil in each hand and played a drumbeat in the air. "If Mr. Seneca keeps you late, you can grab a ride home with me."

"Javier needs to get a ride home with Pat and Feliz— a sweet ride home in that luxury car she drives." Ignacio swatted at Andy's pencils. "Who wants to ride home with *your* mom when a guy can find something much, much better?"

"Don't talk about my momma!" Andy purposely rapped the pencils across Ignacio's hand. "And you know how much I've been dreaming about Feliz Berlanga! Just the two of us on a *smooth* ride."

Javier merely smiled. There was nothing smooth about a car ride with Feliz, but he said instead, "In two weeks, I can drive myself to school."

"Cool! You can give us a ride home after band practice." Ignacio led the way up the steps to the portable building. "My dad told me he'd buy your gas once a month if he didn't have to drive downtown to pick me up."

"My mom would probably pay the rest," Andy said.

Javier would like to drive with his friends, but he knew it wasn't going to happen. "Did you forget those annoying license rules? Just one passenger if you're not related."

"Then it needs to be *me*." Ignacio pointed back at himself with his thumb. "Andy doesn't carry drums home every day. I've always got my trumpet case."

"Ignacio gets his license before I do," Andy replied. "Besides, I live closer."

They walked inside Mr. Seneca's classroom to see it half-filled with third-period students. The teacher had his back to them as he stacked papers on his desk.

Javier walked over to the spot where he sat in first period. His backpack thumped on top of the table. Pat sat at the next table behind it. He glanced up and nodded at Javier.

Ignacio slugged Javier in the shoulder with his backpack. "Too close, Jack. I was forced by Maloney's stupid seating chart into a front desk." He brushed past Pat to claim a table closer to the rear.

Andy followed Ignacio. Javier looked down at Pat. "Want to move back?"

Pat raised an eyebrow. "You're kidding, right? We both know Mr. Seneca's radar for guys in the back. I'm safer here. Always sit in the same place up front and teachers ignore you." He rested his elbow on the desk and planted his cheek against his hand.

Javier heard the creak of Mr. Seneca's crutches behind him and quickly pulled out the chair to sit down. He feared his teacher's impatience more than his friends' annoyance any day.

Other students rushed in. The bell rang. Mr. Seneca took roll and then motioned to Bryce Thayer, another sophomore. "Pass out the papers on my desk, will you? Okay, gentlemen, I'm giving out a quiz. It'll give me an idea of what you already know. If you're totally ignorant, I'll start with assignments like memorizing world capital cities and lessons in latitude and longitude." He said quite calmly, "You have ten minutes."

Row by row, Bryce left stacks of the quiz with each guy in the front table. Javier slipped one off the top and passed the others behind him. If Pat had planned to sleep, it wouldn't happen today. Javier looked down and saw twenty-five rows of multiple choice questions typed in small font.

He heard the shuffle of papers behind him and Pat's pained whisper. "He can't be serious."

Javier felt the same way. He grabbed a pen and started reading. The questions grew more difficult until by the last ten, he was making guesses about conservation efforts in Africa and terrorist activities in Great Britain.

The quiz was all they could talk about as they stood in the lunch line.

"Can a teacher make a guy feel more stupid?" Ignacio complained as he squeezed ketchup across the top of his hamburger patty. "Why didn't he ask more questions about Mexico or South America? I know about those places."

"That's 'cause your mom watches *las novelas*," Andy answered. He grabbed the bottle, smothered his fries with red ketchup, and passed the bottle over to Javier. "And how many did *you* get right? You *always* throw off the test curve for the rest of us."

"The quiz made me feel stupid too," Javier said. "Who knew Lake Victoria was in Africa? I thought it would be in England—you know, named after one of the queens."

After Javier used the ketchup, he followed his friends into the main cafeteria area. He spotted Pat at the end of a table where sophomores often sat. There were several empty chairs around him. "Let's sit over there with Pat."

"Only 'cause it might get me in good with his sister," Andy replied.

Javier was starting to understand why Pat got irritated by everyone's interest in his sister. "Why can't we just sit with Pat because he's in our class?"

"Some things never change," Ignacio said. "Javier always brought home sick birds or lost dogs, and now it's Pat Berlanga." But he walked in Pat's direction anyway.

Javier sat next to Pat. Ignacio and Andy sat across from them.

"Hey, Pat," Javier said and quickly started a conversation they could all relate to. "We were all talking about that quiz Mr. Seneca gave out. What did you think?"

Pat looked around at all of them and just shrugged. "It was okay." He took a bite out of his hamburger and chewed on it slowly.

"Obviously a guy with great conversation skills," Ignacio said, dragging his words along. "So, is this what we can expect tomorrow? Is Javier going to do all the talking?"

Pat frowned. "Maybe." He took another bite and slowly chewed it.

Now it was Javier's turn to frown. Why was Pat acting like he didn't want to talk to them? Earlier he had been friendly, even made Javier laugh. What was his problem?

Andy drummed on his tray with his plastic fork and spoon. "Let's talk about the weekend. Javier, are you coming to the football game?"

"If I can find a ride." Javier just gave the same excuse as last year, but this time he added, "It's not like I can go on the band bus with you two."

Andy shook a spoon at Javier. "Jack, I *told* you back in middle school to play a flute or beat a drum, triangle, cymbals, something! You did Young Astronauts instead."

Ignacio chimed in. "Then you became president of the Junior National Honor Society in eighth grade. Could you be more of a nerd, Jack?"

"Why do you call him Jack?" The question came unexpectedly from Pat.

They all stared at him. Javier was surprised Pat had spoken to his friends.

"It's a nickname from grade school," Andy said. He started laughing and gestured with his spoon as he talked. "Back in fourth grade, we built a pair of tall wooden ramps for our bikes. There goes Javier down the first ramp. Then he tries to make the jump onto the second ramp. He goes this way, and his bike goes that way! Smash, crash, kaboom! Javier totally wiped out! His bike looked like a pretzel!"

Ignacio was laughing too. "He had to get stitches under his eye, and his dad started calling him 'One-eyed Jack'."

"Ha ha ha—so funny!" Javier's voice was thick with sarcasm. "You guys scarred me for life!"

"Aw, well, save it for Brother Calavera." Andy grinned at Javier. Suddenly his eyes widened. "Hey, what if your scar is magnified when you go on TV tomorrow?"

"What scar?" Pat said. He looked curiously at Javier. "You have a scar?"

Javier self-consciously rubbed his cheek. That zigzag scar was visible under his right eye. He felt worse as Pat studied it for a long moment.

"Shoot, that's no scar!" Pat said. "Have a kidney transplant! Now that's a scar!"

They all stared at Pat again. Javier was the first one to say what they were probably all thinking. "Who do *you* know with a kidney transplant scar?"

Pat took another bite from his hamburger. He chewed slowly.

Andy's dark eyebrows tilted as he stared at Pat. "You say something weird like that but don't explain it. What's up with that?"

"What's it to you?" Pat said in a gruff voice and took another bite.

Javier saw Andy draw in a breath and knew from experience his friend was losing his patience. Were Andy and Pat going to start a fight over nothing?

It was Mr. Quintanilla's sudden appearance at the end of the table that changed everyone's next move. Pat put down his burger. Andy stopped tapping the spoon. Ignacio sat up like someone shoved a board down his shirt. Javier felt a million ants scrambling over his feet.

The Dean of Students seemed to tower above the table top. He wore a striped dress shirt and navy blue tie. He placed his big hands on his hips and lowered his head to fix a pointed stare right at Pat and Javier's side of the table. "I understand you two are going to be the first team on Guardian TV tomorrow morning."

"Yes, Sir, that's right," Javier said. At the same time, he jabbed his elbow into Pat's thick ribcage. He noticed Pat's face starting to melt into that blank expression of his, but Javier jabbed him again. Hard.

Pat grunted, but then he raised his chin and said to Mr. Quintanilla in a surprisingly clear voice, "I guess Mr. Seneca told you about us."

"No. Dylan Romo told me." He looked from Pat to Javier. "And what kind of team will the two of you make?"

"The best kind," Pat said, echoing Dylan's words with the same bragging tone.

Javier wanted to strangle Pat. He tried to sound less cocky than his TV partner when he said, "We're going to try our best, Mr. Quintanilla."

"Do that, Mr. Ávila. You and Mr. Berlanga here will set the tone of this program from day one. Everyone in this school watches and learns from you two." One hand whipped from his hip and Mr. Q. pointed directly at Javier and Pat. "I don't understand why a new teacher would choose sophomores over seniors, but you two got selected first string. There's a lot of time and money invested in this new equipment, gentlemen. Do better than your best!"

Javier felt a large boulder drop on his shoulders. He struggled to sit still, his back stiff against the cafeteria chair. "Yes, Sir."

Mr. Quintanilla nodded at all of them, turned his tall frame away, and walked down the side of the cafeteria.

Andy was the first one to speak. "Ha-ha! No pressure! It's like a spy movie with a ticking bomb."

Ignacio picked up his fruit cup and placed it on Javier's tray. "You can do this, Jack—uh—Javier. Remember, just be Mr. Cool." Then he looked at Pat as if he was studying a difficult math problem. "I hope you got his back, Berlanga. There's no falling asleep on TV or pretending you can't talk. Our buddy here needs *you* to step up."

Javier looked at Pat, wishing he knew the guy better, could trust him and depend on him like he could his two best friends. He wanted more time to plan for the bumps in the road. Javier didn't want to wipe out again, especially in front of the whole school.

Pat had picked up his hamburger and looked ready to take another bite. Instead, he turned to Javier and said, "If you need a ride to the game Friday night, my sister can take us. I know where you live. It's no problem."

Javier waited for Andy to say something stupid about getting a ride with Feliz Berlanga, but Andy just nodded. "Cool! You'll be at the game." Then he started tapping on his tray again. "It's about time, right, Ignacio?"

But his friend still watched Pat. Under a sweaty brow, Ignacio's dark eyes could have given Mr. Q some competition in a Most Intimidating Glare contest.

Javier tried to bring Ignacio back to a better mood by saying, "You realize if the freshmen don't perform well at half-time, Mr. Q's ticking bomb might be sitting in *your* lap next."

"You, me, and Andy . . . we can handle the pressure." He raised one eyebrow, still focused on the guy sitting across from him. "What about you, Pat?"

Pat didn't blink an eye. He pointed at Ignacio with his burger as he said, "You're going to have to wait and see what happens tomorrow, just like everyone else."

When Javier entered Mr. Seneca's room after school, he expected to see Kenny standing beside the camera untangling cords. However the sight of his new English teacher, Ms. Maloney, adjusting the camera onto the tripod made him stop and look around for other surprises —like the principal, Brother Lendell, standing behind Landry and Steve at the computers and listening to Mr. Seneca give directions. And who expected Brother Calvin to be sitting beside Pat in the desk area shifting white note cards around on the table like puzzle pieces?

Javier slowly dropped his backpack on the nearest table and walked toward the desk area. He noticed the two microphones already positioned on it. "Am I late? I walked as fast as I could from chemistry class."

Pat shook his head. "No, the rest of us have Brother Lendell's theology class last period."

"Is that why he's in here?" Javier asked, feeling his stomach twist and turn at the extra stress that comes when your school principal's in the room. "To watch us?"

"Yeah. Kenny told him what we were doing after school. We set up pretty quick, didn't we? I put out the microphones but nothing's turned on yet." He was still looking down at the cards in front of him. Some had typed words, and others were handwritten sentences.

"What are the cards for?" Javier asked.

"These are your note cards for tomorrow," Brother Calvin said. "I gathered up the announcements in the front office and put them in a better format." One long finger pointed at a card in the middle of the table. "You must start with this announcement. It's the most important."

"Then it should come later," Pat answered and looked up at Javier. "The guys are still going to be shocked that announcements are on TV. They won't hear the first couple things we say, right, Javier?"

"I disagree." Brother Calvin spoke up before Javier could respond. "I watch the news every night. I've seen the newscasters start with what they call 'the top story of the hour.' This financial aid deadline is very important to the seniors. It needs to be announced first."

Javier frowned, wondering why Ol' Calavera thought he was in charge. Shouldn't he and Pat be working on the order of announcements? He tried not to sound annoyed. "Thanks for your help, Brother Calvin. Pat and I can handle this job, can't we, Pat?"

Pat nodded before he stared at the older man and said, "Actually, you're in Javier's chair. Could you sit someplace else?"

Javier knew he couldn't laugh but he wanted to.

"That was rude, Mr. Berlanga, but I'm a man who knows how to take a hint." Brother Calvin stood up and gave a quick look to both boys. "I still don't understand this pairing. I expected Javier in front of the camera right away, but you, Mr. Berlanga? I'm slightly disappointed by Mr. Seneca's choice to be honest."

Pat's shoulders stiffened against the chair. There was no mistaking the dark glint of hurt shining in Pat's eyes. The unwarranted cruelty made Javier angry. He spoke without thinking about good manners. "Pat and I might not be everyone's first choice, but that doesn't mean we can't do a helluva job." He ignored Brother Calvin's narrow glare. "You'll have to wait and see what happens tomorrow, just like everyone else."

When Pat heard his own words echoed, his eyebrows lifted. Quickly he stood up beside the school counselor and said, "Thanks for your help, Brother Calvin. Javier and I will take it from here."

The man didn't look at either of them as he stepped away from the desk. He wandered toward the computer area, leaving Javier with an odd taste of relief and worry in his mouth. He couldn't wait for the first practice, first broadcast, first *everything* to be over and done with.

Ignoring an itchy tingle inside his shoes, Javier motioned for both of them to sit down. "Okay, Pat, so what do we have for announcements?"

"The usual crap." Pat picked up a nearby card. "No wonder everyone falls asleep during announcements. I never cared until I saw these. They're so boring!"

Javier grabbed a couple of cards, read them over quickly, and said, "Well, we don't have to be *Entertainment Nightly*. We're supposed to get the word to the students. That's all." He sighed. "I just hope our first broadcast isn't a gigantic flop."

Pat crumpled the card in his hand. "If you think we're going to blow it, you might as well quit now." He gave Javier a harsh, angry glare. "I don't plan to look stupid on school TV, so you better get on board with me! I got your back. Do you have mine?"

"Yeah . . . yes," Javier said slowly. Except for the mention of Feliz, he had never seen Pat so riled up. He blinked at his partner as if seeing him for the first time.

Sounds of female laughter made them both turn and look at the camera. Ms. Maloney had laughed at something Kenny had said. Kenny looked like he had scored a three-point shot. He casually draped his arm over the camera and grinned. "Yeah, it's really true. You need to come to the basketball games and watch me play."

Javier didn't know Kenny well, but he could recognize a snake charmer when he saw one. He suddenly felt Pat's elbow poke him.

"Hey, you missed the *real* top story of the hour," Pat said. "I think there's something cooking between Mr. Seneca and Ms. Maloney. She walks in after school and he tells everyone she has experience with media equipment and wants to help get Guardian TV started off on the right foot. Then Mr. Seneca turns all goofy and actually makes a joke about not having two good feet and needing one of hers."

Javier's eyes widened. "He said that in front of Brother Lendell and Brother Calvin?"

"No. They came in later. Just us guys from the broadcasting class heard it." Pat gave a wicked smile as he flattened out the card he had crumpled. "Maybe we'll be writing a wedding announcement before the school year is over."

At that moment, Ms. Maloney called out, "Smile, guys! The cameras are working now. Kenny and I have you in our view."

Pat over-gritted his teeth toward Ms. Maloney like a cartoon character in a dentist's chair.

Javier nudged him and said, "If you and I don't get serious, we'll soon be writing our own obituaries."

Pat replied, "Hey, they'd be a whole lot more interesting than these announcements from Brother Calavera."

Everybody in the room stared with gaping expressions at the desk area. Unfortunately, Ms. Maloney had turned on the microphones too, and for Javier and Pat, this discovery was not funny.

CHAPTER SIX

Fear dried out Javier's throat, burned down his body, crackled across his feet.

Kenny's fingers above the camera signaling: Five . . .

Oh man, Oh man! St. Peter, pray for me!

Four . . .

It's happening. Don't screw up! Don't screw up!

Three . . .

Stare at the camera. Don't look at the guys watching you.

Two . . .

Breathe, breathe.

One!

"Good morning. I'm Javier Ávila. Welcome to Guardian TV and the new version of the morning announcements for Saint Peter's High School here in San Antonio, Texas." He felt like the man in the iron mask as he turned his head toward Pat. *Was he awake?*

Sitting up straight in the chair beside Javier in the desk area, Pat stared into the camera with an easy smile. "Good morning! I'm Patricio Berlanga. You are now asked to stand for the morning prayers and the Pledge of Allegiance."

Using the few seconds it took for students in Mr. Seneca's room to stand up, Landry used the computer to switch the image on the television screen from Javier and Pat to an image of a crucifix. With a slow and steady reverence, Javier read the prayer Brother Lendell had provided yesterday. Then the image on the screen switched to an American flag while Pat read the Pledge of Allegiance in a somber, respectful way.

Silently, Javier counted *one two three four five*, giving students time to sit back down before he started reading the first announcement. He began speaking, his voice trembling with every word. Out of the corner of his eye, Javier saw Mr. Seneca's long arm pointing back and forth from the television to the guys on the computers. Javier slowed his words but didn't stop because Mr. Seneca had warned them at yesterday's practice if the camera was turned on, not to stop talking, no matter what happened. Javier barely finished the first announcement with, "Tickets for the varsity game are now on sale in the business office. Be there to cheer on our champion Guardians."

Pat's voice interrupted quickly. "I know you are still seeing the flag as my buddy Javier is talking. This is one of our new visual images that we can show during the morning announcements. We hope to get digital pictures from the game, all the student activities, and of course, pictures of our cheerleaders! You don't want to just stare at two guys in broadcasting class for five minutes, do you?"

The guys in the classroom laughed but stopped with the next breath when Mr. Seneca slashed his hand across his throat to signal silence. The stern glare he gave the upperclassmen watching and sitting behind Kenny reminded everyone that audio in the room was sensitive to the slightest noise. He had repeated that warning a dozen times the past two days, even saying he was helpless to move and help when the camera started rolling because he knew his crutches made too much noise.

Javier saw Kenny circle his fingers above the camera again, and Pat never missed a beat when he started the next announcement they were supposed to read. As Pat read about the deadline for seniors to mail their college financial aid packets, he sounded enthusiastic and interested in what he was reading. Javier was so impressed he almost forgot to read the next announcement himself, but he read on cue. He tried to sound like he was reading out loud from the most fascinating information ever written.

The whole experience lasted about three minutes, and Javier would never call it "fun," but as Pat ended the broadcast with, "And there you have it! Today's announcements—live! See you tomorrow, Guardians!" Javier felt a swell of pride in the first *ever* broadcast on the school network. He pushed away the nervous worries about doing the whole thing again tomorrow.

"And we're off the air!" Mr. Seneca announced loudly. The guys sitting behind Kenny started clapping and cheering.

Javier grinned at Pat, who had released a sigh that lifted his shoulders up and down with the weight of what they had just done and done well.

"Good save, Berlanga!" Kenny called out. "I didn't know you could think that fast.".

"You made it seem like we wanted to leave the flag image on the monitor," Landry called out from his seat at the computers. "You turned our screw-up into a good thing. Way to go!"

Pat just shrugged and moved his chair back from the desk. "Any of you would have done the same thing." He stood up and looked down at Javier. "You sounded a little nervous when we started. You okay, now?"

"Sure," Javier answered, although he didn't feel as calm as Pat looked. He still felt impressed and surprised by Pat's ease and enthusiasm in front of the camera. Who would have guessed the guy who slept in class had a knack for public speaking?

"Not bad, not bad," Mr. Seneca said as he slowly walked up to the desk area. "You two did well for the first go 'round. We've got a lot more technical areas to smooth out, but we're off to a good start, guys."

Dylan waved off the teacher's compliment. He raised his chest like he had scored the first touchdown. "Just wait 'til the seniors get on TV, then you'll really see something special."

Omar spoke up. "And we won't have any screw-ups, that's for sure."

Mr. Seneca frowned at the three senior football players before he shifted on his crutches, turning his back on them. "Javier, Pat, you two will be our on-camera team through Labor Day weekend. That will give us time for the students to get used to our program and time for everyone in the class to learn the routine." He turned toward the juniors and seniors sitting together in the middle of the classroom. "The next pair on television is going to audition for the job. Since you're all in football, you'll need to practice reading well on your own time. If you guys aren't as good as these two, you'll sit the bench."

"That's not fair!" one of the juniors said. "Football or no football, we shouldn't have to just sit back and watch all semester. Why can't I run a camera or work the computer?"

"Want a job? Then you need to get off your butt and watch and learn from the sophomores during the broadcast," Mr. Seneca replied. "You need to ask questions, learn the routine. Think you can do as well as the guys putting in the practice after school?" Without waiting for an answer, he turned and started walking toward the teacher's desk.

No one said anything to Mr. Seneca, but every upperclassman glared at Javier and Pat. Even Kenny—superstar basketball player that he was—got the mean looks.

For a moment, Javier felt intimidated, but he decided not to let a bunch of football players ruin his good mood. He stood up and followed Pat out of the desk area. They sat down in their usual seats as Mr. Seneca prepared the equipment for everyone to watch the broadcast on tape.

As the media class watched the playback, Javier wanted to hide his eyes. Not only did his skin look yellow, but his ears stuck out. There seemed to be a shadow over his forehead that looked like he had a horn. And his voice! Javier hated that he sounded like a cartoon character. Pat was right—it *was* Bugs and Daffy on TV!

No sooner had the tape stopped when Pat spoke up. "Okay, all that white in the background has got to go. Javier and I look like a pair of sock puppets."

Everyone started laughing, even Mr. Seneca. He turned off the television and maneuvered himself to face the class. "Pat's right. We need to add something in the background. Any ideas?"

"We could get the cheerleaders to draw posters," Ram suggested. "We could hang them up like they do in the main hall."

Javier shook his head. "We can't have words behind us. It would be too distracting."

"Ooooh, distracting! That's an SAT word, right?" Dylan said with a nasty laugh that raised a pitch after Omar offered his hand for a low-five.

Javier ignored them and said, "On TV news, I've seen an outline of San Antonio."

Mr. Seneca looked at the students. "Maybe we could use markers on the whiteboard and outline a landscape."

"That'll take a long time to draw," one of the juniors said. "It's a big space."

"Spray paint would be faster than markers," Pat said.

"You talking about graffiti on school property?" Omar slouched in his chair. "Like Brother Lendell is going to go for that! Man, sophomores are stupid!"

"No, you moron. I'm talking about spray paint on sheets of paper," Pat said, his annoyance with Omar obvious in his tone. "It would be something like that breakaway between the goal posts that you football players run through."

"Pat, are you volunteering to draw an image for the background?" Mr. Seneca asked.

Javier expected Pat to say, "No way," but he didn't.

"I know someone who can do the job with my help. Javier, he can help us too. It might take us all weekend, but I think we can bring in a backdrop for Monday's show," Pat answered in a fairly confident tone.

But Javier wasn't eager to volunteer to draw something to be shown to the whole school. He turned around and gave his TV partner a frown. Unfazed by the look, Pat clapped him on the shoulder. "Trust me, Javier, we can do this."

Javier's feet started itching and didn't stop the rest of the day.

Pat explained his ideas as they walked out of the class-room after first period. "My sister Feliz is a very good artist."

"Feliz?" Javier said, feeling an unexpected rush of excitement.

"Yeah. She can sketch landscapes, draw faces, all kinds of images."

Javier shifted his backpack over his shoulder as they walked down the steps of Mr. Seneca's classroom. He smiled when he thought of spending time with Feliz. "Do you think she'll help us?"

"Sure! She just needs to draw an outline and then we can fill in the blanks." Pat nodded like he was thinking out loud. "You and I can talk to her when she picks us up from school."

"Us?" Javier stopped smiling when he thought of rid-ing home with Feliz Berlanga, the Demon Driver. "Uh, I asked my dad to pick me up today after practice."

"Call him at lunch and tell him you've got a ride," Pat said as they entered the main building. "We'll talk later. Got a test in geometry. Bye!" He hurried off toward the stairs, and Javier made his way to English class.

Ms. Maloney stood by the door to her classroom. She gave Javier a little grin. "Not bad for day one, Javier. By this time next week, it will all be no big deal."

He gave his teacher a half-hearted smile, and thought, *Yeah, right.*

Both Ignacio and Andy gave him a thumbs-up when they took their seats. Other sophomores before and after class commented positively, so Javier graciously accept-ed their praise, although he also knew each broadcast had the potential to go wrong too. He couldn't ever imagine thinking, "no big deal," when it came to talking on television.

When Pat showed up at the lunch table where Javier, Ignacio, and Andy were eating lunch and talking about the first half-time show of the school year, he had a tablet under one arm. "We need to talk about the outline, Javier, so we have something to show Feliz."

"Feliz?" Andy raised an eyebrow as he stared at Javier. "What are you doing with Feliz? Does it involve a launch sequence?"

"Shut up, Andy," Javier said quietly through gritted teeth. Then he said louder, "Mr. Seneca thinks we need a colorful background so it doesn't look so blank behind us when we broadcast the announcements. Pat says Feliz could help us draw it. We're going to talk to her after school today."

Andy and Ignacio exchanged wolf-like grins. Javier knew he needed to get control of the conversation before they said something that made Pat mad. "If I can sit and listen to you two talk band all the time, I think it's only fair that you guys help Pat and me think of something really good for the background."

Pat sat down and opened up a notebook on the table. "I already made some rough pictures. I had some free time during fourth period."

"Wow! You can draw," Ignacio said. He chuckled. "And I thought your best talent was sleeping through Sister Madeline's lectures about the Holy Land."

They all laughed; everyone swore the old nun's voice could shatter glass.

Andy tapped a pencil on the paper near a sketch of the main building. "This one looks good, like the real thing."

"You put all the important buildings into this city out-line," Ignacio commented, pointing to a sketch on the opposite page.

Javier nodded and then got an idea. "Last summer, I saw a city mural at the mall. I remember pointing it out to my little nephew and told him, 'See that space there? That's where my school is. It's downtown too.' Why don't you paint St. Peter's where it belongs in the downtown landscape?"

Pat nodded. "I like that idea a lot, Javier." His brown eyes brightened with a grin.

"And the smart guy does it again! Isn't it great to have smart friends, Pat?" Andy said. He pointed his pencil at Pat and then remarked, "Our friend Javier here is the best of the best. Your drop-dead gorgeous sister would be very safe with our man Javier."

Ignacio let out a squawk then covered his mouth. Javier quickly turned to Pat, ready to apologize for Andy's comments. However, Pat had grabbed the pencil and pulled it from Andy's fingers. "He's definitely better for my sister than you are, Cardona. All the drumming you do with pencils and forks would drive her nuts!" He dropped the pencil and nudged Javier with his elbow. "I'm going to be a real *compadre*. I'll let *you* ask Feliz to help us with the background, okay?"

Javier felt as if he just drank lava. The others grinned and chuckled at the obvious discomfort they had caused. He almost surrendered to the embarrassment, but Pat's response inspired Javier to step up and take a chance. Hadn't he already conquered the first day of speaking on live television? Why couldn't he talk to a girl like Feliz Berlanga too?

Taking in a breath to strengthen his confidence, Javier finally said, "Fine, Pat. I'll talk to Feliz. I'll turn on the charm and convince her to help us."

Ignacio reached out and rapped his knuckles on Pat's notebook. "Okay, now here's the *really* important part. Does Feliz have some hot-looking friends for the rest of us? There's a Homecoming dance in October and none of us have dates."

Wednesday's after-school broadcast practice went smoother. Everyone seemed much more relaxed now that the "first" program was over. Brother Calvin showed up again with his white note cards and demands, and as Javier and Pat walked toward the back parking lot to find Feliz's car, they discussed ways to keep the school counselor out of their way.

"Instead of Brother Calavera's delivery service, one of us could go pick up announcements in the front office," Javier said. He shifted his heavy backpack between his shoulders, trying to take the pressure off his back.

Pat slowed his pace to walk along side Javier. "Too bad we can't use a voicemail system. If you want to make an announcement, call this number."

"Hey!" Javier snapped his fingers. "Why couldn't the clubs and the administration email the announcements to the classroom? Mr. Seneca said that eventually we're going to be reading off computer slides instead of cards, right? Won't it save time if the text's already typed?"

Pat smiled like he felt happy. "Good idea! You know, I'm really starting to like this!"

"Like what?"

"Hanging out with a smart guy! I'm used to the dummies like me in class."

"Pat, you're not a dummy—not the way you think quickly on your feet! You saved everyone from getting embarrassed today. Then you stepped up and volunteered to draw a background so we don't look like—what did you call us? Sock puppets? That's funny!" He slugged Pat's shoulder. "You are way too clever to call yourself a dummy."

Pat shrugged and then pointed. "There's the car. Let's hope Feliz is in a good mood. She can be moody like my dad and say NO to everything."

Javier turned his thoughts to Pat's sister. If the awful August heat wasn't already making him sweat like a marathon runner, facing a pretty girl like Feliz Berlanga would have him soaked to the bone. If only he could talk to her after he had showered or with a cool autumn breeze in the background. Then he wouldn't feel like a grungy, awkward idiot. Where was that "Mr. Cool" guy? Taking a vacation?

As usual, Feliz had the car engine running. Heavy metal music battered the tinted car windows. Pat led the way to the passenger side and opened up the front door to a woman screeching over the music that men were liars and cowards.

Pat yelled, "Hey! Need to talk!" He reached into the car and the music volume suddenly dropped to background noise. "We need to give Javier a ride home again, but there's something he wants to talk to you about, so he's going to sit up front, okay?"

Javier's mouth dropped open, never expecting to sit close to a girl he liked. At the same time, he was worried about riding in the front seat and witnessing firsthand the swerving, speeding, and jerking that came along with Feliz's driving. If it hadn't been for the shove that Pat gave him with his backpack, Javier might have stood like a melting statue in the parking lot. Instead, he slid his own backpack onto the thick carpet and climbed into the front seat.

He turned to Feliz and managed to say, "Hi," and felt even more uncomfortable when she gave him a little smile. She wore black sunglasses, so he couldn't tell much.

"Hi yourself! It's Javier, right?"

He nodded as the back door closed and Pat called out, "He's the guy who lives near Welita."

"I remember." Feliz moved some of her dark hair behind her ear. "It's that old house with the white gate. Welita's house is way old too."

Javier raised an eyebrow. "Actually my great-grandfather built our house in the 1940s. Many homes in that area have historical significance."

Feliz expressed a belittling laugh. "Not Welita's house. It's a tired, run-down shack that should have been torn down years ago. The only thing *historical* is that footed bathtub of hers." She adjusted her sunglasses and then shifted the car into reverse.

Javier immediately reached for his seatbelt and checked twice that it was secure. He grabbed the car door handle firmly with his right hand.

Feliz managed to back out of the parking space without hitting anything, although the seatbelt strangled Javier three times as she sped up, braked hard, and ker-thumped, ker-jumped over the speed bumps in the parking lot. She continued to act oblivious to the car horns as she made her too-wide turn into the busy street around the school. Once she straightened out the car, she had no choice but to slow down and ease along with the rush-hour traffic.

Now that talking wouldn't be a distraction or put their lives in danger, Javier wondered how to start up a conversation. With his sisters, he started with a compliment, but what could he say to a girl in a school uniform? And the throbbing music in the car wasn't something he wanted to mention either, so he decided to make her brother look good instead. "You should have heard Pat this morning. He sounded like a pro on our first broadcast!"

"Broadcast? What are you talking about?" She sighed loudly as the signal light turned red and her vehicle was still eight cars away from the intersection.

Having been raised in a family who took an interest in everything Javier did, he was puzzled by Feliz's ignorance. "It's our new elective: Broadcast Media. Didn't Pat tell you we're broadcasting morning announcements on school TV?"

She shrugged. "Pat doesn't say much. He's asleep all the time."

Javier looked in the backseat. Sure enough, Pat's head leaned against the headrest and his eyes were closed. Javier shook his head. If he was going to get Feliz's help, it looked like he was flying solo.

"Pat and I were the first pair of students to read on TV," Javier said, now giving the pretty girl in the driver's seat his full attention. "Pat and I didn't know each other well, but we ended up making a decent team. Pat reads well and he stayed calm, even when one of the guys goofed on visuals."

"That's so weird. He never wanted to be on TV before."

"What do you mean?"

Feliz took off her sunglasses and looked at Javier. "Don't you know who our father is? Haven't you ever heard of Berlanga Motors? My dad does TV commercials all the time. I've done a few, too, but Pat and my mom never wanted to do them."

Now that he could see her sparkling brown eyes, Javier tried to maintain steady eye contact. He pretended they were already friends and asking her a favor would be easy. "Now that Pat is taking this elective, maybe he'll do a commercial with your dad," Javier told her. "But right now, we need to worry about how we come across on school TV. Pat had an idea to create a backdrop to cover up the whiteboards behind us during the broadcast. He told me you're a good artist, and we hoped you could help us sketch an outline of the city."

Before she could answer, the light changed. Feliz put on her sunglasses and drove up so close to the car in front of her that Javier could read the labels on the boxes in the backseat. Feliz kept up the tailgating and slipped through a yellow-to-red light, only to be stopped again by another light several cars away. She sighed again and reached for the button on the dashboard, probably to turn up the music.

"Feliz, if you draw the outline, we can paint in the rest of the picture." Javier quickly spoke up before tortured voices started screaming inside the car. "Pat sketched an idea that should be easy to follow. You can help us, right?"

Her fingernails tapped an impatient *click-click-click* on the steering wheel. "I have a lot of homework to do tonight."

"No problem. We don't need the backdrop until Monday. We can work on it over the weekend. I'll just walk over to your grandmother's house."

He could see her frown even around the sunglasses. "No, you can't do it at Welita's. There's no room. Besides, Pat's airbrushes are at home."

"No problem. I can get a ride over to your house." Javier smiled at his quick responses. Every word was coming out so easy now.

A voice called out from the backseat. "Javier can just stay over at our house after the football game Friday night. We're going to give him a ride anyway."

Javier whipped around and stared into the backseat. Even with his eyes closed, Pat's smirk revealed his self-satisfaction. Had Pat *really* been asleep, or was he only pretending so Javier had to do all the talking? But it was hard to stay irritated with the guy who just created a good solution to any final obstacles.

Javier looked back at Feliz and smiled. "I guess we could start Saturday morning at your house."

He didn't anticipate Feliz's quick mood change. She sat up straight and looked into the rearview mirror, no doubt at her brother. "You just assume I'll help you with your dumb painting and that I *want* to be your chauffeur, Pat. What's in it for me?"

The voice from the backseat spoke smoothly, as if he was on camera. "You need a friend like Javier. He can help you pass chemistry. He's the smartest guy in the school."

"Really!" Feliz's shoulders slowly relaxed against the leather car seat as she turned to Javier. A wide smile appeared beneath the sunglasses. He was grateful they covered her eyes. Would they filter out the flaming red-ness of his face too?

"Okay, fine! It's a deal," she said before a car horn honked twice behind them. Traffic began moving, and Feliz turned up the music too loud to talk anymore.

Harsh base guitars and shrieking voices shook the car. The singer screamed about love *and* hate, pleasure *and* pain. Some girl had turned him into a real mess!

But Javier could see why that poor guy wailed about different reactions to one woman. Spending more time with a beauty like Feliz could be amazing, but helping her with chemistry could be a disaster. What if Feliz's science skills were as bad as her driving? What if she mixed chemicals like she ignored traffic laws?

He leaned back into the passenger seat, reset the seat-belt across his body, and tried to remember what he already knew about unstable formulas.

CHAPTER SEVEN

Friday night, Javier's dad looked relaxed and comfortable on the living room sofa. He wore a faded Spurs T-shirt, a pair of gray shorts, and some old sandals on his feet. He took off his reading glasses and said to his son, "Are you moving into a college dorm already?"

Javier walked past his father. He knew his collared shirt looked too preppy for a game, but he wanted to look older. He dropped his sleeping bag and his backpack by the front door before he said, "After the game, I'm going to stay over at Pat Berlanga's house. We're working on a school project tomorrow."

"Oh, yes, that's right. But if you're going to watch football, why do you smell so pretty?" He grinned at his son.

Javier ignored the tease and said, "I just showered, that's all."

His dad chuckled. "If you say so."

Now Javier wondered if he had overdone the cologne, but he had wanted to get Feliz's attention, especially if they sat together at the game.

The doorbell rang, and Javier was quick to open the door. "Hi, Pat." Only it wasn't just Pat standing there, but also Feliz and another pretty girl with long red hair, who appeared to be crying. "Oh! Hello, is something wrong?"

Feliz frantically pushed herself inside the house. Javier stumbled backwards like an idiot. No men's cologne was going to help him now.

She had pulled the red-haired girl inside with her. "Brittany's having trouble with her contacts. Can she use your bathroom?"

"Yes, sure." Javier gestured behind him. "It's down the hall. I'll show you."

But the girls didn't wait; they just rushed out, leaving Javier holding out his arm.

"Don't worry. They'll find it," Javier's dad said. He had put aside his book and stood up. "Women have special radar for bathrooms. It's part of their genetic disposition."

"Hi, Javier." Pat closed the door behind him and then shook his head. "Sorry about the stampede. Brittany's been having fits all the way over here. Man, I'm glad I only have one sister."

"Be *very* glad," Javier said. "I have *two* sisters. When they get together, they make us double crazy."

"I usually wear a referee whistle when my daughters are home," his dad said and offered his hand to Pat. "You must be Pat Berlanga. I'm Marc Ávila."

Pat shook his hand. "Hello, Mr. Ávila. I'm glad to meet you."

"Javier said you two have been seen on school TV the past three days. I asked him to steal one of the teacher's tapes so we can see the program, but my son is too honest to do it, I think." He grinned. "Tell me, Pat, do you have any larceny in you?"

Pat blinked rapidly. "I don't know."

"My dad kids around a lot. He doesn't want you to do anything bad, Pat." Javier sighed. Andy and Ignacio were used to Javier's dad, but Pat looked confused. "Besides, if

I got suspended because *my father* wanted me to steal something from a teacher, my mom would kill us both! Right, Dad?"

"Okay, okay." He started laughing and waved toward the sofa. "Pat, come and sit down."

They started to move, but Javier's mom came into the living room. She wore a casual yellow shirt and black shorts. Her eyebrows were raised above laughing eyes. "I'm sure there's a perfectly good explanation why two pretty girls just ran down the hall, one of them laughing and one of them crying." Then she noticed Pat and said, "Hello. You must be Pat Berlanga. It's so nice to finally meet you. I'm Nivia Ávila." She extended her hand and shook Pat's. "I guess you and Javier know about the girls?"

"One's my sister, and the other is her friend with contact lens problems." Pat answered. He shrugged at Javier's mom. "Sorry. They needed to use your bathroom, Mrs. Ávila."

"Oh, goodness! Anyone can use our bathroom. I just wish it was cleaner. I'll start doing some cleaning tomorrow. We're having a big party next week for Javier's birthday," his mom replied. She turned to Pat and asked about his grandmother. Had she lived in the neighborhood a long time? Where was her house? Then the girls came back into the room, and more introductions were made. His mom asked the girls which school they attended. She asked Feliz where she bought her sandals. She asked Brittany about her contact lenses. She questioned Pat again, "How do you like your new teachers this year?"

After an embarrassed sigh, Javier said, "Mom, we need to go. I promised Andy and Ignacio I'd be there for the pre-game concert."

"Who's driving tonight?" Javier's mom asked as she walked them to the door.

"Feliz is driving," Javier told her and prayed she wouldn't start with more questions. "She's given me a ride home before, and it's still daylight outside."

"Do you know where the stadium is?" she asked Feliz.

The girl frowned. "Uh, yeah, it's at the school. I know where *that* is."

"We need to go!" Javier repeated and opened the front door. "Bye, Mom. Bye, Dad."

"Javier, will you call me if you need a ride home? And be sure to thank Mrs. Berlanga for letting you stay over," his mom added. "Do you have some 'goody clothes'? Do you need any money? Did you remember your allergy pills?"

Javier wanted to plop his sleeping bag over his head. He just nodded and felt grateful his parents didn't follow him out to the porch.

The girls giggled all the way down the sidewalk. Javier knew they were laughing at him.

"Gosh, my parents!" Javier said to no one in particular. "Could my mom get any more embarrassing?" He fumbled with the sleeping bag, almost dropping it. Pat caught it and swung it under his arm.

"Your mom's nice." Pat smiled at Javier. "I know a lot of guys who'd love to have a mom like yours."

"Not unless they like to be interrogated every day by the Mom's Bureau of Investigations," Javier replied.

The football game was a disappointment in every way. As soon as they arrived, Feliz and Brittany ran off with their girlfriends to the other side of the stadium. The half-time show was canceled after a man in the stands complained of chest pains. Two police cars, a fire truck, and an ambulance blocked the holding area where the band members and flag leaders waited to go on the field. Then the team from St. Gabriel's trampled across the Guardians, leaving no chance for a touchdown. The final score was 21–0. The only good thing was that Feliz's scary driving didn't kill any of them going to or from the stadium.

After the game, she drove a long time down the interstate. Pat and Javier had seen almost half the movie on the backseat monitors when Feliz finally exited and drove toward a gated community outside the city limits. The winding streets led from hillsides to cul-de-sacs, with a variety of two- and three-story homes and carefully crafted lawns and gardens.

Javier recognized the neighborhood immediately as one where his father's company had built houses. He remembered many summer nights when his father would drive Javier and his mom to a new subdivision in the city and proudly show them what Ávila Construction had built. Once Javier had asked his dad, "Why don't *we* live in one of these beautiful houses?" and his father said, "We live in a house built by my grandfather. Nothing is more beautiful, Son . . . nothing."

Finally, Feliz drove onto a cement path and parked in front of a three-car garage. Javier got out and stared at a modern palace with stone columns and large windows. The girls ran ahead while Pat and Javier took his things from the car. The guys walked up thick granite steps to the open front doors, illuminated by a pair of ornamental lanterns. The girls had rushed up the winding staircase that filled the entryway like a grand waterfall. The rooms had high ceilings, and all the furniture was perfectly matched, but Javier thought he had walked into an exclusive store, not somebody's home.

"Are you hungry?" Pat asked. He left Javier's sleeping bag on the first stair. "Let's see what's in the fridge."

Javier put down his gym bag and followed Pat behind the stairs, through a narrow door, and into a large kitchen. Every appliance was polished chrome, and the cabinets were painted with bright shades of turquoise and brown. A variety of painted clay bowls decorated the countertops and the narrow wooden table with six chairs near the windows. He had never seen such a bare kitchen. Didn't anyone cook or eat in there?

Pat opened up one side door of the tall chrome refrigerator. "Ugh! Way too much diet soda, tofu, and brown rice. But I do see bread, cheese, and—" He paused and unwrapped something in aluminum foil. "Bingo! We got turkey. Want a sandwich?"

"Sure," Javier said. He joined Pat and helped pull out from the refrigerator what they needed for sandwiches. "Man, it's too bad about the game. I'm going to hate announcing the score on Monday morning."

"Even worse, we have to sit in a classroom with angry football players all week." Pat squirted brown mustard on bread. "Poor Dylan and Omar. The defense just ran all over them. And Ram? Whoa! Did he eat dirt all night or what?"

"I feel bad for Ignacio and Andy. I know the band guys practiced their feet off. Lousy breaks for everyone. Too bad about the guy with the heart attack." Javier reached for two slices of bread. "I wonder who he was."

They talked about ways to word Monday's broadcast in a more positive way as they finished making the sandwiches. Pat found two regular sodas in a small refrigerator under the sink and led the way up to his bedroom.

With such thick carpeting, Javier couldn't even hear their footsteps. "Where are your parents?" he asked as they reached the top of the stairs.

Pat shrugged. "Mom's probably in her room reading or sleeping. My dad goes to a lot of meetings. People are always asking him to be on the board of this or that club. He eats it up, that whole big-shot personality."

Javier glanced around at his surroundings and felt a strange chill down his back. He couldn't even sense the presence of Feliz and Brittany in the house—the place was that big and felt *that* empty.

Pat's room, however, had the lived-in comfort of messy and junky. His double bed was neatly made, but there were magazines on the floor, game cartridges and movie cases scattered on the desk, and his school clothes piled up near the closet. The shelves above his computer were filled with books, CD cases, and picture frames in no special order. Sports posters lined one wall, and across the room were several movie posters. It took a moment before Javier realized that every one of them had an autograph of someone famous across the bottom. They ate sandwiches, finished up a bag of chips Pat had hidden under the bed, watched a movie, and fell asleep sometime after midnight.

When Javier opened his eyes and remembered where he was, it worried him that Pat, who could fall asleep so easily in class, might not want to wake up on a Saturday morning. Luckily, Pat murmured, "Hey, you hungry?"

Javier reached for his backpack. If there weren't two pretty girls in the house, he would stay in the clothes he had slept in. He pulled out a green T-shirt and some old shorts.

"You did bring some clothes you can paint in, didn't you?" Pat said, rising up on one elbow to watch him.

"Yeah, I did. I grabbed them from the box my mom calls 'goody clothes'. Comes from a mispronunciation my big brother Eric used when he was a kid . . . never mind. I can't explain it without sounding stupid." He sat up. "Basically, it's a box where we toss worn-out T-shirts that can be still be used for dirty jobs. It comes in handy if your family is in the construction business."

"Do *you* get to build stuff?" Pat asked. He sat up and kicked his sheet off.

"Not me," Javier said, shaking his head. "My job is washing the company trucks or sweeping the job site. Nobody trusts me with tools. I'm a klutz." His face grew warm as he realized what he had said. He quickly started to fold up his sleeping bag.

"So, what kind of things does your dad build?"

Javier felt proud to say, "Big fancy houses like yours."

"No way!" Pat's face opened up with surprise. "Did your dad build our house?"

"He built many of the houses out here. I'd have to ask him."

"That's impressive, Jack. Wait 'til I tell my dad."

When they came downstairs, Javier found it odd not to smell food cooking. His mother always fixed a big breakfast on Saturdays, and it was normal to find his two brothers with some of their kids eating at the table.

They walked toward the kitchen, and the aroma of coffee hinted that someone else was awake. At the table by the kitchen windows sat a woman in a flowing purple robe decorated with swirls of colors. She had short, curly hair and dark skin and when she looked up from the newspaper she was reading, Javier could tell immediately it was Pat's mom. They had the same dark eyes and high forehead.

"Hey, Mom, this is Javier. He's going to help me with a school project," Pat said by way of an introduction. "Do we have any breakfast?"

She nodded at Javier and then looked down at her paper. "Your father hasn't left yet, Patricio. When he goes, I will fix your breakfast."

"Oh, okay. Then I'll show Javier where we can paint. Come on, Javier."

He followed Pat out of the kitchen, feeling strangely out of place in this family's house. He wanted to ask Pat why his mother didn't cook until *after* his father left but caught himself thinking too much like *his* mother with all her questions. They had just arrived back at the stairs when a thin man with wide shoulders came down. He was dressed in white slacks and a light green golf shirt. He stopped when he saw Pat and Javier. His sudden frown was identical to one Javier had seen on Feliz's face. The man had her skin tone and the same light brown eyes.

"Can't you and your friend find something presentable to wear? I know it's Saturday, but you don't have to look like you wear the same clothes you sleep in, Son."

"Dad, this is my friend, Javier Ávila. I found out his dad might have built our house. Do you know if Marc Ávila built this place?"

His father sighed. "I don't keep track of the trade workers who come and go. I do business with architects and engineers." He nodded at Javier. "I'm sure your father is a very handy man. It'll be good if you can learn his trade, Son." He raised his wrist and looked at an expensive-looking gold watch. "I've got to go. I'm golfing with the mayor this morning." He walked through the living room and disappeared.

Pat let out a long breath. "Good, he's gone. My mom can start cooking now. We can go inside the garage after I know he's had time to leave."

If Ávila humor confused Pat, then it was the Berlanga chill factor that perplexed Javier. He had never seen a family like this. Sure, his big sisters demanded a lot of attention, and finding something in common with his older brothers was hard, but they always asked Javier about his schoolwork and came for his birthday parties. Even all the teasing among them was loving and affectionate. Why was Pat's family so different?

When they returned to the kitchen, Mrs. Berlanga had folded up the newspaper and walked toward the refrigerator, coffee cup in hand.

"Do you drink coffee?" she asked Javier.

"No. Do you have milk?"

"We only have skim. Pat, get your friend a glass of milk." After that, Mrs. Berlanga didn't say another word to either of them. She stood at the stove and scrambled eggs with corn tortillas, peppers, onions, and tomatoes that smelled delicious. Meanwhile Javier asked more about the paints they would use for the backdrop and Pat described what he had in mind using a refrigerator box he had found on the curb in front of a new house down the road.

When Mrs. Berlanga set a steaming platter in the middle of the table and only two plates, Javier wondered again about the Berlangas as a family unit.

"Thank you, Mrs. Berlanga," Javier said automatically.

She said, "You're welcome," and left the room with her coffee cup.

"This looks great." Pat reached for the platter. He served himself generously.

"Your mom doesn't eat breakfast?"

"She's always on a diet. Her breakfasts come in the mail." He handed the platter to Javier. "Go for it! My mom's a good cook."

"Shouldn't we save something for Feliz and Brittany?"

"All I ever see Feliz eat is cereal that looks like seeds and twigs with berry yogurt," Pat said. "Take as much as you want, Javier."

J avier watched Feliz walk Brittany to a long maroon car and wave as it drove away. Then she wandered toward the side room off the garage set up with a rack for garden tools, a riding lawnmower, and wide cabinet where the paints were stored. This was the place where Javier and Pat had sliced through the cardboard with box cutters and had primed the cardboard with white paint. All the windows and the two sliding wood doors leading to the back yard were open for ventilation, making the work a sweaty mess and the room hot and uncomfortable. They were taking a break, sitting on the cement ramp and drinking cold water from plastic bottles that Pat had brought from the house.

Javier knew he had paint on his face. His clothes clung to him with sweat, and his legs were dusted with cardboard shavings. Could he look any worse around a pretty girl?

"Do you have some pictures you want me to follow?" Feliz looked tanned and neat as she stepped up to the white cardboard and gave it a once-over. She wore tight red shorts and a tie-dyed tank top that outlined her curves.

Oh man! It took a moment for Javier to trust his voice. "I found an image on the Internet the other night. It was a silhouette of the major city buildings."

She nodded. "That'll work. We're lucky San Antonio has an easy outline." She turned back to Javier and her lips opened with a smile. "Are you an artist?"

"I can paint a wall." Javier chuckled to himself. "I don't think I'd call that art."

Feliz nodded and then wiped her hand across her forehead. "It's way too hot to sketch out here. Pat, why don't you and Javier carry the cardboard into the garden room? Then I can draw without sweating. I'll get my laptop and meet you guys in there."

Javier watched Feliz walk away, knowing her swinging hips and the bounce of her curly ponytail would haunt his dreams for the next year.

"Hey, stop staring at my sister and help me carry this cardboard," Pat said, standing up. He tossed his empty bottle into a green recycling box near the lawnmower.

Javier stood up but avoided his friend's eyes. "Sure. Tell me what to do next."

"Do you want the truth?"

"What?" That's when Javier looked at Pat directly.

"I know you like my sister, and she talks to you like a real person, so that's good." Pat shrugged. "You're a smart guy, so impress her that way. She goes for intelligence so she can look smart too." He turned around and said, "Okay, let's hope this cardboard is dry by now."

The two of them carried the white cardboard down the ramp and across the grass to the back yard patio and deck. They walked past a shimmering swimming pool, a large brick grill, and wrought-iron deck furniture. They went through sliding glass doors that led to an enclosed room filled with plants and wall-to-wall windows. The floor was Mexican tile, and the white wicker chairs and wide ceiling fans gave the room a sense of tropical paradise. Best of all, the room was air-conditioned.

Once they leaned the cardboard against one set of windows, Javier felt way too dirty to be inside and asked for directions to the nearest bathroom. As he looked into the bathroom mirrors, and saw the paint dots across his face and the sweaty clumps of brown hair, he knew he was a lost cause. Still, he washed his face and used some water to smooth down his hair before he returned to Feliz in the garden room.

For the next hour, the three of them made a surprising good trio of workers. Javier stayed on the laptop, finding several city outlines on advertisements that Feliz could copy. Then he moved to the school Web site to get images of the buildings. She sketched what she saw onto the white cardboard while Pat decided what paints he would use. They made small talk, laughed when someone made a mistake, and discussed color and shading, making the whole job seem interesting and fun.

Some time later Feliz tossed the pencil down on the table. "I think I'm done here. The rest is up to you two." She stretched her arms above her head.

Javier tried not to stare at the tanned belly button peeking out between her shirt and shorts. "Th—thanks for all your help, Feliz."

Before she left, she stopped and looked over her shoulder at him. "You owe me some chemistry help, Javier. I'll be calling you!"

He should have grinned happily with the thought of a phone call from Feliz. Instead, he gave a phony smile to hide his worries about teaching her a science he was only learning himself this year. For the first time all day, his feet began to itch like crazy.

After they carried the whiteboard back to the garage, Pat began to show Javier how to use an airbrush. It took several false starts before they got the right pressure on the trigger and the best distance from the board.

"Pat, I'm going to screw this up," he said, feeling a slight tremble in his hand.

"No, you won't, Javier," he replied and lightly sprayed a thin blue streak above the sketches Feliz had drawn. "The great thing about airbrushes is that you work in layers. We'll paint the sky first. If you mess up, the next layer of black will cover it up."

Even though Pat encouraged him the whole time, Javier decided to let Pat do the black outlines of the buildings on his own. He sat on the riding lawnmower and was impressed by Pat's ease with the paints and his skill with the airbrushes. At the same time, Javier felt proud of his own small contribution to a piece of art that would improve the look of the broadcast. Even though it was still rough, Javier knew Mr. Seneca would like it too.

When they heard the sound of a car pulling into the driveway, Pat put down the airbrushes. "My dad's home. I can do the rest tomorrow. Let's get this place cleaned up, and then I'll drive you home in my mother's car."

Javier stood up. "You have your driver's license?"

Pat was looking down, untwisting the nozzle from the glass container of paint. "Yes. I've had it about two weeks now."

Javier continued to be surprised by his new friend. "But why don't you drive to school? Can't you just go pick out a fine car at Berlanga Motors?"

Pat's head shot up to reveal an angry frown. "Just 'cause a guy has a license doesn't mean he gets a car." He squeezed the equipment in his fists. "Do you think you're too good to ride in the backseat of my sister's *fine* car?"

His tone had turned so ugly that Javier could do nothing but take a step back. Then he got mad too. "I just asked a couple of questions. If I was out of line, just tell me. Don't chew my head off."

"Sorry." Pat turned away and walked toward a small double-sink in the corner of the room. "Help me get this place cleaned up, will you?"

Javier busied himself, picking up rags and pushing the air compressors back against the wall. He tried to understand Pat better now that he had met his parents, but having lousy parents was no excuse for dumping on friends. When he turned around and saw Pat reach for the backdrop, Javier stepped up to help him carry it. They leaned the painted cardboard against a rear wall where it wouldn't be in anyone's way. He looked directly at Pat. What happened to that talented guy he was just beginning to respect?

"I was the one out of line, Javier. Sorry." Pat shrugged his shoulders. "Let's just keep this license thing between us, okay? I don't need the guys at school giving me a hard time because I don't have a new car to drive. It's tough when the owner of Berlanga Motors is your father. " His facial expression was weighed down with so much sadness that Javier struggled to find something positive to lift Pat's mood.

That's when he glanced at the cardboard painting behind them and said, "No one's going to give you a hard time after they see this picture on the newscast, Pat. You have a real talent here. I know everyone's going to be as impressed as I am."

Pat stared at the drawing and nodded. "Thanks for saying that, Javier. You're a good guy." He started to walk off, but then he looked back. "And no matter what happens between you and my sister—just remember, it wasn't *my* fault."

CHAPTER EIGHT

Five more days, Javier thought as he stepped off the bus on Monday morning.

Sounded like a kid waiting for Christmas, but he was really a teenager sick of school bus rides and having his parents drive him everywhere. He could apply for his permanent license on Friday, his birthday. He knew there was an old truck parked in Uncle Willie's back yard that would become his in just *five more days*.

He walked across the parking lot and toward the school buildings. He heard a series of car horns, and when he looked around, Javier saw Feliz's dark car parked at the curb and Pat hopping out of it. He gestured at Javier to come over.

Grabbing a chance to see Feliz again, Javier immediately walked toward the driver's side of the Berlanga's car. When the front window slid down, he stopped and smiled at the pretty driver. "Hi, Feliz."

"Hi, Javier," she said, but her head was turned away. "I realized I don't have your number to call you about my chemistry homework. Here!"

Suddenly her hand extended from the car window. She held an expensive phone.

Javier stepped forward and took it from her. His breath sucked tight inside his chest. He stared at Feliz, uncertain what to do next.

She pulled her sunglasses down her nose and sighed. "Well, punch your number in! You don't expect me to do it, do you?"

"Sure, yeah, right," Javier murmured and looked down at the thin silver phone. He might have looked *really* stupid, except it was exactly like his sister Vivian's new phone. *Yes!* He felt very confident as he quickly punched numbers and his name into it. When would Feliz make first contact? His brain buzzed with the possibilities.

"Hey! Need some help back here!" Pat yelled out from behind the car.

"Okay!" Javier called back and slowly handed the phone to Feliz. He tried to imitate that smile Kenny had given Ms. Maloney the week before. "Call me any time, Feliz, anytime at all."

She removed her sunglasses before she took the phone from his hand. "Maybe tonight . . . " Her lips parted with a seductive smile. " . . . if you get lucky."

"Javier!" Pat yelled louder.

The dark window lifted up automatically, and if Feliz still smiled at Javier, well, he couldn't see it. He turned and quickly walked to the back of the car.

Pat had opened both back doors of the sports vehicle. He dragged the folded cardboard toward his body. "I can manage this. Just grab my backpack, okay?"

Javier reached for Pat's backpack that rested on the asphalt behind the car. "Are you sure I can't help you carry the board?"

"No. This isn't heavy—just awkward." He lifted the backdrop into his arms. "Shut the doors and follow me to Mr. Seneca's room, okay?"

As Pat moved out of the way, Javier called out, "Goodbye, Feliz!" When he heard the music go louder in the vehicle, he sighed and shut both doors. He quickly stepped up on the curb in case she backed up and ran over him with her car.

Javier carried Pat's backpack in one hand. It wasn't very heavy—not like the full load Javier had brought home every weekend. Usually he could just walk from the bus into the buildings and the extra weight on his back wasn't too bad. But this morning, he not only walked over to help Pat, but also around the school buildings to the other side of campus where Mr. Seneca's portable building was located. By the time Javier walked up the stairs and opened up the door to the classroom, his back and shoulders felt like he had carried bricks up and down a ladder at one of his dad's job sites.

Inside the room, Landry and Steve were already at the computers. Mr. Seneca sat in his wheelchair, pulling out equipment from the closets. "Good! Two more hands! Pat, put that thing in the corner, and we'll look at it later. No time right now. Javier, come get these mikes. Pat, get the new announcements from Brother Lendell off my desk."

Javier walked to the nearest desk and put Pat's backpack on top. He took a moment to slide his own pack off his shoulders. It dropped to the floor with a loud *clunk*. He turned to his teacher. "Mr. Seneca, can I go to my locker first?"

"Aren't you carrying your whole locker right there in your backpack?" He held out the microphones. "Really, Javier, who studies *that much* on a weekend, huh?"

Javier's face sizzled with embarrassment. What could he say. *I'm a nerd with no life?* He walked to the cabinets and took the microphones from Mr. Seneca and was grateful his teacher didn't say anything else.

When Javier set them down on the desk, he noticed a serious look on Pat's face.

"What's wrong?"

Silently, Pat handed him the paper to read for himself: *We'd like everyone in the school to remember Kenny García's uncle in our prayers. During Saturday's football game, he had a heart attack. He's still in intensive care at Santa Rosa hospital. The doctors are hopeful he will recover soon.*

So Pat and Javier set up the camera as well as the desk area. He was reading over the script that Pat had typed up about the first loss of the football season when all six football players came into the classroom at one time.

Each one moved in a sullen silence, each pair of eyes narrow with a threatening glare. With tense shoulders and a stiff walk, it appeared that any of them would jump the first guy who said *anything* about the game.

Javier glanced at Pat, who shook his head and pulled that sheet of paper from Javier's fingers. He wadded up the paper and shoved it in his pocket.

Pat leaned close and whispered, "Let's just forget to mention the game."

Mr. Seneca was back on his crutches, walking toward the upperclassmen. "Kenny's absent today, so I need someone to step in. Ram, you need to do it."

"Me?" Ram took a step away from the others. His face opened up in surprise. "You want me to work the camera?"

"You aim, you focus, you keep it on the speaker—either Javier or Pat. You've seen a week's worth of shows now. You can handle it." Mr. Seneca turned slightly toward Dylan and Omar. "I want you two to stand behind Landry and Steve this morning. I'm going to put you two on the computers starting next Tuesday." He nodded toward the three juniors. "You managed to get here *early* this morning. What? No little sisters to drive to school? Is there a chicken pox epidemic at St. Vincent's this week?"

The three juniors shifted their feet, their eyes lowered to the floor.

"When you learn to trust me and the other guys trying to put on a good show, maybe you can get promoted from janitor to announcer. In the meantime, one of you will stand with Ram in case he needs direction. I need one of you to stand by the door and turn off the air-conditioner as Ram signals the countdown. Ms. Maloney told me there is a humming in the background, and we think the AC is the problem. And the last guy can study the monitors and decide where we should hang the backdrop later." He swiveled on his feet and called out, "Javier, Pat, ready for a sound check?"

As the football players got busy for the broadcast, Javier noticed how quickly the tension in the room had dissolved. He nudged Pat. "Get that announcement out of your pocket. I think the players would like to know we're always behind them, win or lose."

After a broadcast that was shaky but not disastrous, Mr. Seneca didn't play back the program. Instead, he announced, "Okay, Pat, let's see the backdrop."

"Sure." Pat walked to the corner and carried it closer to the desk area. He unfolded the cardboard and leaned it against the wall by the door.

At first, there was dead silence. Pat's black eyebrows creased together as if he was worried no one liked it.

Javier stared with eyes wide open. Who would have expected a refrigerator box could be transformed from a white, flat surface to a detailed painting of the San Antonio skyline? What stood out most was the center image of the school. Pat had used various shades of gray to highlight and shadow the building to give it depth and dimension.

"Wow! Who painted this?" Landry asked.

Dylan shook his head. "Definitely not Berlanga. Javier, you did this, right?"

Javier had to smile. "I painted the base color and some of the blue sky. Pat is the real talent here." He gave Pat a low thumbs-up that nobody noticed.

"Unbelievable," Omar said. He turned to Pat, who grinned with pride.

One of the juniors said, "This will look great on camera, right, Mr. Seneca?"

Mr. Seneca, who had been standing near the cubicles, nodded his head. He moved on his crutches a few steps and then said, "Alright, you juniors, let's put your long arms to good use and hang this backdrop behind the desk area."

He directed Ram back to the camera and ordered Pat and Javier back into the desk area. They did some practice footage and tried to place the artwork in such a way that it didn't distract from the two broadcasters. Everyone got so involved in positioning the artwork just right, first period seemed to be set on fast forward. Luckily, Steve noticed the clock and all the equipment was quickly taken down and stored because each boy in the room stepped up to help. Except for the backdrop hanging on the side of the room, the classroom was back to normal as the bell rang to end first period.

"I know you worked on a backdrop this weekend. Why wasn't it on TV?" Ignacio asked Javier as they walked toward history class later that morning.

"There wasn't time to hang it until after the broadcast. You'll see it when we get to Mr. Seneca's room," Javier told him.

He enjoyed watching his friends and classmates' expressions when they saw the drawing. And each time someone asked, "Who did this?" Javier found himself grinning as he said, "Pat Berlanga."

The reply was always the same. "You mean the guy who sleeps in class?"

When Pat came into the classroom, Ignacio, Andy, and Bryce started clapping. He looked at the backdrop and then broke into a wide grin. Who wouldn't like so much positive attention?

Unfortunately, Mr. Seneca started history class and explained a short research project due on Tuesday that ruined everybody's good mood. Javier and his friends were still grumbling about the particulars when they met up for lunch.

"What a perfect way to mess up a holiday weekend!" Andy griped as he drummed a beat with his fingers on the cafeteria tabletop. "I'm all set to party at Javier's house, and now I got to research Egyptians."

"Hey, you're lucky! I'm researching Assyrians," Javier replied. He looked at Pat. "And what ancient civilization did Mr. Seneca give your row?"

"I got baloney or something," Pat replied before he scooped beans into his mouth.

"What!" Ignacio started laughing. "Baloney? Don't you mean Babylonians?"

Pat shrugged as everybody joined in the laughter. He swallowed and said, "It's all baloney to me." They all repeated "baloney" again and laughed some more.

"I'd like to know why teachers think Labor Day weekend means more time for homework," Ignacio commented as they continued eating lunch. "We have two essays by Emerson to analyze, and I have a Bible test too. We already have the game on Saturday night, and then the big party at Javier's house on Sunday."

Javier slowly looked at Pat. Even though he had spent all day with Pat on Saturday, Javier hadn't said anything about his party. Ignacio and Andy had come to Javier's birthday parties since they were in kindergarten together. By now, the family treated his best friends like two more *primos*.

He felt he should extend the invite now that Ignacio had mentioned the party, so he slowly said, "My birthday party is Sunday around four. Would you like to come, Pat?"

Andy pointed a fork across the table. "The bigger question is, can you bring your sister to the party?"

"Yeah, right!" Javier quickly glared at Andy. "You know how crazy an Ávila birthday party can be—little kids crying over piñata candy, my uncles arguing about the Cowboys, my sisters and *tías* singing to *Tejano* tunes after they drink margaritas."

"Yeah, but your dad barbecues three briskets," Ignacio replied. "It's so good!"

"And your Tía Celia makes *aguas frescas* and—oh, man—your mom makes that chocolate cake of hers!" Andy waved his fork like he was conducting an invisible band. He stopped and gave Pat a wicked smile. "Every year, I hear Javier's Uncle Willie say eating the chocolate cake was better than having sex. Of course, the man's in his seventies, so I'm sure he isn't getting much sex anymore."

What if Uncle Willie says that in front of Feliz? Javier thought. Could he take back the invitation? Maybe Pat wouldn't want to come, and surely a girl like Feliz had lots of plans on a three-day weekend. When he looked again at Pat, the guy was smiling, something similar to the expression when everyone liked his painting.

"Yeah, Javier, I'll go to your party. And I'll ask Feliz to come with me."

Javier adjusted the driver's seat in his mother's car to leave more leg room. He positioned the rearview mirror and then glanced at both side mirrors. The only thing he didn't check was the expression on his mother's face so he wouldn't get nervous. He backed the car out of the driveway, grateful that her constant questions were often silenced when they drove together.

"You're a good driver," she said after he had made the tricky left turn onto the busy intersection toward the grocery store. "Eric and Leo were so impatient. Every time your dad drove with either of them, he came home and asked for a beer." She laughed. "And your sisters! Oh, don't get me started on *their* driving. Your Uncle Willie had to hammer the dents out of the car bumpers at least once a month!"

He immediately thought about Feliz. With the way she liked speed and got so close upon the car in front of her, did she ever cause an accident? Pat didn't drive like a demon, but he also played loud music that interfered with conversation. They made him wonder about his own driving habits once he would drive alone.

Javier glanced at his mom and said, "Mom, it's not a problem if I invite a couple more friends to my party, is it?"

"Who's coming? Do I know their parents?"

"No, not the parents, but you met Pat and Feliz last week."

"What about contact lens girl? Don't you want to ask her?"

"No way," he said. If Feliz had Brittany with her, she'd totally ignore Javier. When it had been just the three of them working on the backdrop, Feliz had acted very friendly. Not that he expected anything to happen at the party with *la familia* watching, but at least he wouldn't be competing with one of Feliz's girlfriends for her attention.

"Javier, you know two more people won't make a difference to me. Besides, I like meeting your friends." She pulled her purse onto her lap and started looking for something inside it. "But with so much family around, I probably won't have much time to talk to them."

"That's okay, Mom." Javier said, relieved. The last thing he wanted was his mother's FBI questions to scare away Feliz.

That night he waited for Feliz's phone call. No luck. As he fell asleep, Javier repeatedly called himself stupid for not asking Feliz for *her* number. Extra chances to see her evaporated quickly when his dad said at breakfast,

"Son, I'll pick you up after school this week so you can get more driving practice. I'd like to see how you handle the downtown traffic before I let you drive to school by yourself. "

A sharp itch stung the top of Javier's feet. He wiggled his toes inside his shoes. "Dad, don't you think it's time to park Uncle Willie's truck at our house? I'd like to practice driving it. I know it will handle differently from driving Mom's car."

His father looked over at his mother, who quickly picked up her coffee cup, rose from the table, and said, "I need to get ready for the office." She left the kitchen.

Javier's dad reached for the sugar. "It's time to live in the real world, Son. That old truck couldn't make it around the block. Uncle Willie was nice to make you the offer, but your mom and I don't think it would be reliable transportation, especially getting on and off the expressway and driving it in downtown traffic."

Disappointment stuck to his body like a wet towel. "Dad, please don't tell me I'll be riding the school bus the rest of the year." He looked at the breakfast cereal floating in the bowl in front of him. For the past two years he had told his friends he would have Uncle Willie's truck to drive. Sure, it was old, but Andy's cousin ran a body shop. Andy and Javier had been looking at paint books since last summer, planning how they might fix up the truck. Javier had saved his money to buy new tires. All that time they had spent imagining ways to improve the look of that truck. Now nothing! Gone! ¡Nada!

His father stood up and clapped him on the shoulder. "You can be my chauffeur this week. Once you have your license, you can teach the bus driver how to drive, eh?"

Javier nodded. What could he say? If Uncle Willie's truck wasn't a piece of junk, wouldn't the old guy still be driving it? How dumb was it to want an old truck that sat in your uncle's back yard for the past five years?

He brooded on the school bus as he sat alone and ignored everyone around him. He had no truck to drive, Feliz didn't call him, and he had two tests today! And he hated the fact that he still had to put himself on school TV that morning and pretend to be excited about the cafeteria hot dogs or senior photos. He would love to announce, "I think sophomore year sucks!" Why couldn't he say *that* on school television?

Few students were in the hall when Javier dropped off his books at his locker and grabbed what he needed for the morning classes. As he walked toward the media classroom, his dismal mood hung over him like a rain cloud.

Setup in Mr. Seneca's room was moving quickly when Javier came in. Even Kenny was back, adjusting the camera tripod so it would be more comfortable with his height. "Javier, sit there by Berlanga. I'll need to focus in a couple of seconds."

Javier dropped off his backpack and headed to the desk area where Pat sat at the table, reading over the announcements.

"Hey," Pat glanced up from the papers in his hands. "Kenny's uncle is out of danger now. Mr. Seneca wrote up something about it you need to read over."

"Great," Javier said as his body sank heavily into the chair beside Pat.

"You look like a ray of sunshine. Did somebody run over your cat this morning?"

"Very funny. It's just been a lousy morning so far," Javier said. "Oh, and by the way, I don't need a ride home this week. My dad's picking me up after school so I can do more driving. Although why I need to practice driving seems pointless now." He sighed and reached for the papers on the desk. "I thought I was getting my uncle's truck to drive, but my dad said it's not . . . " he paused to add extra sarcasm " . . . *reliable*."

"Dads! They sure know how to ruin your life, don't they?"

Javier nodded, but at least his dad wasn't like Pat's. And he wasn't really mad at his father, just disappointed about not driving his own vehicle sooner. "At least I'll have a license by the end of the week. That's the main thing."

"So I'll call my sister after school and tell her to pick me up. No big deal." Pat shrugged. "Any chance your parents will buy you a new car for your birthday?"

Javier frowned at him. "Yeah, right!"

"I know the feeling, man," Pat replied. He sighed and picked up his script.

Javier shook his head, trying to push the lousy feeling out of his head before the live broadcast began.

"Javier! Javier, wake up. You have a phone call."

It took a few seconds to realize his mom's voice wasn't part of his dream. He opened his eyes. In the light that came into his bedroom from the hall, he saw her standing in her white robe beside his bed. She carried his cell phone in her hand.

"Someone wants to talk to you at this late hour. It's a girl."

Immediately he was awake and reaching at the phone. He cleared his throat before he said, "Hello?"

"Hi, it's Feliz. I need help with some chemistry vocabulary words."

"Oh! I—uh," He stopped and sat up. "Hold on, Feliz. Please."

"Who is it?" His mother still stood in the room, tapping an impatient rhythm with one foot. Her facial expression and messy hair only emphasized her displeasure. She looked as if she might have fallen asleep watching TV in the den, only to be suddenly awakened by Javier's cell phone, which he obviously had forgotten there.

"Mom, it's Pat's sister. She has a question about chemistry," he told her.

"Doesn't she know it's after midnight?" Her annoyance seemed to make her slippers clap even louder against her heels as she walked out of the bedroom, leaving the door open. "And it's a school night, remember?"

Javier turned on his lamp and rushed to the door to close it as quietly as possible. Instinctively, he sat at his desk and said, "Sorry. Now what was your question?"

"We just got done with that stupid periodic table. We've moved on to hippo genius and homo-something-or-other." Her voice sounded frustrated.

"Do you mean homogeneous and heterogeneous mixtures?" Javier replied.

"Yeah. My teacher wants our own definition and examples of each mixture, so what do I say?"

"Feliz, it's after midnight," he said groggily.

"So? This is due as a quiz grade tomorrow. I thought you said you'd help me."

"I can, but—"

"Okay, so I'll wait for your call back." And the phone call ended.

Javier sighed, turned on his computer, and went looking for his chemistry book. It took him forty-five minutes to search for and think of definitions and examples that would sound like Feliz had thought of them herself. Then he called her back.

She answered with, "Do you know the answer?" No greeting or anything.

He explained the mixtures with examples of Jell-o and chocolate chip cookies. She asked him to clarify two points and then paused a long moment. Then she said, "Thanks, Javier. I owe you one!"

Surprised and encouraged by her friendly tone, he got up the nerve to say, "Feliz, my family is having a party for my birthday on Sunday. I wanted you and Pat to come. Did he tell you about the invite?"

"No. He never tells me anything."

"Oh. Well, can you come? It starts at four—this Sunday." He felt he was stumbling over his own tongue. "My dad barbecues . . . uh, Mom bakes chocolate cake, and uh—" he stopped and thought immediately of Uncle Willie. He groaned.

"Maybe. Later!"

The abrupt end to the conversation wasn't what he wanted, but at least he had her number in his cell phone and well, that was one step closer than before.

Ironically, homogeneous and heterogeneous mixtures were the main focus in Mrs. Alejandro's chemistry class the next day. The guys in sixth period looked confused when she asked for common examples. When Javier presented the answer so easily, all the guys and his teacher were visibly impressed.

"How do you do that?" Andy rapped him on the back of the head with a pencil as they gathered up their books to leave the lab. "Man, it kills me how smart you are!"

Javier turned around and rubbed his head. "I just got lucky."

Ignacio walked around the table and said, "Lucky works for women and money, Jack. *You* got extra brain cells or something."

"Way more cells than the whole class put together!" Andy added.

Lately their praise made his itchy feet worse. "Really, guys, it's not that hard." He stepped closer and almost admitted the truth, but then he'd have to tell them he talked to Feliz last night. He didn't want to hear teasing from Andy or get a lecture from Ignacio, and they both would say, "Didn't you invite her to the party, Jack?"

And even though he did it, she had only given him a "Maybe."

No, he decided as he followed his friends out the door, *it's better to look like a chemistry geek than a fool.*

CHAPTER NINE

Fifteen didn't feel any different from sixteen when Javier woke up on his birthday. Even the smell of waffles, an Ávila birthday tradition, seemed more familiar than special. When he walked into the kitchen, his mother stood at the counter checking the steaming waffle iron. She wore a colorful blouse and dark skirt for work. His father sat drinking coffee at his usual spot. He wore his denim work clothes like any other morning.

"Happy birthday, Javito!" his mother exclaimed before she gave him a tight hug. "My baby is sixteen! Sixteen!" Then she held him at arms' length and smiled into his face. "Marc, can you believe our baby is sixteen?"

"In some countries, a boy can buy his own goats at sixteen," his father commented, slowly standing. "Perhaps I should arrange a marriage with the father of that girl who likes to call our son at midnight! But only if her father has the right number of cows and chickens for her dowry."

"Very funny!" Javier replied before he walked into that affectionate embrace his father easily gave away to everyone he loved. Their hug felt tight and real. Then his father clapped him across the back and let him go.

Javier felt inspired as he said, "Dad, if you're going to negotiate for livestock, shouldn't you get me a horse I can ride to school?"

"You're getting as clever as your old man." His father laughed. "Watch out!"

"Sit down for breakfast, Javier. Your dad is going to drop you off at school today so you don't have to rush for the bus."

Javier nodded, his parents did the same thing last year. He had even told the bus driver that he wouldn't be waiting Friday morning.

"I wish I didn't have to go to school," Javier said after he took a couple of bites from the delicious waffles his mother had baked. "Why can't it be a holiday?"

"But today is the pep rally. That'll be fun!" his mom said as she sat down with a plate at the table. She reached for the syrup bottle as she said, "I'll pick you up on time, okay? I promise! Then we'll go over to the DPS office like you want."

"Thanks, Mom. Getting my permanent license is the only thing I *really* want for my birthday," he said, hoping sixteen would feel different from fifteen once that license was in his hands. He ate a few more bites as he had turned over a question in his head. "Do you think that I can borrow your car and drive to the game by myself?"

He looked up from his plate to see his mom and dad exchanging a private message in the way their eyes locked together and their eyebrows raised. He assumed mental telepathy developed as a couple's sixth sense; something about living together for over thirty years!

"Is the game at the school?" his mother asked, looking back at her son.

"We're playing at Alamo Stadium," Javier said. "I'll just drive down Hildebrand to get there, Mom. There's not as much traffic as downtown, and I won't get lost because it's the same way we drive to Uncle Willie's house." After living with his parents for sixteen years, he had to learn how to read minds too. He knew exactly what their concerns would be, and he had already planned what to say. How could they say no?

"Let's take it one day at a time. License first, then we'll talk about my car," his mom said. "It's not even Saturday yet. I might need my car to shop for your party."

"Okay," he sighed. Reading his parents' minds was *never* as easy as he hoped.

"Good morning. I'm Javier Ávila, and these are today's announcements."

After two weeks of speaking to the camera, he didn't feel like his face was concrete or that he acted like an eight-year-old trying to read a hard word in a dictionary. He had learned a lot about his own presentation watching the replays, and as his confidence grew, so did his creativity.

"Mr. Seneca, wouldn't it be interesting if we did the Spanish club announcements in Spanish?" he had said Wednesday during afternoon practice.

The teacher had merely raised an eyebrow. "Your translation had better be perfect, or Mr. Montejano will be in here using two languages to yell at you!"

Javier not only translated the Spanish club announcement, but also let his parents proofread it and practiced it with them a dozen times the night before. He had to deliver it perfectly. After the broadcast, students in the class, random students in the hallway, and all of Javier's teachers complimented him—especially Mr. Montejano.

Meanwhile, Pat's backdrop was a sensational hit. Pat's enthusiasm in front of the camera was also the source of many compliments, especially from so many who were surprised he could be so entertaining with his ad-libs between announcements.

"Man, if Javier and Pat keep it up, the rest of us are going to look like dopes on TV," Dylan Romo had announced after the broadcast on Thursday morning.

"They just set the bar very high," Mr. Seneca replied as he set up the tape for the replay and discussion that usually followed every broadcast. "All of you guys need to work hard to reach it."

So, on Friday morning, Javier's self-confidence was strong as he and Pat smoothly delivered the announcements. As they were reaching the end, Javier felt an unexpected thrill when Pat reminded students of the three-day weekend ahead. Javier's sudden grin was inspired by his plans to get his license, but to the students watching the broadcast it appeared he seemed very excited to tell them, "Mr. Henley needs all band members to remain after today's pep rally for a mandatory meeting in the band hall."

Pat added, "Because of last week's medical emergency—and by the way, everybody in the school is happy that Kenny García's uncle is going to be released from the hospital on Monday—we all know that no one saw the band's half-time show. One member of the drumline bragged to me just yesterday that this week's show is *guaranteed* to give us twice the entertainment. Ha ha, no pressure!"

Javier started chuckling but quickly tried to swallow it. He rolled his lips inside his mouth to hold back the urge to keep laughing. Pat had moved on to the last two announcements about soccer practice and the cafeteria menu, but when Pat said, "Hey, students, it's chili-bean burritos on the menu today! And a special happy birthday wish goes out to our cafeteria manager, Mrs. Burrito—uh! Burriola! Mrs. Burriola, I mean!"

Mrs. Burrito? Javier started laughing again. He wanted to breathe normally, but a cough-laugh sound escaped, and he couldn't stop the giggling sound that followed. Pat made the mistake of looking at his partner with an amused grin. It made Javier feel as if a whiff of laughing gas had made him high and crazy. When Pat cracked up with laughter, too, Javier's condition only got worse.

Desperately, Pat nudged him with his elbow and said, "Man, you're killing me here! Cut it out!" That's when every guy in the class caught the bug and started chuckling and giggling. Mr. Seneca tried to look stern, but his face reddened. He twisted his lips like a deranged scarecrow, struggling against the natural urge to laugh out loud.

"Okay, okay, I can do this!" Javier said, gasping between words. He turned his watery eyes toward the camera to say, "This is Javier . . . no wait . . . " He paused for more laughing and said, " . . . this is Javier Ávila . . . "

"Oh, man, this is P-P-Patricio—whatever!" Pat waved his hand like he couldn't remember his name. He dropped his head into his arms, laughing into the top of the desk.

Javier knew he had to salvage the sign-off and jumped in with, "This is Javier and Pat giving you today's announcements . . . " His voice shook like Jell-O. "And giving you some laughs too. Oh, man!" He had to wipe his eyes but quickly pushed out, "Have a . . . " He paused to catch his breath, but felt helpless when his words jiggled humorously. "Have a g-gr-great weekend, G-g-guardians!"

Then Javier pantomimed a slit across his throat, hoping Kenny, Landry, and Steve would end the broadcast quickly. In record time, Kenny yelled, "And we're off the air!" only to break into gut-busting laughter that set off the whole room again. It was so contagious that Mr. Seneca had to sit down before his laughter knocked him off his crutches.

Javier kept laughing at his own inability to *stop* laughing. He followed Pat's example and dropped his head into his arms on top of the desk, and laughing until he thought his stomach would explode from the exertion.

Javier finally raised his head when he heard Dylan say, "Javier, thanks for this! You two clowns make me feel so much better." The senior football player was still wiping his face and chuckling. "Not just 'cause you made us laugh, but because you two *finally* messed up. At least now the broadcast team that follows you next Tuesday won't look too bad if they screw up too."

Mr. Seneca rubbed his hand across his chin, still chuckling as he said, "I guess we all needed to release a little pressure this morning." He straightened up in his chair. "I'm not sure how today's broadcast will sit with the administration, but we'll just shoulder the responsibility as any team would and share the good with the bad." He looked directly at Javier and Pat, and while he didn't look mad, his voice was deadpan serious when he said, "If either of you do that again, you're toast. Got it?"

Javier nodded and didn't dare look at Pat for fear of laughing again.

The teacher clapped his hands. "Alright, gentlemen, let's start looking for our next two-man team. Everyone can audition with the scripts from today's broadcast."

"But what about football practice after school?" one of the juniors asked.

"Looks like everyone will need to get to school *extra* early so we can practice before school instead." Mr. Seneca's stern mask quickly dropped into place. He stared hard at the trio of football players from the junior class. "Does anyone sitting in the room have a problem with that?"

As Javier attempted to walk down the main hall for second-period, he felt a heavy hand grip his shoulder. It didn't take a guy with a 4.0 to know who stood behind him.

"Mr. Ávila, did you have a mental breakdown this morning?"

"No, Sir." He turned around slowly and faced Mr. Quintanilla. He looked up and tried to stand steady under the hard gaze the Dean of Students gave him. "I'm sorry."

"What are you apologizing to me for?"

Javier glanced around at a variety of students who paused to stare at him with curiosity or sympathy as they moved through the crowded hallway. "I'm not sure . . . whatever I'm in trouble for, I guess, Sir."

"A few minutes ago, I told Mr. Berlanga that I expect him to apologize to Mrs. Burriola," Mr. Quintanilla said.

He looked more intimidating than usual with a solid black shirt, gray tie, and black slacks; an angel of death would look just like him. "I also expect a public apology on Tuesday morning on the school broadcast."

Javier started to tell him that it would be a new team on the air—in fact, it would be Ram and Dylan who had delivered a promising audition twenty minutes earlier, but something in this angel of death's glare made Javier just nod and say, "Yes, Sir."

"Get to class," he growled, and Javier obeyed, walking quickly down the hall.

Ms. Maloney stopped writing on the whiteboard when Javier came in. "Got all that funny business out of your system now?"

"Burrito, burrito, burrito," whispered some voice from the back of the room.

Javier's face burned red hot, but he only said, "Good morning, Ms. Maloney," and walked quickly to his assigned seat by the windows. He slumped down in the desk and wanted to disappear. Nothing seemed funny anymore.

"Hey, Jack," Andy said cheerfully as he headed toward his desk, which was three seats behind Javier's. "You got everyone's attention this morning, didn't you? Even Mr. Henley cracked up! It was hilarious!" He stopped at Javier's desk to say, "But you better watch out with Mrs. Burriola! That's one big woman! If she slaps you silly, she could send you flying across the cafeteria."

"Thanks a lot." Javier gave him a look to match his sarcastic tone.

Only seconds later, Ignacio came running into the classroom and broke into a sweaty grin when he saw

Javier. "Hey, I didn't know you two wrote reality TV shows. You should call it *Burrito and Berlanga*!"

Javier was never so glad to hear the bell ring! He knew there would be no more comments once Ms. Maloney started class. She had sent so many students to detention the first week of school that no one acted up in her classes much.

As she took roll, he let himself think over the crazy broadcast this morning. Why laughter took over like a demon possession still mystified him. It was too bad they embarrassed Mrs. Burriola, but he would also apologize when he saw her at lunch. In his head, he began composing an apology that Dylan could read on Tuesday.

"Javier Ávila, did you hear me?" Ms. Maloney's sharp tone startled him.

As the other students started chuckling, Javier sat up in his seat and looked at his English teacher. "I . . . guess not. I'm sorry, Ms. Maloney."

She stood at the whiteboard, her open palm under the words she had written on it. "Javier, I asked if you could start the class discussion on this quote by Ralph Waldo Emerson. What does it mean to you?"

Javier read it out loud. "Every sweet has its sour; every evil its good." His eyebrows wrinkled together as he studied it a moment and then nodded. "For me, it means nothing's perfect. Even good things can go wrong, and sometimes with really bad things, there is some goodness to be found." Javier looked at Ms. Maloney with new curiosity. Did she pick that quote on purpose after she saw the broadcast? Or was it just a coincidence?

She gave no indication as she walked to her desk and picked up her textbook. "Let's open our literature books to page forty-one and discuss Emerson's mood when he wrote it."

"Well, what happened?" Andy asked as Javier and Pat sat down at the lunch table. "Did Mrs. Burriola spit on your burritos?"

"That's disgusting!" Javier said, scowling at his friend.

"Mrs. Burriola accepted our apologies, no problem," Pat told them. "She also told us we made the cafeteria ladies laugh all morning. When I said it is also Javier's birthday, she gave him an extra burrito." He pointed at his tray. "Then she gave me an extra one too. I should make a mistake every broadcast, right, Javier?"

Javier felt annoyed and embarrassed all over again. He couldn't wait for the school day to be over. Apologizing to Mrs. Burriola came easy after all the teasing he got from strangers in the halls or the peers in his classes. He looked at Pat, surprised by the calm humor he showed about the whole situation. "Why is it that you look happy and I'm getting all the harassment?"

"Don't you get it?" Pat had picked up one of the burritos. "It's like what Dylan said in class. It makes the rest of us feel good to see that you can screw up too. You are so perfect all the time!"

"I'm not perfect!" He spit out the word like it was an insult. "I mess up all the time." He gestured across the table at Ignacio and Andy. "These two love to point out my screw-ups. Just ask them."

Ignacio leaned across the table and said, "Do you want to know the best thing about what happened this morning? It was that you laughed, Javier. You laughed like you had been holding it in all your life." A grin spread across his damp face. "Admit it! It felt good to let loose!"

Once he looked his friend in the eye, Javier surrendered into a smile. All that laughter in the morning had made him feel like somebody escaping from a straitjacket. Why was he trying so hard to put it back on?

Andy had started to snicker again. "It was *really* funny the way you couldn't stop laughing; like some crazy wind-up toy."

"Or like a hyena on steroids!" Ignacio added, chuckling and laughing too.

Pat swallowed what he had been eating and said, "So what if the guys give you a hard time today. If you make a joke out of it, then they're laughing with you, not at you." He nudged Javier with his elbow. "Besides, who knows what'll happen at today's pep rally. Everybody will stop teasing us if Andy or Ignacio mess up in front of the whole school. And what if the whole band screws up tomorrow at the half-time show?"

"Hey!" Andy and Ignacio said in chorus, both of them suddenly frowning at Pat.

Javier chuckled and said, "Ha ha, no pressure!"

Last year, Javier hated school pep rallies. Students were smashed together on crowded bleachers in the gym. All the loud music, rowdy pushing, and continuous yelling seemed pointless. Even the fact that girls from St. Monica's were welcome on campus for the pep rallies wasn't worth the pounding in his head when it was over.

He was already anticipating the first headache of the season as he followed other sophomores who had left last period and moved toward the gym. Then he heard someone shout his name. He turned to find Pat walking with another group of sophomores behind Mr. Seneca's motorized wheelchair on the sidewalk.

Javier slowed down to wait for Pat. Now he had a friend at the pep rally.

"Hello, Mr. Seneca," he said politely when his teacher passed.

"What am I in for, Javier?" Mr. Seneca had stopped his chair and raised an eyebrow. "Should I have brought the earplugs I use at the rifle range?"

Javier couldn't resist a laugh. "Yeah, probably!"

Mr. Seneca gave a rare smile and then rolled forward in his chair. Javier and Pat walked behind him into the gym.

"My sister's supposed to come today," Pat told him. "She'd better, 'cause I need a ride home. I told her you have stuff to do after school."

"Feliz is coming to the pep rally?" Javier's feet had itched all through chemistry class, but he had blamed it on applying for his driver's license. He should have guessed that his feet were warning him about something else. "Maybe she's already inside." Even though Feliz wasn't a cheerleader or a member of the band, friends and siblings often attended pep rallies. He was anxious to find her among the visitors.

It was crowded and noisy as the sophomores took their seats in the bleachers. Javier got whacked on the shoulders by Landry and Steve, who were already in a rowdy mood. He took a seat by Kenny, who grunted and then turned to talk to a couple of other basketball players. Javier nudged Pat, and they both laughed at the freshmen students across the gym. They sat smashed together near the locker rooms because the school band sat in the middle on that side of the gym.

"So much better than last year," Pat said.

It was the last comment Javier heard. Andy and his drumline struck up a loud cadence that rolled into the opening notes of the school fight song. Pat pulled Javier up to join with all the students jumping up, yelling, and clapping as the football team and the coaches entered the gym. They made their way into the middle of the gym, where metal chairs were set up. Once they stood in place, everyone was supposed to sing.

Pat nudged Javier hard in the ribs. Pat had started singing the words at the top of his lungs like he wanted the freshmen across the gym to hear it. Javier laughed and decided to join in. Both of them also started laughing at how off-key they sang, "Guardians, the rock upon, we stand so strong . . ." *Who cares?* Javier thought. Every guy around them sang terribly too!

The song ended, and everyone cheered as Coach Delgado took the microphone and introduced the football players.

Javier genuinely clapped and cheered for Dylan, Ram, and Omar since he knew them personally. He did the same for the three juniors from broadcasting class too. Who would have guessed the pep rally would be more fun because of that elective?

Once the team was introduced, the school band played a song that featured Ignacio and the rest of the brass instruments. The next song featured the drummers, and Javier yelled and clapped for his friends when it was over.

Everyone whistled and yelled when the cheerleaders danced to a popular melody. The guys around Javier didn't yell out stupid comments and risk Mr. Quintanilla's wrath, but they said plenty among themselves about the girls. Javier still looked around for Feliz but couldn't find her.

To end the pep rally, the cheerleaders led the classes in a cheer competition. The pretty girls in their small, tight outfits were divided among the four classes. Each group rallied the boys before them.

Landry and Steve pounded on Javier's shoulders until he joined in with Pat. They yelled like maniacs with all the other sophomores. Finally, they jumped up and screamed even louder when the girls chose the sophomores as the "Most Spirited Class."

As the pep rally ended, Javier's throat was raspy and sore, and his head still hurt, but it was better than last year, thanks to new friends from the broadcasting class.

Pat was suddenly tugging at his sleeve. "Look, there's my sister," he said.

Javier spotted Feliz at the far end of the gym. She stood among a group of girls who were walking out with the cheerleaders. He glanced at his watch. He was supposed to meet his mom in the parking lot soon. All day he had hoped his mom would be on time; but now, he prayed his mom would run late so he could talk to Feliz.

But first, they had to walk back into the building and fight their way down a crowded hallway to get to their lockers. Once that was done, Javier followed Pat to the parking lot and talked casually about his birthday party and getting his license.

"You know getting your license is no big deal, right?" Pat said as they walked toward the parking lot in the rear of the school. "The big deal comes later when you drive all by yourself for the first time. I took my mom's car, and I was gone for two hours—just driving where I wanted to go. It was my freedom on wheels!"

"I can't wait to drive alone," Javier told him as he scanned ahead looking for Feliz's vehicle. "I already asked to borrow my mom's car to drive to the game."

"What did she say?"

"What else? 'We'll see . . . maybe . . . ' the usual parental answers." He smiled when he saw the shiny sports vehicle with the tinted windows parked in one of the closer spots. He smiled wider when he didn't see his mom's car in the lot. "There's Feliz's car."

"Yeah, I see it. So, if you don't get the car, do you want a ride to the game?"

Javier chewed up the smile quickly. Would Feliz be more impressed if he wasn't just another boy needing a ride? But if he took his own car, would he see her at all? Unexpectedly, the driver's window slid down, and Feliz leaned out the window. "Hey, Javier, I got some great news. I passed my chemistry quiz today!" Her dark glasses hid her eyes, but her smile and voice revealed her happiness well. Her long hair slipped down her shoulder and arm. The shiny brown hair looked like it would feel like silk.

The attraction to this girl felt like magnets gripping his insides with a tightness that made swallowing painful. An inner voice screamed at him to loosen up and laugh. So, he latched onto the personality he became on school TV, the guy who could act enthusiastic about the most boring school announcements. He gave her his most televised smile. "Congratulations, Feliz. That's great." His voice didn't even shake. "Did you like the pep rally?"

"It was okay." She turned away for a brief moment as Pat climbed into the front seat of the car and slammed the door.

"Tell Javier 'happy birthday', Feliz," Pat called out. He leaned around his sister and grinned at Javier. "He's been laughing like a happy man all day today!"

"Laughing?" Feliz pulled off her sunglasses and looked right at Javier.

He shrugged and smiled. "Yes, your brother helped me look like a fool on school TV this morning, but it's all good now." He was pleased by how easy it was to talk to her.

"Well, happy birthday, Javier," she said, her dark eyes staring right into his. "I hope the rest of today is all good."

"It is now," he said without thinking, blinking, or feeling embarrassed.

Her eyebrows lifted at his reply, but she was still smiling at him. She laughed softly and sat back in the seat. "Good-bye, Javier."

"Call me later, okay?" Pat called out.

Javier stepped up quickly and put his hand on the door before she could lift the window. "Feliz, don't forget about my party on Sunday, okay? It starts at four."

"It's all good, Javier." She gave him a wink and then put on her sunglasses.

He wondered, *Does "It's all good" rank higher than a "Maybe"? Why didn't she tell me one way or another if she is coming to my party?*

There was no time to clarify anything because he saw her hand swiftly move toward the window controls. Javier reacted quickly to pull away his fingers before they got caught. As the dark window lifted between them, he walked away. Like another pathetic guy waiting on his mom for a ride, Javier took a spot by a line of students waiting beside the fence.

CHAPTER TEN

"**F**ine! Look like a hoochie-mama at Javier's party! Do you *always* have to look so desperate?"

"Well, at least I'm not glued to my cell phone waiting for some guy I met in an airport last week to send me a message! You're *so* pathetic!"

They're home. Javier sighed as he opened the back door. His big sisters sat at the kitchen table eyeing each other like suspicious cats. Both were curvy women with layers of highlighted brown hair. An open bottle of beer sat in front of each one.

Javier wanted to turn around and walk back outside, but his mother had tugged on his arm, pulling him into the kitchen. Her voice grew louder with each sentence. "You two live in two different houses now, but you still fight like you share a bedroom. And are you drinking your daddy's beer? Why didn't you come home with your own six-pack? And have you even told your baby brother 'happy birthday'?"

Both women jumped from the table and screamed, "Happy birthday, Javito! Congratulations! Happy birthday to our little Javito!" They stumbled toward him.

Suddenly Javier's arms were smashed against his chest as both sisters crushed him between them. One pair of cold beer lips smacked his cheeks, and another left his forehead with a slippery residue. If he ever wanted a chance to drive away on wheels of freedom, it was at this moment.

"Go change your clothes, but come back downstairs," his mom said as Javier pulled away from his sisters and started to leave the room. "Then you can tell your big sisters all about your new TV class."

TV class? Javier suddenly felt six years old again. He looked back at Vivian and Selena and set his shoulders straight. "I have a new elective this semester. Broadcast Media. We do the announcements on closed circuit television every morning. My friend Pat and I were the first team to go on the air." He felt satisfied by the way he sounded: confident and mature. Sixteen.

"I bet you look so cute on TV," Selena said. She actually pinched his cheek. "It's good you got Daddy's dark eyes and straight nose, Javito. I bet when all the girls see you on TV, they think you're so hot."

"Selly, don't be stupid! He goes to an all-boys school!" Vivian exclaimed.

"So what? It's not a school for wannabe priests! He can still go out with girls." Then Selena raised one carefully drawn eyebrow at Javier. "You can date girls, right? I mean, you *want* to date girls, right?"

"Yes, I date *girls!*" Javier couldn't believe his sister just said that.

Vivian was laughing now. "Of course he does. He's super-smart, not gay."

"Oh, man!" Javier sighed and walked away feeling helpless to say what he was *really* thinking. The age gap still made a difference. Would he ever feel like an adult around them? Life had to be easier when brothers and sisters were closer in age like Pat and Feliz.

After Javier came back downstairs in a green T-shirt and khaki shorts, he avoided the loud voices in the kitchen and settled in the den to watch television. When his father found him later, he was laughing at a classic *M*A*S*H* episode.

"You're watching one of my favorite shows," his father said and sat in the chair beside him. "Nowadays there's nothing but reality TV on every channel. There's even an episode of *Ávila Women Gone Wild* going on in our home!"

"That's why I'm hiding in here," Javier answered, grinning at his dad.

He reached over and clapped his son on the knee. "Forget the TV. I have something to show you." They walked back into the kitchen, and Javier was relieved it was empty. His father opened the back door, and Javier walked out to the back porch.

"Surprise!" A trio of female voices echoed around the back yard.

A small blue truck with a wide red ribbon on the hood was parked behind his mom's car. Javier's body ignited like a bottle rocket when he saw the gift.

His father slapped him on the back. "Happy birthday, Javier!"

Javier howled and spun in a quick circle. "Wow! This is so cool!"

He ran down the steps. The truck didn't look brand new, but it was a sporty design with black detailed fenders and doors. He saw bucket seats through the front windows, and when he opened the driver's door, a gold number sixteen hung from the mirror. He should have been totally annoyed by the tacky ribbon and the cardboard numeral, but they only made him laugh at his sisters' sense of humor.

"Is this all a dream? Does this fine truck belong to me, really?" Javier slid his hand over the fenders as he walked around. He threw the bow at Vivian. "Here!"

When he reached his mom, he hugged her tightly. "I love you, Mom!" He wrapped his arms around his father and crooned, "I love you, Dad! Thank you both so much! This is the best birthday gift of my life!"

"Happy birthday, Javito! Happy birthday!" his sisters proclaimed and jumped in for a group hug of suffocating proportions. It took a while before Javier could untangle himself and stand alone by the truck, still stunned by the birthday gift he never expected.

His mom put her hand on his shoulder. "I'm glad you like it. We hadn't planned to get you a vehicle, but one of your dad's workers needed some quick cash." She squeezed his shoulder gently. "If we take care of insurance, you can cover gas and maintenance with your money, right?"

"I can handle that," Javier said, glancing at the tires that still looked new.

His dad spoke up. "I really wanted to buy you a horse, but your mom didn't have enough garden space to use up all the manure."

When Javier looked at him, his dad winked, and they laughed together. Then Javier headed toward the driver's side of the truck. "I'm going for a ride!"

His mom asked him, "Don't you want one of us to come with you?"

"Nivia, give the boy a break!" his dad exclaimed. "He's sixteen now."

Javier turned on the ignition and smiled at the way the engine sounded. He tugged off the silly numeral, flipped on the air-conditioner, and set the radio on a station he liked. He waved at his family and backed out of the driveway. The truck ride wasn't as smooth as a car, but he enjoyed the more masculine feel of a truck as he drove around Woodlawn Lake, wishing he could honk at somebody he knew.

He drove up Cincinnati Avenue toward St. Mary's University, where he drove around the athletic fields and gym. He saw a trio of pretty girls walking toward the gym and bravely waved at them. When they first waved back and then craned their necks to see who was in the truck, he smiled like they were old friends. He tapped the horn, then circled around the lot and headed out the rear gate. Sixteen fit him so much better than fifteen ever had. He breathed in a sigh of happiness now that he owned his personal wheels of freedom.

"You realize your dad made it hard for the three of us to go anywhere together? It's too bad this model isn't an extended cab with a backseat," Andy remarked on Sunday afternoon. He sat behind the wheel of Javier's truck. It was parked behind his parents and sisters' cars and blocked in by four other family vehicles. "It's still a good little truck, Javier." His fingers did a drumroll on the steering wheel.

Ignacio sat in the passenger seat, opening up compartments on the console between the seats. "You're so lucky. Can we trade parents?"

"Yeah, right!" Javier chuckled as he stood by the open passenger door. He was thrilled to show off the truck to his friends. "I still can't believe it's mine!"

Andy got out, and as he walked around the truck bed, he told Javier, "You should have driven it to the game last night, Jack. Why didn't you go?"

"I wanted to, but I felt I should help my dad around the yard. It was the least I could do after my parents got me the truck." Javier stepped aside so Ignacio could get out and then he closed the door. "I'll drive it to the game next weekend."

The three of them stood around the truck talking about the game when Javier felt anxious hands tugging on the back of his shirt.

"Uncle Javito! Uncle Javito! Can we hit the piñata now? Please! Please!"

He looked down at his nephew Trey. The boy kept tugging and pleading.

His sister Laura had dragged along the stick decorated with rings of colorful paper. "I want some candy. It's time for the piñata."

"No piñata yet. Not all the little cousins are here." He reached out and grabbed the stick from Laura. "I thought Grandma hid this thing in the house."

"We found it!" Laura planted her fists on her hips. "I want to keep it."

Javier laid the stick inside the truck bed. "Go away! You'll hit the piñata later."

As the kids stomped off, Ignacio whined, "Uncle Javito, you're so mean!"

Javier started to say something, but he forgot all about it when he saw Pat and Feliz walking up the driveway. Feliz wore a strapless white top and white mini-skirt that exposed her perfectly tanned shoulders and legs. Her brown hair was gathered in a loose braid that trailed over one shoulder. She carried the straps of a white purse in one hand and moved with a sway of her hips that was almost illegal.

Liquid heat roared up and down Javier's legs. From behind him, Ignacio whispered, "I can die a happy man now."

Happy birthday to me! Javier walked down the driveway to meet her. He felt confident in a striped collared shirt and new shorts instead of ordinary jeans shorts and plain T-shirts like Andy and Ignacio. Earlier, they had teased him about "dressing up" but he had wanted to make the effort *just in case.*

"I'm glad you came." Javier smiled directly at the girl he wanted to impress. Were his itchy feet forecasting that today could be the day? "Feliz, you look very nice."

She smiled like she was glad he noticed. "You look nice yourself, Javier."

"Aren't you going to tell me I look nice too?" Pat said with loud sarcasm. "I put on clean underwear and everything!"

The guys all cracked up, but Feliz rolled her eyes and stepped away like her brother smelled bad. Javier cleared his throat and said, "The party's this way."

Everyone walked back up the driveway to glimpse the activity going on in the back yard. Children ran over the grass with a soccer ball, older relatives sat at the patio tables talking over iced tea and cold beer, and a trio of uncles sat under the pecan trees strumming their guitars. Trey and several other boys were trying to jump up and touch an embarrassingly huge piñata shaped like a big blue truck that hung high in one of the taller trees.

Javier paused by his real blue truck so Feliz could understand the connection to the silly piñata. "This is mine—a birthday gift from my parents. I was totally surprised."

"A *great* surprise!" Pat said, slapping the rear fender. "When you said your dad wanted you in a reliable car, I pictured a tank of some kind."

"Nice truck, Javier." Feliz nodded in approval as she looked over the vehicle. "It looks fun to drive. Let me drive it downtown sometime."

The Demon Driver behind the wheel of his new truck? Javier struggled to keep a look of horror off his face. Instead he said, "Umm . . . Feliz, you know everybody, right? This is Andy Cardona and Ignacio Gómez."

"Sure, hi," she said without looking at them. She walked away from the truck.

Seeing the frowns on his friends' faces, Javier felt embarrassed. He thought maybe she was just nervous around them. He tried to appear casual and friendly as he caught up to her. He said, "Regardless of when September fifth arrives, all of my family gets together Labor Day weekend to celebrate my birthday. When I was little, I used to care about exact dates, and some years I wanted two parties, but it doesn't matter to me anymore."

Feliz waved her hand in front of her face. "If it doesn't matter when you celebrate your birthday, why don't you pick a cooler month?" Her eyebrows creased slightly. "Maybe we could go inside, huh?"

"Well, I guess so," he said, glancing behind him as Pat, Ignacio, and Andy walked up. "You guys want to go inside and shoot some pool?"

When they agreed, Javier led the way into the house through the back door.

They dodged the aunts and cousins moving food from the stove or gathering bowls out of the refrigerator to take into the dining room. That's where Javier's mom and sisters were arguing about the arrangement of the many bowls and platters on the table. Javier's mom glanced up and said, "Hi, kids! I hope you're hungry!"

But Vivian walked around the table when she saw Javier with his friends. She looked very pretty with her layered hair pulled back with sparkled combs and wearing a yellow sundress. Javier could see why men in an airport asked for her phone number.

She took a moment to stare at her little brother. What would she say? It was the first time Javier had invited a special girl to the party.

He wiggled around his itchy toes as he attempted a casual tone. "Vivian, these are my friends, Feliz Berlanga and her brother, Pat. I told you Pat and I are in that new television broadcasting elective, remember?"

"Hello." Vivian nodded, but her stare remained on Feliz. "You look hungry." She cleared her throat. "Umm . . . the food's ready. Javito, why don't you and your friends serve yourselves before the rush starts?" With the back of her hand, she whacked Javier's upper arm and gave him a wink before she walked back to the kitchen.

Meanwhile, Selena had circled the table and told Feliz, "You have a great tan, girl. Where did you spend your summer vacation?"

"Well, we go to Acapulco every August." Now it was Feliz's turn to stare at Javier's sister. Selena wore a shiny purple halter with a plunging neckline. Her white Capri pants were tight on her hips. Her lipstick was the color of dark wine.

Javier hated to admit that Vivian had been right about Selena's appearance as a "hoochie-mama". He could just imagine what Ignacio, Andy, and Pat were thinking right now. He turned to his friends and said, "Let's eat, huh? I'm starving!" He hoped they'd think about food and not his sister's breasts. And, it was a good reminder not to gape at Feliz either. "Mom, can we serve ourselves before the crowd comes inside?"

"Yes, go ahead." She had been rearranging bowls so Aunt Liz could put a watermelon filled with chopped fruit on the table. "Selena, bring me two more spoons."

Javier led the way to the plates and plastic utensils wrapped in napkins. The guys shared positive comments about what was on the table and used every available corner of their plates to put a scoop of everything. He looked over his shoulder and noticed that Feliz put a small spoon of watermelon pieces, a few sticks of raw vegetables, and one scrawny chicken wing on her plate. Even six-year-old Laura ate more than that!

"There's more room to eat outside. Is that okay with everybody?" Javier asked, but he looked uncertainly at Feliz. "There are ceiling fans hanging from the patio cover."

"Go for it!" Ignacio called out, and Javier decided to ignore Feliz's pout. Besides, his mom expected everyone to eat outside where tables had been decorated with small vases of fresh flowers from her garden.

They sat together under one of the fans at a large round table. Javier was glad to sit beside Feliz, but she didn't talk to him. She was quiet when the guys agreed how great the food tasted. Since she had so little food on her plate, she had nothing really to talk about. When Andy and Ignacio started talking about the football game, she said nothing because she and Pat didn't go. At the last minute, they had to attend a wedding with their parents.

"I'm just glad we won the game," Pat said, wiping his hands with a well-stained napkin. "Can you imagine Ram and Dylan doing the announcements on Tuesday looking mad at the world? Now they won't be embarrassed to show their faces on TV."

"I'm waiting to see what they do with Brother Cala-vera's boring announcements," Javier replied. He turned to Feliz and said, "I don't think those guys in class realize how much Pat and I rewrote everything so that the announcements were more interesting."

She fanned herself with a napkin. "School announce-ments are *never* interesting."

"I think you're wrong," Ignacio stated. It was the first time he had talked directly to Feliz. "You should see how much fun it is watching Javier and Pat do announce-ments."

Feliz shrugged. "I wouldn't know. I don't go to your school, do I?"

When Ignacio's eyes started to narrow, Javier spoke up quickly. "Hey, Andy, you never told me about the half-time performance. Did the freshmen mess up or any-thing?"

As Andy began telling funny stories about mess-ups and cover-ups by the band during the game and at the half-time show, Ignacio relaxed. There was laughter and good-natured teasing among them, except for Feliz, whose passive expression didn't change.

As they finished eating, Javier's big brothers came up to wish Javier a happy birthday. He politely introduced Feliz and Pat, but she didn't extend her hand or say hello. Pat was quick to shake hands and smile.

Eric told Pat, "You're the guy on TV with Javier, right? He told me you can ad-lib with the best of them. Javier seems to be having fun in the class. That's great!"

Leo told them, "I always figured Javier would be on TV someday when he gets a scholarship to Harvard. I never thought he could be the guy with the microphone doing the interview. I'd tell everyone to watch my brother on TV. How cool is that!"

It was so rare to hear his brothers offer positive words about an activity that wasn't a sport. Javier sat up straighter, feeling happy for doing something that didn't require a high GPA. He smiled in Feliz's direction. She still looked bored and hot, and it was starting to get on his nerves. *Why can't she join in and try to have some fun?*

Javier couldn't dwell on the answer because his mom appeared and encouraged them all to get second helpings. Pat, Ignacio, and Andy all stood up quickly and headed back into the house. He took the chance to speak to Feliz without an audience, and unfortunately he said the first thing that popped into his head. "Did you get enough to eat? There's plenty of food." As he glanced down at the one-bite leftovers on her plate, he felt stupid. "Uh, would you like something else to drink?"

Feliz sighed as she looked around the patio and out into the yard. He followed her gaze. Javier saw his parents walking among tables to catch up and share news, his old *tíos* looking content under the trees in their circle of chairs, and his sisters serving margaritas to the ladies. Eric was lining up the children under the paper truck piñata. This was his *familia*, and he felt honored to share them with her.

Javier looked back at Feliz, his lips trembling into an uncertain smile. "I'm glad you decided to come to the party."

"Well, Javier, I was thinking I would leave now." She looked back at him, and her eyes narrowed like she had a headache. "It's been a nice party and all, but my head hurts. Well, thanks for inviting me." She slid out of her chair and stood up.

"Don't go." Javier popped up right beside her, so close he could almost touch her rigid shoulders. "I can get you an aspirin. Would that help?"

She rubbed her forehead. "Not really." She walked around the table completely opposite from where Javier stood. "I'll find Pat and tell him we're leaving."

He followed her inside the house where they found Pat at the kitchen sink, wiping a wet dish towel down his light blue T-shirt. A long stripe of barbecue sauce ran from his chest to his stomach.

"What happened?" Javier asked, ready to start laughing.

"The brisket fork slipped out of my grip and did a number on my shirt," Pat said, chuckling at his own clumsiness. "I almost jabbed Andy too. You should—"

"Pat, I want to go home now."

"What?" Pat turned and looked down at his sister. "You want to leave? It's a great party. What's wrong with you?"

"It's just Javier's *family*." Feliz spoke like it was a bad thing. Her voice lowered to a whisper. "I thought more older guys from school would be here."

Pat twisted the dish towel between his large hands. "Feliz, don't start!"

"Start what? I just want to leave, that's all. Let's go, Pat."

No warning itch, just a flame of anger made Javier's feet clench against his sandals. "Pat, I can take you home later," he said, but he wasn't sure Pat heard him.

"I don't want to waste my time here." Feliz whined just like Laura who couldn't hit the piñata when she wanted to. "If we leave now, I can catch up with Brittany and the other girls going to Sea World tonight for the concert."

Pat's glare looked intimidating, but Feliz didn't seem bothered by it.

"I'll just stay with Welita tonight." He threw the dish towel on the sink and walked out of the kitchen as he said, "You are such a pain! Man, I hate you!"

"Whatever!" Feliz stomped her foot and turned away. She was out the back door in a flash.

Javier knew he should walk Feliz to her car, but what kind of a friend would he be if he didn't go talk to Pat? He felt like a man on a rack, his body pulled in two painful directions at the same time.

"Oh, Javito, there you are!" Selena had come into the kitchen with an empty margarita pitcher in her hand. "That girlfriend of yours is leaving." She frowned at Javier. "Or did you already know that?"

"Yes, I know. She wants to meet her friends and go to a Sea World concert with them." Javier explained quickly, hoping to conceal his pain over Feliz's choices. "She'll probably have a good time there." He must have failed at hiding his emotions, because Selena quickly put down the pitcher and placed her arm around his shoulder.

"Javito, that girl is way too high maintenance. I know. I was just like her . . . well, okay, I still am, and so is Vivian." Selena had started giggling. "Go find a girl that is totally *opposite* of your sisters, okay?" She squeezed him close and let him go.

Javier felt like the dumbest guy alive. Even his sister saw the stupidity of trying to impress a girl like Feliz. He wanted to hide in the kitchen, but he heard a burst of laughter coming from his friends in the dining room and knew he had to face them.

Trying to find that don't-stop-talking-no-matter-what-happens attitude Mr. Seneca promoted, Javier forced a smile onto his face before he walked into the next room. There, he found Ignacio, Andy, and Pat standing around the food table talking with Javier's cousin Natalie and two other girls. Could he trust a sudden flicker of hope that his party wouldn't be a total wash-out?

No one had seen Natalie since they were all eighth graders. Javier was surprised to discover that the chubby girl with thick braids and big rabbit teeth had slimmed down into a nice figure. Her shoulder-length hair now framed her face in a prettier way.

"Hey, Javier, happy birthday!" Natalie proclaimed with a big grin that revealed a mouthful of braces decorated with hot pink rubber bands. She gave him a quick hug and turned to introduce the other girls. "This is Carrie, and this is Amanda."

Carrie was a tall girl with a long black ponytail and an interesting collection of small earrings pierced all over both ears. Amanda had short brown hair highlighted with blonde streaks and gray-blue eyes that turned bluer when she smiled at him.

"Natalie said your mom's cake is fabulous!" Amanda said with laughter in her voice. "So we're crashing your party! I hope you don't mind, Javier."

Ignacio slapped Javier on the back "The boy invites *everyone* to his parties! Pretty girls especially!" He grinned mischievously when Javier looked at him.

"Should we play pool?" Natalie turned to her friends. "Andy was *always* an easy way to earn ten bucks!" Then she raised an eyebrow at Andy. "Are you game, drummer boy?"

"You're on!" Andy called out, pointing a carrot stick at Natalie.

Ignacio and Andy quickly picked up their plates. They followed Natalie and her friends into a side room where Javier's parents had set up a pool table four years earlier and had since bought other games to entertain the family and friends who visited.

Pat stayed behind at the dining room table. He was piling some tortilla chips on his plate and spooned some salsa on top. Javier waited for Pat, wondering how to salvage the party spirit for both of them. He said, "My cousin Natalie went to grade school with us. She always makes us laugh."

Pat shrugged and then finally looked up. His dark eyes shimmered with anger. "Feliz doesn't care about anyone but Feliz. Get used to it."

Javier remembered what Selena had said and offered Pat a wry smile. "I'm not sure I need the extra stress of a girl like Feliz in my life."

Pat had dribbled salsa on his fingers and paused to lick it off. Then he said, "That's too bad." He was walking around the table toward Javier. "All my life when my friends crush on my sister, I'm always the one who gets dumped."

"Not this time." Javier shrugged helplessly. "Besides, your sister . . . well, she made it pretty clear today . . ."

He paused, hating to admit the truth. " . . . she's not interested in me."

Pat stepped up to Javier. "Don't take it so personally. She's just one girl, and there are plenty others." Suddenly his face brightened with a friendly grin. "Come on, Jack! Let's go party with some girls who came because they *want* to have fun."

CHAPTER ELEVEN

"Friendly girls and good food. Great party, Jack!" Pat sighed in a happy way.

Javier had just backed his truck out of the driveway and slowly started driving down the street. He smiled and said, "Natalie and her friends made my night!"

"Carrie put her number into my phone. That made *my* night," Pat replied and then pointed. "Turn up there. My grandma's house is on Mistletoe." He settled back into the passenger seat. "I'm going to enjoy riding in this truck to school every day, Javier."

"Every day? What about going home?"

Pat turned away to stare out the truck window. "I've been staying with my grandma for two years. It helps keep peace in the family." He chuckled to himself. "And it makes Feliz mad to have to drive me around, so that's a bonus."

"I know where your family lives, Pat. That's a lot of gas for Feliz to run you back and forth, isn't it?"

"My dad said if I make straight As this first quarter, he'll get me a car." Pat shrugged, still looking out the window. "I don't think it's worth the hassle."

"You should go for it, Pat." Javier flipped on the truck blinker. "I can help you with schoolwork! Why don't we work together on our history paper tomorrow?"

"Tomorrow is a holiday, Jack. Who does homework on holidays?"

"People like me who need As, that's who," Javier answered. "Who would I be if I wasn't the smartest guy in the class?"

"I don't know," Pat replied and finally turned to look at Javier. "Do you want to be the guy who sleeps in class? I can teach you all the tricks."

"What, and take away your fabulous reputation?" Javier replied. He was starting to really enjoy hanging around with Pat, whose honest, funny answers made Javier feel it was good to be the same way.

Javier began scanning the neighborhood, admiring some of the restored brick homes. "Which one is your grandmother's?"

"Three houses down, where the porch light is on. Welita knows I'm coming."

When Javier parked at the curb, he couldn't believe he had the right place. Having seen the Berlanga's expensive home, it seemed weird that Pat's grandmother lived in a tiny house with narrow windows and a cracked sidewalk.

"This is where my mom grew up." Pat leaned forward to look through Javier's window. "The house needs a lot of work, but my dad says it would be a waste of money. He keeps telling my grandmother to move out of the neighborhood."

"Why doesn't she just live with your family in your big house?"

"Welita wouldn't like living there. Hey, *I* don't like living there." Pat sighed. He unbuckled his seatbelt and opened the truck door. "Thanks for the ride, Javier."

"Hey, no problem." Javier rapped his fingers across the steering wheel. "Call me tomorrow. If you're staying here, I'll pick you up for school on Tuesday."

Pat nodded. "Thanks. I had fun tonight, Javier. I'd love to have a family like yours." He looked very serious as he said, "Do you know how *really* lucky you are?"

"Yeah, I'm starting to figure it out."

It took the prep camp kids from schools around the city to make him realize that he was *very* lucky to have the family he did. His parents and siblings were older than most, but they were always loving. Sometimes he felt like they would *always* see him as "little Javito," but it was just annoying and nothing bad.

Javier sighed as he watched Pat getting out of the truck. Here was a good guy whose family life seemed complicated and unfair. Pat slept in this old house to watch over his grandmother, but his father, who owned two of the biggest dealerships in San Antonio, wouldn't buy him a car?

Quickly, he pressed the button to lower the truck window and called out, "Hey, if you want some help to make straight As, just let me know, Pat."

"And if you want some pointers about sleeping in class, just let *me* know!" his friend called back before he walked up the sidewalk toward the lonely porch.

Javier waited until Pat went inside the house and then drove away.

"Forget her, Jack," Andy told Javier as they worked together on algebra problems Monday night at the Cardona's kitchen table. He tapped his pencil against Javier's notebook. "Feliz might look hot, but she's a real ice queen."

"Pat tried to warn me." He raised one eyebrow as he looked at Andy. "Next time I'll listen to *him* instead of you guys."

Andy shrugged. "At least Natalie and her friends were nicer than Feliz."

"Feliz was so rude at the party. I can't figure her out," Javier replied. He grabbed Andy's calculator and compared the answer with the one written on his paper. "And obviously, I can't figure out this problem either."

Ignacio walked back into the room. "It doesn't look good for the Cowboys tonight." He sat down at the table where he had abandoned his book ten minutes ago.

"It doesn't look good for us on tomorrow's test," Javier said. "Forget the game and help us figure out the last two problems."

"What? You don't have the answer yet? Last year you were a wiz at math," Ignacio replied, wrinkling his eyebrows. "You know we depend on you to explain stuff. You're the smart guy, remember?"

Now it was Javier's turn to frown. He was sick of those expectations, especially from guys who were supposed to be his friends. "I'm not a computer, Ignacio. I don't have all the answers. Stop putting that kind of pressure on me."

"You're crazy." Ignacio scratched his head and stared down at his textbook. "You're the only one sitting at this table with a 4.0. What are you complaining about?"

"You're just grouchy 'cause you struck out with Feliz." Andy's drumming pencil bounced from Javier's book to his calculator. "When you ace tomorrow's test, you'll feel ten times better."

How could his old friends be so blind? Javier sighed. "Never mind. Let's just put our heads together and try to finish the last two problems, okay?"

Javier thought driving to school with a friend would be interesting and fun. Even though the skies were still charcoal-gray when he drove on Tuesday morning, this early ride with Pat would give them a chance to talk about the media class and predict what new jobs Mr. Seneca might give them. He assumed since rush-hour traffic hadn't started yet, driving on the interstate into downtown would be easier. What he didn't expect was the guy in the seat next to him falling asleep before Javier drove around the corner and how many big eighteen-wheelers got an early start on their deliveries. His shoulders felt like they had been twisted in a vice by the time he parked his truck. The student lot by the gym was dimly lit, but he recognized Ram's jeep and Omar's old Ford.

"Hey, Pat, wake up!" he said probably louder than he needed to.

"Huh?" Pat's dark eyes fluttered open, and he straightened up in the seat. "Are we here already?" He yawned and unbuckled his seatbelt. "You've got a comfortable truck, Javier. I didn't even feel you start and stop. Feliz drives so jerky compared to you."

If Pat had meant to compliment Javier, it did nothing to stop the irritation he felt. "Let's go, Pat. I don't need Mr. Seneca yelling at me this early in the morning."

Javier stepped out of the truck. He lifted his heavy backpack from behind the driver's seat and hung it over one shoulder. He looked around, unaccustomed to arriving at school when the lots and fields were empty, security lights beamed around the buildings, and the classrooms looked dark and creepy.

Pat trudged along beside him, quiet except for yawning. Javier said nothing.

"Look around and see what needs to be done," Mr. Seneca said when Pat and Javier walked into the media classroom. He leaned heavily into his crutches as he spoke with Dylan and Ram in the desk area. They wore identical grim faces, as if the football team had just lost the Homecoming game to a rival school.

Everyone gets nervous in different ways, Javier thought, relieved his feet were itch-free this morning. He dropped his backpack on the first desk in the middle row and saw Pat already walking back to the cabinets to find the microphones.

Both Landry and Steve stood behind the juniors who sat at the computers. They looked busy as they answered questions from the upperclassmen. Kenny stood by Omar discussing the camera. Javier glanced around, but it looked like everyone was working, so he decided to go over to Mr. Seneca's desk and take a look at the announcements. There was still time to change words or rewrite them completely before Dylan and Ram went on TV.

When he got to the plastic tray on the desktop where Mr. Seneca kept the new announcements, though, it was empty. He turned around and realized the papers were already in the hands of the senior football players who had rearranged the chairs and looked ready to practice. Had they read them at all? Did they know how much rewriting Javier had done to make the announcements interesting?

"Javier, you need to stand by the air-conditioner switch. Turn it off and turn it back on. That's your only job now," Kenny García said to him in a superior tone. Omar and the three juniors laughed. Even Landry and Steve grinned.

His earlier irritation at speeding truckers and a sleeping friend resurfaced as an angry stare at the guys around the computers. He knew the time would come when he'd have to do something menial for the broadcast, but it wasn't easy to accept it after two weeks in front of the camera. He had actually enjoyed all the stressful excitement as a broadcaster on Guardian TV, but now what?

Javier turned his back on the juniors and walked toward the desk area. Maybe he'd give a little advice to the new broadcast team. Two weeks ago, he would have been grateful for someone with experience to tell him what to expect. Dylan and Ram were taking their seats behind the desk. Mr. Seneca had moved toward Omar and Kenny at the camera.

Pat, who was setting up the microphones, told them, "Don't forget, no matter what happens, don't stop talking."

"We know what we're doing, Berlanga!" Dylan said with a pit-bull snarl.

"I hope so, Dylan." Javier stepped from behind Pat and spoke from experience. "You two are up front and personal with the whole school. Everybody has a do a good job or all of us look bad."

"We're seniors. We don't make mistakes like dumb sophomores," Ram said, shuffling through the papers he held. "We can handle this ourselves. Go away!"

"Sure, fine," Javier replied, still annoyed by everyone around him. "I'm going to enjoy watching instead of sweating. Come on, Pat. We're in charge of turning off the air-conditioner. It used to be a junior job, but I think we can handle it."

"Yup, I think so, yuck, yuck, yuck," Pat replied in a comical way that should have lowered the stress factor for Javier but didn't.

They walked toward the door where the thermostat was located. Javier hit his fist against the wall. Then he crossed his arms and leaned against it.

"You okay, Javier? You seem a little tense," Pat said in a low voice.

"It's nothing."

"No, it's *something*. I can tell. You've been like this since we got out of the truck. What's going on?"

Pat's persistence only made Javier feel angry again. He glared at Pat and said, "Okay, do you *really* want to know?"

"Yeah, I do." His dark face appeared curious and serious at the same time.

"Well, I'm mad at the guy who expects a ride and then falls asleep in my truck like an old dog. Great conversation we had coming to school this morning, Pat!"

"Oh!" Pat took a step back. "Right . . . uh, sorry!" He shrugged and tossed up his hands. "Hey, you know I can fall sleep anywhere."

"The school bus stops in my neighborhood, Pat. If you stay with your grandmother, you can catch a ride and sleep on the bus like all the other guys do." Javier's face burned, but it still felt good to tell the truth. "I gave you a ride because I wanted a friend along. I don't need to watch you sleep."

Pat's black eyes widened as he said, "I really am sorry, Javier. I was looking forward to riding with you, too, but . . ." He stopped and licked his lips; pausing, as if to say something embarrassing. " . . . Welita always wants me to stay awake with her and watch TV all night." His voice lowered to a whisper. "It's why I fall asleep in class."

"Okay, everybody QUIET! We need to run through this RIGHT NOW!" Mr. Seneca's voice sounded like a death threat.

Javier spun around and turned off the thermostat. It kept him from staring at Pat with a pitiful apology on his lips. No guy wanted that. Pat had been a real friend at the party after Feliz had ditched them. Pat didn't embarrass Javier then, and now it was Javier's turn to return the favor. Each had their say, and that was good enough.

As the tape of the broadcast ended, Ram dropped his head into his hand. "That was so bad. We looked like there were poles shoved up our butts."

"We sounded like fifth graders." Dylan turned in his chair and glared at Javier and Pat, who sat behind each other in the middle row. "You two made it look way too easy."

"It's not easy. It'll never be easy." Javier still felt annoyed by the seniors' earlier attitude. He felt ready to tell off the great Dylan Romo. "You know, it doesn't take a genius to do a job well—just someone willing to work hard."

Dylan gave him another killer glare before he turned back to Mr. Seneca. The teacher stood by the television, a frown as deep as a cavern marking his features.

"You need to keep Javier and Pat on the air until football season is over," Dylan told him. "It's not fair they get all the extra time to practice and we don't."

"If you think it's all about an hour of practice, you're sadly mistaken." Carefully, Mr. Seneca took a few steps forward. "Javier and Pat read ahead of time and then rewrite what needs to be said. You and Ram grabbed the announcements off my desk and read them cold. Did you even listen during practice? I knew it was going to be bad."

"Why didn't you tell us?" Ram said. "Why didn't you make Javier rewrite the announcements first? We looked so stupid this morning!"

"If I had tried to warn you, would you have listened to me?" Mr. Seneca replied, slightly lowering his chin to stare directly at Dylan.

"It's not fair. I don't know nothing about writing." Dylan's voice got a notch louder. "Why can't Javier just keep writing all the announcements? Why do the rest of us have to look bad because we aren't all super-brainiacs like Javier Ávila?"

"So you're going to insult Javier and then expect him to help you?" Pat quickly jumped into the heated discussion. "We wanted to help you this morning, but all you did was blow us off and brag about yourselves. Face it . . . you two messed up! You owe my friend here an apology and a *polite* request to help you with the writing."

No one said a word. Who knew sleepy ol' Pat had grown a backbone?

"Okay." Ram slowly unclenched his teeth and looked at Javier. "We can use the help, Javier. Can you do some of the writing so we sound better tomorrow morning?"

Javier liked the feeling of power he held in his hands. It was hard not to smile as he said, "I don't mind becoming a scriptwriter for other broadcast teams, but you need Pat's help too. I might know a better way to structure a sentence, but Pat can coach you on ways to work together." He hoped the guys in the class finally understood that even non-athletes could appreciate teamwork.

Mr. Seneca cleared his throat loudly. "Javier and Pat shouldn't have to bail you out every day, gentlemen. All of you need to get better at rewriting and speaking on camera. No more excuses." He started a lecture on media ethics, and just before the bell rang, he announced, "Attention, sophomores! Today after school, we'll meet so I can demonstrate how to insert video clips into the broadcast. Plan to stick around until five."

"We get here early, and he *still* wants us to come after school?" Javier complained to Pat after they walked outside after first period. "He's getting us coming and going, isn't he?"

"Yeah," Pat replied. He rushed his hand through his short dark hair. "And there's still a lot of equipment in those cabinets we haven't used yet. We could be here *every* day for the rest of the semester. Don't you just love the surprises in an elective class?"

Javier shrugged. "I don't know. I've never been in an elective class."

"What?" Pat's eyes widened under his raised eyebrows. "Are you kidding me?"

"I'm dead serious. In middle school, I took classes to get me ahead for high school. Now I am doing pre-AP classes and taking junior-level courses as a sophomore. I never made time in my schedule to take an elective."

"Then how did you get into this one?"

"It was Brother Calvin," Javier said, shifting his backpack on his shoulder. "I know old Calavera put this class on my schedule because I wasn't involved in any school clubs. All last year he'd tell me, 'There's more to life than studying twenty-four-seven.'"

"Amen to that!" Pat said with a laugh. "Why not have some fun? You only get one life, right?"

"Yeah, I guess," Javier replied, feeling the itch of uncertainty slide inside his shoes.

But even if he had wanted to change his thinking, there was no time for it. He walked into a pop quiz on Emerson in English, had to lead the discussion on the Assyrians in history class, and felt as if the rest of his teachers had spent their Labor Day weekend figuring out ways to add more work to their students' lives. As he pushed his way through the crowded hallway after last period, Javier wished he could go home and get started on papers, problems, and projects. Only Mr. Seneca had other plans for him.

Javier sighed as he opened his locker and started to load up his backpack with books he would need later. He had actually finished all his chemistry definitions in class and felt tempted to take the book home to read ahead, but he didn't have the extra time anymore. He left two other books behind, closed his locker, and started walking down the hall. He had just reached the area leading out of the building when he saw Brother Calvin coming inside the door.

He gave Javier a grin that only made the old man's face look even more like a cardboard Halloween skeleton. "Hello, Javier. I missed seeing you on Guardian TV this morning. You have developed a great on-air persona."

"It's time for Dylan and Ram to take their turn on the broadcast. I'm working behind the scenes now." Javier wasn't expecting his voice to sound cold, but it suited the mood he felt. He was tired and suddenly resentful of the man's interference.

"Learning a lot, are you?" Brother Calvin clapped Javier on the shoulder like they were long-lost *compadres*. "You know, it was like working a jigsaw puzzle to fit that elective into your schedule."

Javier took a step back, shrugging off the man's bony hand. "I don't think it was fair to put me in that elective without telling me first."

"If I had asked you about it, what would you have told me?"

"I would have said that I'd think about it."

"Think about it? Maybe? Last year, Javier, every answer you gave me was indecisive."

"I'm decisive," Javier answered. "I made a decision to work hard on my academics when I came to this school."

"I respect the effort, Javier, but I'd like to know if you're satisfied with that decision. Are you happy with it?"

"Why is 'happy' relevant? I can't believe the school counselor could be complaining about my high grades." His eyes burned with anger. "Shouldn't you be more worried about kids who are failing?"

Brother Calvin crossed his arms like adults do when they think they're right. "You know, Javier, there are other ways to fail besides getting an F on a report card. What about failing to try something new? What about failing to discover something to feel passionate about?"

"Passionate? I'm passionate about my schoolwork. I kept a 4.0 all last year."

"There's a difference between passion and obsession. I think you are so caught up in school academics that you forget you should be enjoying your life."

"Why did you assume this elective was going to let me enjoy life? Media class takes up all the extra time I used to have for reading and studying."

"So you don't like the elective?"

Javier stopped in mid-reply. He wanted to tell the old man, "No, I hate it," but the truth was, that class had taught him a lot. But he didn't want Brother Calvin to know it. He said, "Mr. Seneca's giving me a lot of work to do after school because of this new elective you put on my schedule. I'm late now. Excuse me, Sir."

He stepped around the school counselor and headed out the door. And while he still fumed as he walked inside the media classroom, it didn't take long before Javier forgot about grade points and school counselors. As soon as he watched Mr. Seneca load up the first broadcast and explain how the switcher could make announcements even better with video clips, Javier felt excited and inspired. "Mr. Seneca, can you teach us more about the cameras in your cabinet? What good is the switcher if what we film looks like an amateur did it?"

Kenny grunted and said, "Speak for yourself, Javier. I know what I'm doing behind the camera."

"That's good, Kenny. Then *you* can teach the other guys," Mr. Seneca said. He leaned over and unhooked his keychain from his belt. "Javier, open up the cabinets and get out the cameras we have in there. Pat, help him carry them over to the desk area so Kenny can take over for a while. I'll be back in about ten minutes."

As Javier and Pat walked away, Kenny said, "Any idiot can aim and focus. Just be sure to press the ON button before you screw up and got nothing to show for it."

"I'd rather get a tooth filled than learn from Kenny García," Javier said quietly to Pat as he opened the cabinets. "I'll borrow the manual from Mr. Seneca, okay?"

"You *are* a nerd, Jack," Pat replied. He laughed before he said, "I'd rather get a tooth filled than read a manual."

After listening to Kenny's I-know-it-all-and-the-rest-of-you-are-idiots lecture, Javier took home one manual and convinced Pat to read a different one. By the next day they started to film inside the band hall. Javier shot close-ups of the drumline. Then Pat filmed the brass section and did close-ups of Ignacio playing his trumpet and Mr. Henley conducting the band. Finally, they did a wide shot with most of the guys waving or pumping their instruments over their heads, hamming it up for the camera.

Inside the media classroom, the real work began as they uploaded the raw footage and worked with the editing software for the rest of the week.

"I'm glad I told Kenny to film tomorrow's game," Mr. Seneca told Javier and Pat on Friday afternoon. They had been sitting at the computers the past two hours. "You two have a better sense for editing."

"That's 'cause Javier is so crazy about details," Pat told his teacher. "He's also a perfectionist. Javier does everything over and over and *over* again."

Mr. Seneca chuckled, but he also tapped Javier's shoulder and said, "Attention to detail has its place. Look at the big picture too. Details are only as good as the whole message they create."

"Yes, Sir," he answered, a bit thoughtful about Mr. Seneca's advice. He looked at the image on the computer screen in front of him. It was Andy leaning over his drum, his blurred hands beating a rapid cadence. His face beamed with a toothy smile of undiluted joy. But when Javier looked again, he saw the rest of the drummers angled behind Andy and the horn players in front of him, also engrossed in their own music making. In the bigger image, he discovered creative expression and collaboration. It was the difference between random noise and a thing called music.

He began to wonder what would happen if he used music behind the film clips they showed during the broadcast? *What if we filmed more student activities besides the band and the football team? What about taking the camera to the next pep rally? What about interviews?*

"Let's call it a day, gentlemen." Mr. Seneca's order interrupted Javier's musings. "It's almost five-thirty, and I'm beat."

Javier reluctantly shut down the computer. He liked to experiment with the sequence of images and think about ways to present them. He hadn't enjoyed anything like this since his grade-school Science Fair days. That was the last time he recalled using new skills and his own creativity to solve a problem.

It wasn't until they had walked away from the building that Javier said, "I hope Kenny gets good video from tomorrow's game. Maybe we can set it to music."

Pat nodded but didn't comment. They had walked closer to the parking lot before he said, "Did I tell you Carrie's coming to the game tomorrow night?"

"Pat!" Javier stopped walking and stared at his friend. "Have you been talking to Carrie since my party?"

"Yeah, but that's not all." Pat smiled like the Big Bad Wolf about to eat up Little Red Riding Hood. "Carrie's bringing Amanda too. You ready to try again, Javier?"

"Try again?" Javier replied, though he knew *perfectly* well what Pat meant.

"Don't play dumb!" Pat told him. "Maybe Amanda's not the girl of your dreams, but you can help a friend out and be nice to her, right? I need you to be my wing man."

When Javier just stared back, Pat's eyebrows furrowed over his dark eyes. "You're not still hung up on my sister, right? She left you hanging, Jack! I wouldn't wish my sister on anybody—except maybe Kenny García."

Javier responded, "A match made in hell, right?"

"See? You can be funny too, Javier." Pat shook his head. "You were so freaking serious last year. You reminded me of a robot, and I kept wondering who was pushing the buttons on the remote control?"

Javier stepped back. The robot comparison stung, but it was truthful too. "I guess I used to be a robot, Pat, but not anymore."

"That's good news." Pat laughed. "Humans make much better friends."

CHAPTER TWELVE

"**F**irst time I met you, I thought you looked familiar, but I didn't figure it out until after your party," Amanda told Javier as they stood together under the bleachers. They were waiting for Pat and Carrie to buy soda at the concession stand across the yard. "You went to the same science camp I did two years ago."

He shifted his weight as if he had stepped on a hot sidewalk. "You went to prep camp, Amanda?"

"Yeah, well, I quit after the first month." She shrugged and gave him a little smile. "Prep camp interfered with my swim team practice. I like math and science, but I had the chance to train with an Olympic swimmer, so I dropped out."

His feet started to cool down. If Amanda didn't remember that stressed-out phony he had been there, maybe he had a chance to make a better impression. "With that choice, I might have done the same thing. Have you always liked swimming?"

She laughed easily. "My friends swear I was a mermaid in my past life."

Javier smiled. Amanda wasn't drop-dead gorgeous like Feliz. She didn't wear make-up, and her streaked hair had been cut way too short to be attractive. Still, she had been nice at his birthday party after he thought Feliz had ruined it. He decided he could be a wing man for Pat and be nice to Carrie's friend tonight.

"Swim team is one of my favorite things about school," she was saying. "What about you, Javier?"

He remembered awkward conversations with girls because he had never done anything but study, but now he could happily say, "I'm taking a new elective this semester in Media Broadcasting. We televise the school announcements every morning."

"Oh, yeah. We do that where I go to school," Amanda said. "They even show student films. Have you made any movies yet?"

"I've got a lot to learn before I can do that," he answered honestly and then smiled at her again. "I seem to be a pretty good scriptwriter and editor, but I hope to get more experience shooting film too."

By then, Pat and Carrie had come back. They all walked up the ramp into the section of the St. Peter's football stadium where the students sat. Javier felt relaxed as he climbed up the bleachers behind Amanda, Carrie, and Pat. It was always better to sit with girls. They stopped midway and settled in among other sophomores to watch the game. It wasn't too crowded, so they had space to sit together comfortably.

"Look, there's Kenny," Pat said, pointing toward the field.

As the referees lined up with the school captains from both teams for the coin toss, Javier also noticed Kenny standing on the sidelines. Kenny spun the camera on the tripod as he talked to an older man with an even bigger camera.

He leaned around Amanda to tell Pat, "I bet that's a TV sports reporter. Can you imagine what Kenny is probably telling the man?"

"That he's the *only* one in our media class who knows how to work a camera."

"Do you think Kenny knows he has to pan the camera to follow the moving players?" Javier said. "He can't just point and focus like he does during a school broadcast."

"I guess we'll find out," Pat answered and then jumped up with the rest of the students when the band began playing the school fight song.

Sadly, the Guardian football team didn't provide any outstanding plays, and by the second quarter, they were losing 28-3. When Javier saw the band lining up for the half-time show, he also realized Kenny wasn't on the field anymore.

Javier turned to Amanda. "I'll be back. I want to be sure someone films the half-time show for our morning broadcast." He stood up and started to pass in front of the girls. He got past Amanda, but he tripped over Carrie's feet and toppled toward her.

"Aw, man!" Javier gasped just as Pat's strong hands pushed up and kept him upright. Here he was with two nice girls, and he looked like a stupid klutz! Ugh!

"Where are you going?" Pat asked. He had stood up to keep Javier from falling.

Javier felt grateful to have a buddy with quick reflexes. He glanced down to be sure he didn't trip again before he stepped forward. Then he looked up at Pat. "Kenny's not on the field. Just because we're losing doesn't mean he can take off."

"Wait . . . I'll come with you." Pat gave Carrie a smile. "We'll be right back."

The two of them quickly walked down the bleachers in search of Kenny García. They found him at the concession stand, drinking a Coke and talking to a couple of the senior basketball players. The zipped camera case hung over Kenny's shoulder. The tripod was leaning against a trashcan.

Javier walked purposefully toward him. Only for a moment, he feared the confrontation with Kenny; his desire to present an entertaining broadcast was stronger.

"Kenny," he said when he was close enough to be heard, "aren't you going to film the half-time show?"

"What?" Kenny turned and frowned. "What's your problem, Ávila?"

He attempted to keep his tone even and reasonable. "Kenny, I know there hasn't been much to film tonight of the football team, but the half-time show's about to start. Don't you need to get back on the sidelines and film that too?"

Kenny straightened up to his full six-foot-three height and glared down at Javier. "My job's done. The game's over, man. It ended two touchdowns ago."

"That's a loser's attitude," Pat said, stepping up beside Javier. "You don't have much faith in our football team, do you?"

"I got Omar kicking the field goal," Kenny snapped out his words. "That's good enough." He turned to the two tall boys beside him and gave them a grin. "We'll have great highlights when our season begins, won't we?"

Javier ignored the conceited chuckles and said, "If you're done for the night, Kenny, then let me have the camera." He heard the referee's whistle that ended the first half of the game. The band would march onto the field in the next few moments. There was no time to be polite.

"Kenny, you can't show up on Monday without highlights." His voice held firm. "If we can't show the team making a touchdown, then we'll show the band marching or show pictures of the cheerleaders. So, if you can't do the job, get out of the way and let someone else take over."

One of the seniors jeered. "Man, you gonna take that?"

That's when Kenny's tone grew nastier. "So when did Mr. Seneca die and put you in charge?" He kept up his intimidating stance, but Javier didn't let it faze him.

"You just can't stop filming because it doesn't interest you, Kenny. That's not the way it works! How would you feel if someone stopped filming *you* because the basketball team was losing?"

Kenny rolled his eyes. "Fine! I'll get back on the field and get more footage."

"Good! Do that! Now we need to leave. Two pretty girls are waiting for us. Come on, Pat. Let's go." He turned away with a smile of self-satisfaction. With Pat at his side, he walked away from Kenny and the others. He couldn't believe what had just happened. Brother Calvin was *so* wrong about his lack of passion.

"That was great, Javier," Pat told him. "I don't think Kenny knew what hit him. And when you mentioned the girls? That was genius."

"It wasn't genius—just the truth. Kenny had a job to do, and you and I have girls waiting for us in the stands." He tried to sound like it was no big deal, but on the inside Javier was jumping around like his nephew Trey on Christmas morning.

As they reached the top of the ramp, the band played its first number and marched across the field. Kenny was running across the track, camera and tripod in hand.

Pat clapped Javier on the shoulder, and both of them started cheering for their friends. The band played well as they began an intricate pattern of circles on the field.

There was a lot of moving around in the stands during half-time as parents got up to stretch or visit with others and kids ran for the concession stand. Even the cheerleaders came up to mingle with their friends. Javier walked behind Pat, half-watching the half-time show and trying not to trip over his own feet.

When they climbed the steps and got back to their seats, they were surprised to see Javier's cousin Natalie sitting between Amanda and Carrie.

"Okay, now what kind of *primo* are you that you don't call me and invite me to the game?" Natalie scolded, wagging her finger at Javier. "I got to hear it from my girl-friends that this game's the place to be tonight. What's up with that?"

Javier jerked his thumb toward Pat. "He set this up, not me. Blame him."

"Can't!" Natalie jumped up and hopped over to give Javier a quick hug. "He's not family. I can blame *anything* on family." She laughed and grinned, her braces now striped with blue rubber bands. "Remember how I used to tell Miss Canales you were the one stealing the pencils off her desk?"

"You stole pencils from my locker too. Nat, you stole pencils from everybody!"

She laughed and playfully pinched his arm. "I've missed you, Javito. We could have some really good times if you went to my school."

"You'd probably have me sitting in detention with you," Javier answered, breaking into an easy grin. He enjoyed how relaxed he felt—no itchy feet, no fear of feeling like an idiot. He slipped into the row without tripping and sat down beside Amanda. He smiled at her, thinking *She has pretty eyes and good taste in friends.*

Javier looked out the backseat window of his mom's car. They were on their way to eleven-o'clock Mass, his father taking the route he favored around the lake toward the basilica. How many Sundays they had followed the routine of church, cooking hamburgers on the grill, and the family eating together, and watching the Cowboys football game. He didn't know how to tell them he had other plans for the afternoon.

An uneasy itch crawled down his back and he rubbed it against the backseat. He tried to recover the positive feelings from last night. Even though the team had lost, he had come home feeling like a winner. His showdown with Kenny made him proud, and having a girl beside him at the game felt good too. Natalie's presence helped take pressure off Javier and Amanda to act like a couple, especially when Pat and Carrie took off and stayed out of the stands for most of the fourth quarter. Natalie had kept them laughing with stories about elementary school, and when Pat and Carrie finally came back, it was Natalie who had a suggestion for getting together again.

"Be sure to invite Ignacio and Drummer Boy!" Natalie had called out before she walked away with Amanda and Carrie after the game.

Javier smiled as he thought about his funny cousin and suddenly remembered what Natalie had said. *You can blame anything on family.* "Hey, Mom, did I tell you that Natalie was at the game last night? She invited me to a Diez y Seis festival. I told her I'd go downtown later and meet her."

"Just you and Natalie?"

"Ignacio and Andy are going to meet us there. Pat too."

His mom lowered the visor as if she was checking her appearance in the mirror. She ran her fingers through her brown hair, but Javier saw her sharp gaze checking out the backseat. "And those girls Natalie brought to your party? Will they be going too?"

"I suppose," he said, shrugging like it was unimportant.

His father suddenly straightened up in the seat. He glanced into the rearview mirror as he called, "Has Natalie gone into the matchmaker business on the side? Do I need to start negotiating for goats with another girl's father?"

Javier swallowed his embarrassment, thought quickly, and replied, "If you can't get at least six horses, don't make a deal. Mom wants to plant a bigger garden next year."

When his parents laughed, he gave a confident smile to an invisible TV audience.

And it was a good thing he kept practicing that TV audience smile, because on Monday morning when Javier walked into the media classroom, he was told to substitute in the anchor chair for Ram, who had a terrible cough. After Mr. Seneca told Ram, "You can't be coughing during the broadcast. Go to the library and come back after announcements are over," he told Javier to take his place beside Dylan.

"But what about editing the film and using the switcher?" Javier replied.

The teacher merely raised an eyebrow. "Get your priorities straight, Mr. Ávila. We can add bells and whistles later. Get busy on the scripts now."

Javier took a deep breath and mentally switched hats from editor to broadcaster. He walked over to the desk area and started reading over the announcement papers. He didn't even notice Kenny had come up to him.

"I shot all that film, and now you're not going to use it?" he complained.

Javier felt his own irritation coming to the surface. "I've got something else to do this morning. I'll get to it after school."

"Why can't Porky do it?"

"What did you say, you jerk? You can't be talking about my friend Pat, can you?" Javier's head shot up. His eyes burned holes into Kenny García. "Omar's letting Pat work the camera this morning. We'll get to it after school. Now go away."

He looked back at the announcements, ignoring the string of profanity Kenny muttered under his breath as he walked off.

Dylan came back to the desk area with other papers. "Okay, Ávila, let's do this right. My team lost the game. I don't want to look like a loser on TV."

"That makes two of us," Javier answered, sounding more efficient than he felt. "Let's start practicing, Dylan. We're going to be the first sophomore-senior team, and I want us to sound good." He glanced over at Pat and saw him listening intently to Omar. He whispered a prayer to Saint Peter and took his seat beside a new partner.

"You and Dylan weren't too bad on announcements this morning," Ignacio told Javier as they walked with Andy out of the building after second-period.

"Except he's tall and you're not," Andy said. He gestured with his pencils, pointing one of them below his knee. "Jack, you looked *really* short on TV."

Javier let the teasing go because as soon as he had seen himself on tape, he knew how to fix the visual imbalance. "Tomorrow we're going to lower Dylan's chair and raise mine so we're equal height on the screen. Pat should have spotted that during rehearsal, but it was his first time on the camera," Javier replied. "Dylan's reading better, and the juniors got all the visuals right this morning."

"Didn't Kenny shoot film at the game? When are you going to use it?" Andy asked as they climbed up the steps of Mr. Seneca's classroom.

"Pat and I are going to edit this afternoon." A secretive grin appeared on Javier's face. "We have a surprise for morning announcements tomorrow . . . just wait."

Kenny had started basketball practice after school so it was only Javier, Pat, Landry, and Steve who worked together on editing for Tuesday's broadcast. They planned carefully how to use rock music behind the film clips. The next morning, Javier expected to feel like he had stepped into a scorpion's nest, but sitting beside Dylan, he felt tall and proud, and not just because their chairs were better balanced, but because the team of sophomores had produced a music video.

"Cool highlights!" a freshman said as Javier walked down the hall after first period, and he even gave Javier a quick high-five. So did a half-dozen other guys.

"Javier, what a great video you sophomores made!" Ms. Maloney told him when he walked into English class. "Did you know there are student film contests you can enter? You could win a scholarship."

"Your video was so good that nobody noticed that the team lost!" one of the football players told Javier and Pat at lunchtime.

Compliments from random students and all his teachers about the new-and-improved look of announcements on Guardian TV left Javier smiling all day long.

Ram was back in the anchor chair by Wednesday, and he asked Javier, "What do you think of me and Dylan taking a camera during first period and interviewing Coach Delgado about the next game? Can you use that for Friday's announcements?"

"Why can't we show the girls running for Homecoming Queen on Guardian TV?" one of the juniors asked after Wednesday's broadcast. "We could make a video of them."

"If we do that, I know the perfect music we could use for audio," Landry said.

"Nothing too loud," Mr. Seneca replied. He almost smiled when he said, "Brother Lendell said that music we used on Tuesday almost took the paint off the walls."

"Alright!" they all cheered, slapping each other on the back.

"We should start painting a new backdrop," Pat said as they left Mr. Seneca's room that afternoon. "Javier, can we haul the compressor and my paints in your truck over to my grandma's house this weekend?"

"Sure," Javier replied, learning to welcome new ideas as fast as they appeared. His cluttered mind shuffled between visuals images, script writing, and new technology, as well as algebra problems, chemistry equations, American poets, ancient cultures, and world religions. He always did his homework, but any "extra" time now involved reading about new software or watching amateur films online.

As Javier sat in front of a big chemistry test on a Thursday afternoon, he tried to clear his head of the funny film showing chimpanzees riding miniature ponies. He had described it in detail to Pat, Ignacio, and Andy at lunch. He began to read the exam directions. Mrs. Alejandro had given them a two-part test: a section of multiple-choice questions and the major part that began with one large reaction that had to be repeated with different concentrations of reactants.

He tapped his pencil against the second page, flipped back, and got started on page one. The teacher's multiple-choice questions stumped him at first, but he felt confident about all but two of his answers as he completed Part One of the test. He turned to page two and started reading. He wrote down a couple of numbers, shook his head, and erased them. He nodded when he had settled into a comfortable pace for working through the chemical equations.

When Mrs. Alejandro called for the tests at two minutes before the bell rang, Javier ignored the itch between his toes and told himself, *Even if I missed a couple of questions on page one, I should still get a high grade. No worries.*

Andy's pencil tapped his shoulder and he turned around to see his friend frowning. "I hate those kinds of tests when it's all or nothing. What if I didn't start with the right equation on the reaction? It'll screw up everything."

"Don't worry about it. Mrs. Alejandro's one of those teachers who gives extra points when you show your work," Javier answered, offering his usual pep talk.

For as long as they had been friends, Andy's grades had been up and down, but he usually pulled off a solid B average at the end of the year. Ignacio was the same way.

He knew both guys wanted a music scholarship to get them into a major Texas university. Andy and Ignacio worked hard enough to earn decent grades but took their true enjoyment from band instruments they played so well.

As the bell rang to end sixth period, Javier realized he finally understood his friends' attitude. Now that he had felt the excitement of writing words people listened to and putting together images that told a story, he couldn't wait to do again. It had to be the same feeling when Ignacio and Andy played an instrument or when Pat painted with his airbrushes. He walked out of the classroom feeling like he had stopped thinking in only black and white. Shades of color, light, and sound had filtered into his mind as different options to explore, combine, and discard in any way he wanted.

Javier was in a great mood when he walked into Mr. Seneca's room and couldn't wait to get started on the next project for Guardian TV.

"Ignacio, you think I can *read* that lab report? Maybe Mr. Seneca knows about hieroglyphics, but I don't. Erase those numbers and start all over!" Mrs. Alejandro's loud voice echoed around the chemistry lab. "And you two juniors better have your calculations right this time, or I'll make you both buy new calculators!"

"Man, she's in a bad mood," Andy whispered as he stood beside Javier working on a chemistry lab Friday afternoon. "You think it's PMS?"

"Shut up," Javier mumbled as he wrote down the results of the experiment the two of them conducted. At least he had gotten that stupid penmanship award in fourth grade, and he used a new scientific calculator that he won in a raffle at prep camp. He and Andy usually had no trouble with Mrs. Alejandro.

She came around to their table, glanced at their lab report, and then grunted. She said, "Well, at least there's hope. I wondered after what I saw on your test last night."

As she walked away, Andy looked like he might wet his pants. "I knew it," Andy whispered. "I blew it on the test. My mom's gonna kill me."

"It can't be that bad," Javier spoke very quietly, "and it's only the first test. Come on . . . let's get this finished up. Just tell your mom you can always raise your average with good lab grades."

Minutes before the bell rang, Mrs. Alejandro started passing back the tests, turning them face down in front of each student. She started with the juniors in the back and moved up to where Javier and his friends sat.

At the next table, Javier saw Ignacio wipe the sweat off his forehead before he turned over his test and sighed, "Seventy-two. Well, at least I passed." And Javier had to smile when he saw Andy receive his test, look at it, and suddenly flop his upper body across the top of the lab table with relief. "Thank you, God, an eighty!"

Then Mrs. Alejandro stopped in front of Javier. On the first day of school when Javier had helped her with the microscopes, she was quick to carry on a friendly conversation, and she always seemed pleased with his answers in class. But at this moment, staring at Javier with her dark eyes peering over her pink reading glasses, she didn't look friendly or pleased. "I'm incredibly disappointed, Mr. Ávila." Her words clicked like high heels on a hardwood floor. "I can't believe you could be this careless—you, of all people." She set the paper face down with a firm thump on Javier's desk. Her red polished nails rapped upon it as she said, "I expect corrections first thing on Monday morning." Then Mrs. Alejandro said even louder, "I expect all of you to turn in corrections to me before first period on Monday, and those who *failed* this exam know my policy. Your parents need to sign the test." She gave his paper one last tap and walked away.

Javier sat frozen to his chair, unable to move. He stared down at the test paper, trying to ignore an imaginary drumroll in his head. *Ready . . . aim . . . fire!*

The sound of the bell almost shook Javier off the lab stool. Several guys around him started laughing. Others commented as they left the room.

"Whoa, Javier flunked a test!"

"The smart guy got shot down!"

"How does it feel to be like the rest of us flunkies?"

It felt like he had a relapse of the chicken pox, that's how it felt. He reached out with an itchy hand and finally turned over the test paper. He stared at a two-inch red 45.

"Jack, that's an Ignacio grade, not a Javier Ávila grade." Andy stood next to him.

Ignacio had come around the front of the lab table. "What happened?"

"I don't know," he said and scanned the multiple-choice questions. He had missed the two he thought he might, but there were five wrong answers he didn't plan for. When he flipped to the second page, he groaned at the sight of all the red marks. He guessed that the equation for the initial reaction was balanced incorrectly. That meant all the other answers that followed it were wrong too.

"It was like you said, Andy—all or nothing on page two," Javier told him as he stood up. He folded the test in half and stuck it inside his chemistry book.

"I can't believe how I lucked out," Andy said before he sighed with relief. "Mrs. Alejandro was mad at your test grade, not mine. As for you, Jack, so sad, too bad."

Ignacio clapped Javier hard on the shoulder. "Man, Javier, this is a first: you *flunking* a test. Who knew the smartest guy in the whole school could get tripped up by chemistry? And you did all that science camp stuff too. Man, Javier, it sucks!"

"Yeah," Javier replied, frowning at his friends for stating the obvious.

"You're lucky that your dad isn't like my dad. When my father has to sign a test that I flunked, I catch all kinds of hell. Your dad just makes jokes," Ignacio replied.

"He won't joke about this," Javier said. "That F doesn't stand for funny, you guys. It stands for failure."

CHAPTER THIRTEEN

F rustrated by his own mistakes, Javier stomped his way down the noisy hallways and headed for his locker. Andy and Ignacio had gone straight to the band hall. He was glad; their comments had just made him mad. Neither gave him any sympathy, or even tried to understand how he felt, even after all those years he helped them with homework or said something positive when they got low grades. But instead of doing the same for Javier, they made stupid comments.

He reached his locker and started working the combination lock. What would his parents say when he showed them that chemistry test? They wouldn't yell like Andy's mom or swear like Ignacio's father, but he knew how disappointment cooled his mother's gaze. His father grew quiet when people let him down. For years, Javier gave up fun so he could make them proud. What did it get him? Half a scholarship and two miserable summers in a program he only attended to look smart. And what about the constant backache from carrying home all his books every night?

Javier stood there, still brooding at his open locker, when Pat walked up.

"Hey! Mr. Seneca sent me a note during seventh period," Pat said. "He wants me to pick up the camera for tonight's game. I guess Kenny doesn't want to film it."

Javier heard the excitement in his friend's voice. He nodded but still frowned at the pile of textbooks that had his attention. "That's good, Pat. You know what to do."

"Javier, what's wrong?"

Before Javier could answer, someone slapped him on the back. When he turned, he saw one of the juniors from chemistry class with a big grin on his unshaven face.

"Hey, Ávila, I gotta thank you. You flunking that big chemistry test really made me laugh." Before the junior walked off, he added, "Don't forget! Have your mommy sign the test."

It felt like he had inhaled burning chemicals during lab. Javier turned around and yanked his canvas backpack from the locker. He couldn't even look at Pat.

"You flunked your chemistry test?" Pat stepped closer. "Really, Javier, how bad was it?"

"What does it matter?" he spit out.

"Well, if it's above a fifty, there's good chance that a few nineties will bring it up to a C average. A couple of hundreds can let you pull out a B by the end of the semester." Pat spoke in that earnest tone he used when he made announcements. "If it's below fifty, you need to ask for extra-credit work."

Javier Ávila asking for extra credit? He shoved his chemistry book and his lab folder into his backpack. He put his math book and paperback copy of *Walden* on top of that. "I got a lot of homework this weekend, Pat. Don't expect me at the game tonight."

"What?"

"You heard me. I'm busy. Besides, I don't need everybody at the game talking about my chemistry grade either! Word travels fast—probably at the speed of light if your face has been plastered on school TV."

"Jack, you're talking crazy. It's just one F."

"Hey! Why don't we put me on the announcements? Then my chemistry grade could make everyone laugh!" Angry sarcasm burst out like a flash fire. "We could set it to music and show me on my knees begging Mrs. Alejandro for extra-credit work. We can put Brother Calvin dancing in the background. Won't that be hilarious?"

"Stop it, Javier!" Pat banged hard on the locker door. "Just stop it!"

Javier stepped back. His breathing slowed as that insane mood started to leave him. He stared at his friend, wishing he could start the whole conversation again. What was Pat going to think about his TV partner turning into a crazy moron? "Sorry."

Pat shook his head but didn't frown. "Javier, you're now sitting in the same boat with normal people who screw up. Didn't you say you don't want to be a robot anymore? That means you get to flunk tests like the rest of us guys, okay?"

"You know, Pat, all my life, I wanted to be like the rest of the guys," Javier said, surprised he actually said it out loud, "but I can't run or pitch a ball without looking like an idiot. I play no instruments and can't draw. School is the only thing I do well, so now what?"

"Javier, you need to do what Mr. Seneca said and look at the bigger picture."

Look at a bigger picture? Right now Javier felt like a blind man.

"Come on, Jack. Forget about chemistry," Pat told him. His enthusiastic tone had returned. "We'll go to the game tonight, and we'll take turns on the camera and get some great footage. And who knows? Our next video could make us famous!"

That's when another junior from chemistry class walked past them and called out, "Tough luck, Javier. Looks like you'll need to suck up to Mrs. Alejandro big time. You better pucker up!" Three loud kissing sounds followed.

"Man, juniors are idiots," Pat said. "Remind me not to turn stupid next year."

Javier had to laugh. "Yeah, me too." He looked inside his locker again. With Pat watching, Javier couldn't add unnecessary books and not feel pathetic. He had already gathered what he needed for homework, so he closed the door. He lifted his backpack by the handle and carried it easily in one hand.

"Do you need a ride today?" Javier asked as they walked out of the building.

"Yeah. I'll go to my grandma's tonight and go home tomorrow morning. If I'm not there every once in a while, my mom takes it personal," Pat replied. "If my dad's not around, it's so much better for me."

"Do you realize how strange that sounds?"

Pat gave a hollow laugh. "You got a dad who cares about you, Javier. My dad is all about the show. He loves to present his good-looking daughter to everybody, but his son? I'm like one of the used cars he keeps in the back lot of the dealership."

"Have you even told him about your elective? When I asked Feliz to help us with the backdrop, I could tell she knew nothing about what you do in school." Javier shook his head. "Do you know that on the first day of school, my mom grilled me like the FBI, and later I heard her on the phone with my brothers and sisters telling them all about my elective? My dad's still asking me to steal a copy of the show and bring it home."

By then, Pat and Javier had walked up the steps of Mr. Seneca's building. Pat reached for the door and said, "Why don't you just ask Mr. Seneca to let you borrow a tape so you can show it to your dad?"

"I will if you will," Javier said, hoping to make things better for Pat at home. *How could Mr. Berlanga not be swayed by his son's sense of humor and his on-camera persona?* "I bet if your dad saw a tape, he'd be just as impressed as everybody in this school has been." He let Pat open the door, and they walked inside.

No one expected to see Ms. Maloney leaning against Mr. Seneca's desk. He stood very close in front of her, with only the awkward position of the crutches providing space between them. Under the spell of whatever they were saying, it took a moment for them both to turn toward the door.

Ms. Maloney's blue eyes widened, and Mr. Seneca's wide brow wrinkled. She gasped and straightened up, trying to sidestep her way around him. He shuffled back in a crooked fashion and wobbled so uncontrollably that Ms. Maloney grabbed onto his arms. One of the crutches slipped out and crashed to the floor. His upper body swayed like a large balloon losing its air.

"Oh, my God!" she cried out as he started to fall backwards. "Help him!"

Javier tossed the backpack out of his hands and ran. Pat had moved even quicker to come up from behind their teacher and press his wide shoulders against Mr. Seneca's back to keep him upright.

Javier went for the crutch, whipping it up and letting Mr. Seneca grab it. Javier covered his teacher's shaking hand with both of his and pulled the man toward him. He strained against the weight of the bigger man. Even with Pat pushing from behind, Javier pressed his own legs to the floor and held his back and shoulders firm to keep Mr. Seneca and his own clumsy self upright.

"I got it, I got it," Mr. Seneca whispered through panting breaths. "I'm up. I'm not going to fall. Frances, I'm okay." He stood straight on his feet, but he leaned unevenly toward the side of his body where his fist tightened around the metal crutch.

"Are you sure, Mr. Seneca?" Pat stood behind him, his hands spread across his teacher's shoulders. "I got your back, Sir. Lean against me if you need to."

"Get your bearings, Win. Take your time." Ms. Maloney's voice reminded Javier of the way his mom would soothe him after she applied a Band-aid or an ice bag.

Ms. Maloney guided Mr. Seneca's arm through the cuff like it should be, and that's when Javier realized this wasn't the first time she had helped him with his crutches. He almost smiled, only he saw the embarrassment quickly narrow into anger in Mr. Seneca's dark eyes. Javier let him go and quickly stepped away now that his teacher had the crutches to hold himself steady.

"I told you we weren't going to work after school today." His gruff voice sounded like a monster's from an old movie. He pressed his hands into the handle of his crutches to shift himself in Javier's direction. "What are you two boys doing in here?"

Pat stepped around Mr. Seneca and said, "Sir, you sent me a note during seventh period, remember? I'm supposed to pick up the camera to film tonight's game. That's why Javier and I are here. The note said to come after school."

Mr. Seneca's jaw slowly unclenched before he nodded silently.

"I'm sorry if we startled you." Javier knew they had interrupted a personal moment they probably shouldn't have seen. "I guess we should have knocked first. We're very sorry."

"No harm done," Ms. Maloney said, tugging at her yellow sweater and smoothing it over her striped skirt. She kept her eyes down. "You two were lucky to be here when Win . . . uh, I mean Mr. Seneca almost . . . well, I guess I should leave . . . uh, so you get the camera."

Javier squeezed his fingers behind his back. "No, Ms. Maloney, don't leave. Just let Pat and me grab the camera and tripod, and then we're out of here."

Pat extended his hand. "Can I borrow the keys, Sir?"

"And can we borrow one of the replay tapes?" Javier asked, taking advantage of Pat's word choice. "Our parents want to see what we're doing in the class. May we take a tape home over the weekend?"

"Take a tape home?" Mr. Seneca blinked like he wasn't sure he heard correctly.

"Why not take home a tape of the broadcast with the music video? That was impressive too," Ms. Maloney said in a voice that sounded more like her old self. She had moved closer to talk to her students. "If Mr. Seneca trusts you with school property, I'm sure he can trust you with the class tapes he's made."

At this point, Mr. Seneca grabbed the keys from his belt. His chin lowered before he said to Pat, "I expect you both can be trusted with anything inside this classroom. Do you know what the word 'discretion' means, Mr. Berlanga?"

"Yes, Sir." Pat took the keys from Mr. Seneca's hands. "It means Javier and I came for the camera. I haven't seen Ms. Maloney since fifth period. And except for Javier flunking his chemistry test, nothing out of the ordinary has happened today."

"Shut up!" Javier jerked Pat's arm. "Didn't the man just ask you if you knew the definition of discretion? What's wrong with you?" He pulled him toward the back cabinets before Pat could tell his teachers anymore embarrassing news.

"Hey, I was just trying to take the edge off." He grinned all the same.

Javier let it go. If everybody had agreed to discretion, his teachers couldn't mention failing a test either. Besides, he could bet that Mr. Seneca wanted them to find the camera equipment and get lost.

"There's a box on the bottom shelf!" Mr. Seneca called after Pat had opened the cabinet door. "I labeled the tapes as I made them. The August/September dates would be the two of you. Don't lose it. I haven't had time to make copies."

Javier found their tape but also grabbed the broadcast with the music video too. Meanwhile, Pat pulled out the camera bag and the tripod. They had the cabinet locked and were walking back to return the keys to Mr. Seneca in no time.

Ms. Maloney stood at one of the maps on the wall reading it with apparent interest. Mr. Seneca sat at his desk, shuffling papers.

Javier placed the keys on the desktop and said, "Thank you, Mr. Seneca. Have a good weekend. You too, Ms. Maloney."

"Good-bye, gentlemen," he said quite abruptly and didn't make eye contact.

Ms. Maloney turned around to offer a weak wave of one hand. "Have a good weekend, guys. I hope your parents enjoy the show."

"Thanks. Bye." Javier grabbed his backpack and followed Pat outside.

Pat waited until the door closed behind them before he let out a gigantic sigh. "Okay, I'm going to rank that as one of the worst moments of my life!"

"I learned a whole new definition for awkward that won't be on any SAT test." Javier walked to the railing and rested his backpack on top. He unzipped the middle compartment and put the tapes inside. He surprised himself by smiling. "Look on the bright side, Pat. We can't tell anyone what we saw today."

"That's too bad." Pat lifted his eyebrows and grinned. "If everyone started talking about Ms. Maloney and Mr. Seneca messing around, then who'd care that Javier Ávila got an F on his chemistry test?"

In all the excitement of a failed test and the sight of two teachers in a romantic moment, Javier had been too busy to check the messages on his phone until he arrived in his own driveway. Both his parents had called about working late. His father wanted to finish the roof on a restored building in Universal City in case of rain, and his mom was meeting with auditors at the office. So he wouldn't have to deal with their reactions to the chemistry grade right away, and he couldn't bring it up while his big brothers and their kids were piling on the pancakes tomorrow morning or before they showed up for hamburgers and the Dallas game. He'd wait until Sunday night, which was usually a quiet time in their house. His mom would be reading the newspaper at the kitchen table; his father would be watching TV in the den; and Javier would be in his room doing homework. It was the perfect time to break the news to them.

Javier glanced at the camera bag Pat had left on the front seat and decided to follow his buddy's advice: "Just enjoy the game tonight and forget about the F."

But not before he went over the test. Javier had to know why he had made such careless errors and knew he wouldn't enjoy anything until he had the answer. He'd leave corrections for later, but now that he was all alone, he wanted some time to read through the test, figure out the mistakes, and plan ways not to repeat them.

Later, as he drove with Pat to the football game, Javier tried to explain what he had learned, but it was obvious Pat was more concerned about his phone messages from Carrie than whatever Javier was saying. That's when Javier realized he had left his phone at home. He wondered if Amanda had left *him* any messages. *Probably not.*

"Carrie can't make it tonight. Says she has to babysit. Do you think it's the truth?" Pat was frowning at his phone like Carrie could magically see him on her phone screen.

"Why do you think she's lying to you?" Javier asked him as he glanced in the sideview mirror to check traffic as he drove onto the expressway. "Did you do something wrong?"

"I don't know. Last weekend was the first one we spent together. I think she liked me better online." Pat sighed. "I was going to ask her to Homecoming. Figured you could ask Amanda, and maybe if Andy asks Natalie, we could have some fun."

"What about Ignacio?" Javier replied. "We can't leave him out."

"Don't you have any other cousins?"

"Do you?"

Pat chuckled. "Well, let's hope Natalie has one more friend."

Once they got on the football field sidelines and started to work with the camera, both guys forgot about anything else. They had to concentrate hard as they tried to follow the game from the sidelines.

Javier was used to watching football games on television where a commentator's analysis and instant replays tracked the movement of both teams. But standing on the field, it was hard to distinguish patterns of offense and defense. Football players tangled up quickly; spotting the ball became a guessing game. Javier and Pat tried a variety of places to stand: behind a goal post, on the opponent's side of the field, and near the trainer's table. They managed to film a Guardian touchdown and the extra point by accident, not by planning.

By the end of the first quarter, Javier had a better understanding of Kenny's bad mood at the last game. It was not that the Guardian football team was losing tonight, but it was extremely frustrating to focus on key plays and capture them on film.

"I can't believe someone as impatient as Kenny García could film a game," Javier commented as they waited for the official's whistle to start the second quarter. "I have new respect for the cameramen who bring us football games on TV."

"Well, on TV, it's not two goofy sophomores who don't know what they're doing," Pat replied. He stopped checking the sight through the lens and looked at Javier. "It's a team of camera people shooting from different angles and some director in a booth watching the monitors and putting them in order. I think I want to be *that* guy."

"I don't like sports that much. I'd like to be the guy who makes a documentary that helps people think," Javier said. "Or maybe take a book and make it into a movie."

"Aren't you mixing up your jobs? Do you want to make movies or write scripts?"

"Why can't I do both?"

The whistle sounded, and they both started paying attention to the game again.

They lucked out catching another touchdown on film. When Javier saw the band lining up at the opposite side of the field, he told Pat they should go to the top of the bleachers and film half-time from a higher vantage point.

"I think we should ask Mr. Seneca to buy more cameras," Javier said as Pat untwisted the camera off the tripod. "It would be great to have someone on the field and someone up in the stands. Editing could be more fun too."

From the top of the bleachers, they took turns filming the band. They also panned the camera across the crowd for other images to use.

The third quarter had just begun when the drizzle started.

Pat muttered several curse words. "Rain . . . just what we need. If this equipment gets wet, Mr. Seneca will kill us."

Javier was already reaching for the camera bag. He handed it to Pat and then started to fold up the tripod. "Let's go under the bleachers. If the rain stops, we'll go back on the sidelines."

But the drizzle became a steady rain, and while it could have made for great film to show highlights from a mud bowl, Javier and Pat decided it was better not to anger Mr. Seneca, and neither one of them wanted to pay for damaged equipment. Besides, the Guardians were winning against Temple 18-3.

As the fourth quarter started, almost half the people had already left the stadium.

Javier and Pat agreed that it would be dumb to spend any more time standing under the bleachers, especially as thunder rumbled in the distance. Pat put the camera bag under his shirt, and Javier folded up the tripod into its smallest size and carried it in one hand against his chest. They ran to the parking lot, trying to sidestep watery potholes, and trying not to fall on the slippery parking lot.

They were both wet and panting when they finally sat inside the truck.

A clap of thunder was followed by streaks of lightning above the stadium lights.

"That's it. They'll end the game now. The refs won't let them play in lightning," Pat said, positioning the camera bag between his legs. "Man, I'm soaked!"

Javier shivered from the wet T-shirt clinging to his body. He rubbed down his wet arms and wiped his hands on his damp jeans. His face pinched together nervously as heavy rain pummeled the truck cab. Inside the small space, the noise sounded like stones fell from the sky. "I've never driven in a storm like this," he said to Pat.

"Me neither. Do you want to sit here for a while and see if it stops?"

"No. I'll just take it slow. If it gets worse, I'll pull over."

As Javier drove out of the stadium parking lot, he was grateful to follow the line of red tail lights in front of him. Even though it was hard to see between the hard rain and the whipping windshield wipers, Javier enjoyed the warmth from the defroster. Pat said nothing as he checked his phone again, and except for a frustrated grunt, he stared out the window silently. Javier didn't want to try to talk and drive in the storm at the same time, so he was quiet too.

By the time he reached the exit for the Woodlawn Lake neighborhood, the rain had settled into a thick drizzle, but the thunder and lightning seemed to be over. It was good to be off the expressway and driving down a wet, but familiar street toward home. There were only a few cars on a usually busy street. All the houses looked dim and gray. Few house lights were on, and a church he passed looked empty and dark.

"I'm anxious to see the pictures we shot tonight," Javier said. His hands relaxed on the steering wheel when he drove past his house and up the side street to drop off Pat. "I hope I didn't shake when I took pictures of the band."

"It's too bad we can't get together tomorrow and work on this film," Pat replied. He had flipped open his phone once more and then sighed. "You know, Javier, I've been thinking. What if my parents buy me the same editing software we have at school? My mom can usually guilt my dad into something I want, especially if I can use it for school. I'll talk to her tomorrow. Maybe I'll even squeeze a new laptop out of the deal."

Javier would never think to "squeeze" anything out of his parents. Pat's attitude made Javier's feet itchy, or maybe it was his wet socks. Regardless, he had to say, "You know, Pat, I have plenty of homework right now. I don't know if I can afford to spend my weekends working on film."

"That's just the F in chemistry talking, Jack. I know you love what you're doing for Mr. Seneca's class. You should see the excitement on your face when you sit at the computer or when you tell us at lunch about the films you watched online."

"Maybe I do like the class," he said as the truck neared Pat's grandmother's house. "But I need to get serious, concentrate on my other classes before that F in chemistry burns a big hole in my GPA."

"Who cares? So what if your GPA drops two or three points?" Pat replied, looking out his window. His voice hardened with more sarcasm. "What? You think your parents won't love you if you don't make As all the time?"

"Just shut up, Pat! You don't know what you're talking about." Javier's anger hit him like a whip. He felt the sting from his head to his feet. "Just because—"

He never finished his sentence because Pat had started yelling. "Welita's house! It's on fire!"

CHAPTER FOURTEEN

"For God's sake, stop the truck!" Pat repeatedly pulled the lever on the truck door. "Let me out! Now, Javier!"

"I can't just stop in the middle of the street!"

"Then pull over, dammit!" His frustration made him angrier. "Damn, these doors! Javier! Stop the truck! Pull over! NOW!"

Javier jerked the steering wheel. The truck veered to the curb in front of the house next to Pat's grandmother's. He stomped on the brakes. They both shot forward and then slammed back into their seats. Javier did a quick shift into PARK so the truck doors would unlock. Pat whipped his door open, only to be lurched back by the seatbelt. His shaking hands tugged and pulled at the silver latch. He screamed and cursed.

"Pat, calm down!" Javier spoke in that same firm tone he used when Trey started to act like a crybaby. "You can't help anybody if you freak out!" He quickly reached over to press the release button on Pat's seatbelt, and then his own.

Pat stared at Javier, his dark eyes wild and frantic. But then he tossed over his phone. "Okay . . . here. Call 9-1-1. I'm going inside and get Welita out of the house." He bolted out of the truck and ran toward the front porch.

With stiff fingers, Javier punched in the emergency number on Pat's cell phone. He pressed it against his ear, and with the other hand, he opened his door. He got out and stood in the street. Thick drizzle veiled by a gray mist carried the stink of smoke and fire. When he looked directly at the house, Javier saw short tufts of reddish-orange flames spreading across the roof. As Pat got the front door open and ran inside, Javier's fears shivered under him like a second skin.

His footsteps were heavy as he crossed the front yard. The male voice on the phone asked him for the nature of the emergency. Javier stopped and said, "Hurry! There's a house on fire on Mistletoe Drive." He called out the plain black numbers hanging from a wooden sign above the porch.

"A fire truck is on the way. Don't go into the building," the man told him.

Javier snapped the phone closed. He looked around for help. Not one house had a light on. *Are they gone? Asleep?*

Where is Pat? He shouldn't have gone inside! Javier started running but tripped over the cracked sidewalk and fell. His shins slammed against the concrete. The palms of his hands scraped across the sidewalk. Despite the stinging pain, he got up and jumped over the small step on the porch. He pulled open the screen door. "Pat? Pat!"

A dense curtain of black smoke filled the doorway. He covered his nose and mouth but started coughing anyway. He used his arms to wave away the smoke. He tried to put his head inside, but the smoke blinded him. His eyes stung, his nose started running, and he yelled in the house, "Pat! Pat?! Can you hear me?!"

He pounded on the door frame, but it just made the smoke come out faster. He started coughing harder and leaned back against the front window. *Around the side of the house,* he thought, *They'll have to use the back door or climb out a window.*

He limped off the front porch and around the house to the side windows of the bedrooms. "Pat! Pat!" he yelled. The rain was cold, but his body sweated heat. He was breathing so heavily that he felt like he was running laps in gym class.

Javier banged on the window frames with his fists. One of the rooms had to be where Pat would find his grandmother asleep and where Javier would find them together. *Oh, please, God, let them be there. Keep them safe*, he prayed.

"Pat! Pat!" he yelled and paused to catch his breath. He must have swallowed smoke, because his throat hurt. He pounded on the last two windows. "Pat, can you hear me?" He clenched his fists and pounded harder. His nose ran, and his eyes watered. *Where is that damn fire truck?*

He was about to step away and try the back door when he heard the scraping noise of an old windowpane lifting open.

"Javier! Javier! We're in here!" Pat's voice sounded raspy and hoarse.

"*Ayúdame*," groaned an old woman's voice. "Help me."

Javier pressed his hands against the screen. "Hang on, Pat! The Fire Department's on the way." He could barely make out his friend's shape and didn't see Pat's grandmother. "Are you okay?"

"Dammit, Javier! Get us out of here!" Pat's voice screeched with panic. "The bedroom's full of smoke. My grandmother's going to suffocate! Me too!"

There wasn't time to wait for firemen. "Open the screen," Javier told him, back to giving orders to keep Pat calm. "Unhook the latch at the bottom."

"It's stuck! It won't open!" Pat cried. "Both of the latches are stuck!"

"They're probably rusted shut," Javier replied. He had dealt with his share of old windows when Uncle Willie used to take him along to help the painters.

Javier couldn't see for the drizzle in his eyes, but he pounded on the bottom of the windowsill, hoping to shake the hook from the latch. "You need to find something to hit the latch and loosen it. Hurry, Pat!"

"*Ayúdame.*" The old woman kept coughing and gasping.

Javier jabbed his fingers against the bottom of the screen, hoping to poke a hole. He felt sharp little wires pricking his fingers, but he kept prying at the screen, trying to make an opening.

Hard tapping, metal on metal, came from inside. Pat groaned, coughing, and cursing. Javier coughed too. The smoke sailed through the window, and he had to step back to catch his breath. He wiped his nose, but burning soot filled the air.

A siren wailed in the distance, but Javier was scared they'd be too late. "Keep trying! You need to get the latch open. Pat, don't stop!"

"I got it!" Pat gasped. "It's loose!"

Then he pushed open the screen—right into Javier's forehead. Firecrackers seemed to explode in his eyes. Javier stumbled back, but he grabbed the bottom of the window screen and pulled himself upright. He couldn't fall now.

Javier held on, and by an instinctive knowledge that came from helping his brothers on remodeling jobs, he knew to lift up so the screen popped off its hinges. Then he tossed the whole thing over his shoulder.

Pat's grandmother had already lifted a leg out of the window. One bare foot dangled off the windowsill. Javier stood up on his toes and reached in to grab the old woman's body and pull her through the window. She was so much lighter than Mr. Seneca had been that afternoon, but he felt off-balance and clumsy as he tried to keep a grip on her. His wet hands slipped over her thin cotton gown. His fingers pressed against the soft flesh of her stomach. He put another hand at her head, scared she might hit it against the window pane.

"Let me help! Let me help you!" said a man's voice behind Javier, but Javier didn't turn around for fear he would drop Pat's grandmother. "Señora Mendiola! I'm here to help. It's me, Tomás, your neighbor."

Javier was so grateful for the neighbor's help not only to get her out, but also to carry her away from the house. Once Welita looked safe in the older man's arms, Javier turned back to the window and called inside, "Pat! Pat, can you hear me?" Smoky ghosts answered, making him cover his mouth and wheeze.

Then he felt Pat's grip on his arm. "I can't breathe," he whispered.

"I'm here. I won't let you go." Javier reached in with both arms. He tried to pull Pat's heavy body out into the rainy, smoky night. His hands reached higher, grabbing Pat by the shoulders. He groaned, pulling and tugging.

"No, you can't do this." Pat's raspy words sounded tired and weak. "I'm too big . . . you can't . . . get real, Jack."

"Help me! Use your legs! Come on! Friends don't give up that easily." Javier felt as if he was sobbing. Every inch of him was determined not to be clumsy and to step up in every way possible to save his friend.

Javier took a deep breath and pulled again. Pat pushed himself forward, and Javier gripped so tightly that he thought his arm muscles might explode. Using the leverage of the windowsill and gravity itself, he tugged and shifted Pat's body down and out. He tried to catch Pat, but the bigger guy came down on him like an avalanche, and Javier toppled over. Pat's full weight landed on Javier's chest and legs, knocking the wind out of him. Javier surrendered to the empty black feeling that released him from the pain of his aching body.

From out of that dark place, someone grabbed him and lifted him up, and when his eyes fluttered open, Javier saw two moving legs, the muddy ground. He was being carried on someone's shoulder, away from the smoke and the burning house, but closer to loud voices, sirens, and flashing red lights.

Then he felt the wet ground against his back, but this time, two arms braced his fall like hard cushions around his shoulders. Then he was released, and when Javier opened his eyes wider, he saw Pat's body slump down beside him.

Javier had never been so grateful for his mom's FBI personality than he was that night in the emergency room. He felt invisible; no one would tell him anything.

When his parents arrived, he sat upright on a hospital bed inside a curtain enclosed cubicle. He was affixed to a clear thin tube with two prongs that went inside his nose, providing him with fresh oxygen. A nurse had covered him with a blanket. She stood at his bedside taking his blood pressure when his mom's questions began. Then, a young intern got the same treatment a few minutes later. They told his parents Javier had suffered from minor smoke inhalation which a few hours of oxygen would help. He'd be released and could go home in three or four hours.

His dad had stood silently on the other side of the bed. He had grasped Javier's hand, and after several minutes of listening to the nurse and doctor, had still not let it go.

When they were alone again, his mom looked at Javier, her dark eyes blinking back tears. She leaned down and kissed Javier's forehead. *"Gracias a Dios."*

His dad slowly released Javier's hand. His smile trembled as if it was hard to wear it on his mouth comfortably. "Nivia, do you remember when Selena threw Vivian's doll into the barbecue pit? It looked like Javier's smoky face, *verdad?"*

When his mom laughed, Javier smiled and started to relax, but when he tried to talk, he barely recognized his own voice. "I'm okay, but what about Pat? No one will tell me where he is, what happened to him, nothing." He wasn't crying, but because of all the smoke, his nose kept running and his eyes watered. Also he couldn't stop his voice from shaking since he felt wet and cold. His shivering never stopped, even with the thick hospital blanket on top of him.

His mom cleared her throat and stepped back. She rubbed Javier's shoulder. "Don't worry . . . I'll find out something for you." Then she looked at her husband. "Marc, call Eric and get him to go to our house and bring Javito some dry clothes. Son, you need to rest. I promise I'll be back with news about Pat." She pushed the curtains aside and left.

His father's expression was very solemn as he called Eric. Javier watched his dad, listening while he walked around the bed and kept assuring Eric that his little brother was going to be okay. It had been a while since Javier had paid attention to the wrinkles around his father's tired eyes, the thickening of his chin, and the small bald patch on the back of his gray head. Tonight, his dad really looked sixty years old.

After his father ended the call and turned back to look at him, Javier said, "I'm sorry, Dad. I hate to make you and Mom worry like this, but I'm going to be fine."

"I know." He nodded like his neck was stiff. Then his dad sat down on the edge of the bed. "Why don't you tell me about what happened tonight, Son?"

Unlike his mother, who questioned every detail, his father listened intently as Javier took the time to describe the night's events, but his dad wasn't without his sense of humor. "And what if there had been burglar bars on the windows? Did you two think you were the Hulk and Spiderman?"

Javier smiled, but he had thought the same thing earlier. So many houses in the neighborhood had iron bars on the windows. He knew it was lucky this wasn't the case tonight. "But you know what really helped, Dad? I knew about old windows. Thanks to those spring breaks when you made me work with Uncle Willie, I could help Pat get his grandmother out."

His father squeezed Javier's arm. He nodded and smiled. "Not just book smart, but sensible smart too. Although I'm not so sure getting your head in the way of an open screen was such a smart move. You're going to have a nasty bruise in the morning." Then his lips straightened into a fine line, and his eyes darkened. "But you wear that bruise proudly, Javit . . . uh, I mean Javier. Tonight you saved Pat and his grandmother's lives—" The next words caught in his throat. He blinked several times and swallowed hard before his said, "No man could be prouder of his son than I am right now of you, Javier. I love you, and I'm so grateful God gave me this chance tonight to tell you. You have *always* been our miracle, our blessing. Do you know that?"

Javier's heart swelled inside his chest, into his throat, and up to his head until it burst from his eyes in relieved tears. All his life, Javier had been hugged by his father, but tonight's *abrazo* made him feel like he gave back to his father as much as Javier took from him.

When they finally released each other, Javier wiped his face with the back of his hand. His dad rubbed under his eyes and then grinned like his old self. "This is your mother's fault. She makes us watch those silly *telenovelas*. Those *hombres* cry if they lose their hat."

Javier had to smile. "Yeah, what wimps!" he said. "Why don't they do something really masculine like run into a window screen?" It felt good to be talking and laughing with his father for a while.

But he felt overwhelmed by the emotional waves crashing his heart and his head when *both* his big brothers arrived at the hospital thirty minutes later. After tight hugs and relieved sighs, his brothers helped Javier maneuver a change of clothes, despite the oxygen tubes and his own shivering hands. His feet were ice cold, and wiggling his toes around in dry socks helped him relax.

After he changed, Javier felt warmer, especially when the nurse brought him a heated blanket. He leaned back against the pillows and dozed to the familiar sounds of his father's quiet voice explaining to Eric and Leo what had happened. It was his mom's voice that pulled him awake, especially when he heard her say Pat's name.

"Mom, is Pat okay?" His words felt thick and dry upon his tongue.

"Yes, Javito," she said, rubbing her hand over the blanket covering his chest. "Pat's suffering from smoke inhalation, but the doctors are optimistic since he is young and has no conditions like asthma. They said he needs two or three days in the hospital and a week's rest at home." She looked at her husband and two older sons. "I met Mrs. Berlanga in the waiting room. She looked so lost, the poor woman. I'm glad I could help her get some answers from the doctors."

Javier frowned. "Wasn't Pat's father there?"

His mom shook her head. "Mrs. Berlanga said her husband was with the chief of police and the fire marshal, surveying the damages to the house."

"What about the old woman?" Leo asked. "Dad said Javier helped pull the grandmother out of the burning house."

"She's fine. Mrs. Berlanga said she'll take her mother to their house tonight." She smiled down at Javier. "I told her that you and Pat are true heroes."

"Why wouldn't our little Javito be a hero?" Eric pressed his hand on Javier's shoulder. "Javito's just like me and Leo. We're all brave men when the pressure's on."

"Thanks," Javier said, touched by the comparison, but as he looked up at his big brother, he also said, "And can you stop calling me *Javito*? It makes me sound like a little kid—like Trey or Laura."

"Javier's right," his father said. "I named Javier after my father, and he was one of the finest men I ever knew." He stepped up behind Leo and put his hands on his oldest son's shoulders. "Every man should be so lucky to have three smart sons like mine."

Javier's mother pushed open the door to the hospital room where the nurse told them Pat would be. Javier knew it was past two in the morning and all of them were worn out, but he had begged to see Pat before he left the hospital. With a few pointed questions, his mom had learned his hospital room number. Javier felt embarrassed when he saw the wheelchair, but once he sank into it, he was glad he didn't have to walk.

The fifth floor was quiet except for the subtle humming of machines. Javier's dad pushed the wheelchair inside the dim room. Two vertical lights on both sides of the bed were set on low, so Javier could see his friend under the white sheets.

Pat lay there with a plastic mask on his face. A monitor with green and red numbers and lines was attached to his arm with wires. A plastic IV bag with clear liquid was also connected to him. His eyes were closed, and his chest seemed to be breathing heavy. His dark face had been washed, and his usually spiked hair was combed back from his wide forehead.

The sight of Pat's vulnerability made Javier start shivering again. He clutched the armrests of the wheelchair. His raw emotions resurfaced, and he was scared he might lose it in front of his parents. So, he breathed in and out, over and over, pacing his rhythm with Pat's until he felt he had regained control.

"Why is he all alone?" his mom whispered. "If this were Javier, I'd be in that chair by the window watching him through the night."

"I'd be there beside you," his father replied, "even if I had to blow up an air mattress to sleep on the floor."

"Pat, I'll be back later." Javier spoke in a normal tone just in case Pat could hear him. "You need to get out of this hospital. We have film to edit, and we need to partner on Guardian TV again. Don't you leave me hanging, Pat."

He wanted so much for Pat to open his eyes, to say something back, but Pat just kept sleeping. Then Javier remembered that when it came to sleeping, Pat was an expert!

As Javier rode home in his mom's car, he finally thought to ask about his truck.

"Leo and Eric already picked it up and drove it home. Don't worry about anything but resting," his mom told him. And when they got home, Javier was relieved to see the school camera and tripod on the kitchen table, safe and sound. He was happy to carry them to his room, but at the same time, he couldn't stop thinking about his good friend back at the hospital.

After a hot shower and deciding his scrapes, bumps, and bruises were nothing new for a clumsy-but-brave-guy, Javier finally relaxed in his own bed and fell into a dreamless sleep.

He awoke to his mom's cool hand on his cheek. It was a gesture that usually annoyed him, but he suddenly recalled last night's dramatic events, and her touch was a welcome comfort. He struggled to open his eyes. "No fever, Mom. I'm okay." He couldn't remember when he felt so tired and sore.

"Are you hungry? It's almost one o'clock," she replied. Her hand traveled through his hair. "You've got an interesting bruise. It looks like a purple stripe."

"That should look *great* on Guardian TV," he drawled. Sudden thoughts of his TV partner made Javier's eyes pop open. "Have you called the hospital to check on Pat?"

His mom walked around the room, gathering up dirty clothes. "Yes, Pat's still there, but I'm not driving you to the medical center today. You need to rest." She rolled his jeans, shirts, and school uniform into a ball. "Pat's mom will be taking care of him like I'm going to take care of you. If he's still there tomorrow, we'll go visit, okay?" She walked out of the bedroom as if there was nothing left to say.

Javier sighed, but he knew arguing wouldn't help. And in a way, he was glad he didn't need to go any place. He felt like he had been trampled by elephants and wanted to do nothing but lie around and sleep.

Later, though, when he was eating a turkey sandwich in the kitchen, he started worrying about Pat all over again. He tried to call Feliz, but only got her voicemail. He left a message but doubted she would call him at all. He also left a message on Andy's and Ignacio's phones to call him when they got back from the band competition in Waco.

He spoke to each of his sisters when they called to check on him and then spent a couple of hours on the den sofa, flipping through channels on the television. He never realized how many college football games, corny Westerns, and cooking shows filled up Saturday afternoon TV. He started to turn on the computer in his room when he saw his backpack by the desk. He remembered the two tapes he and Pat had borrowed and thought maybe he'd watch them now. Javier pulled them out and saw the chemistry test paper caught between them.

He sat down on his bed and unfolded the paper. His gaze fell upon the red 45. He frowned, feeling a sharp sting from the bruise on his forehead. It reminded him that getting an F on a test wasn't the worst thing that could happen to a guy. Suddenly, he felt foolish for ever giving his school grades that much power over him.

"How are you feeling, Javier?"

He looked up to see his father standing in the doorway of the bedroom.

"I'm fine, Dad, just tired. Mom said you went to check on the Universal City job. Did you find much damage from the storm?"

"Nothing too serious," he said. He walked toward the bed.

Instinctively, Javier folded up the test paper and slipped it under his pillow.

"At least nothing got hit by lightning." He sat down beside Javier. "I've been wondering if lightning set Mrs. Mendiola's house on fire. I drove by it today. It's beyond repair. Hopefully, the old woman had good insurance and can build a new house."

"Pat's father won't do it." Javier sighed. "He wants to move her out of the neighborhood. Pat lived there to keep peace in the family. Now I guess he'll go back home and live with his parents. Man, I'm going to miss driving with him to school."

His dad leaned forward, resting his arms on his thighs. "How can a guy who owns a car business not buy his own son a car? I'm sure Mr. Berlanga has his reasons though."

"Who knows? I don't get Pat's family at all, but they make me appreciate my own family even more," Javier replied. He loved the quiet conversation between his father and him—no teasing, no jokes, just talking.

His dad nodded and turned to look at Javier. "It's always good to be reminded of what's really important. Last night we all got a reality check. I think it's still sinking in today, what we might have lost. Right, Son?"

"Yes." Javier chewed on his lip. He thought about Pat, just starting to fit in well with Javier, Ignacio, and Andy as friends. He pushed Javier to loosen up and enjoy life. Thanks to Pat, Javier had become a guy who was a real person—not a fraud, not a robot, not the smartest guy in the whole school. Javier was looking at himself within a bigger picture now.

He turned around and pulled the test paper from under the pillow. "I have something to show you, something you need to sign." He unfolded the paper and with a slight tremble in his fingers, passed it over to his father.

His dad sat up and whistled. He held the paper at arm's length since he didn't have his glasses on. "Okay. I can see that grade, Son, but am I missing anything else?"

"It's chemistry. I flunked the test."

His dad frowned. "That's a *low* grade for you, Son." He finally looked at Javier. "Maybe your mom can help with your chemistry homework. I'm the guy who didn't finish college, remember?"

Javier actually laughed. "I'm not eight years old, Dad. I don't need Mom's help with my homework." He flicked his finger against the corner of the test paper. "I already know how to fix all the mistakes. I just did a wrong calculation that messed up everything else. It was a dumb mistake, that's all."

"Hey, you come by that naturally. Ávila men make mistakes all the time." His father smiled and gave Javier a wink. "But Ávila men are always smart enough not to make the same mistakes twice." He handed Javier back the paper. "I've always thought a man learns more from a mistake than he does when he gets everything right all the time."

"I wish you had told me *that* in fifth grade," Javier said in a sarcastic way.

His father stood up. "What do you mean? What happened in fifth grade?"

"Never mind." Javier tossed the test paper back on his desk and picked up the broadcast tapes. "I've got something else from school to show you, and you're going to like it much better than signing a sorry test paper."

Then he stood up and proudly gave the tapes of Guardian TV to his father.

CHAPTER FIFTEEN

F amily came through the kitchen door like a Fiesta parade. Trey and Laura bounded into the room with a pair of balloons that proclaimed, "Get Well Soon!" They were followed by Leo's twin sons and his daughter carrying more balloons and waving posters that read "We Love You, Javito." Their moms and dads brought in pizza boxes, grocery bags with sodas and beer, and a two-layer-coconut cake for dessert.

"We brought pizza for Uncle Javito," Trey exclaimed. "We got five of them!"

"How about pizza and a show?" Javier's dad suggested in a loud voice. He held up the tape over his head and said, "Everybody grab some pizza. We'll eat in the den. We're all going to watch Javier on television."

Javier's itchy feet were no match for the prickling heat spreading over his face. He never expected anyone but his parents to see that tape, and it was one thing to watch himself on Mr. Seneca's twenty-inch classroom TV, but looking at his face on the big screen television in the den? *Oh, man! Help me, St. Peter!*

His nervous heartbeat kept thumping away during the time it took to settle the children onto the floor of the den with their lap trays, for his brothers to bring in a few extra chairs, and for all the adults to get their own pizza and grab a beer or soda, and settle down to watch the tape.

Once Javier stood at the cabinet beside the television, put in the tape, and pressed PLAY, he remembered how Pat used humor to get people on his side.

Javier turned around and said, "This show might be better if everyone drinks three beers first!"

When the adults laughed, it helped him relax. He sat on the floor by his dad's chair and took a couple of bites from the pizza before he saw himself on the screen. He had forgotten how stiff and scared he looked that first day. He expected teasing from his brothers or his father, but they watched with great interest.

Javier couldn't help but laugh at Pat, whose humorous ad-libs and great timing added so much personality to the broadcast. He was reminded again of what a great television team they had created. And who wouldn't be amused by the whole burrito-Burriola screw-up and their on-camera laughing fits? All the children begged to watch that one broadcast three more times!

When everyone saw the music video made from highlights of the football game, Javier received more compliments and quickly gave Pat, Landry, and Steve their share of the credit.

"Has Pat's family seen that tape?" his mom asked Javier as the adults stood around the table while Leo's wife cut into the cake she had baked.

"No," Javier said. "I really want them to see it." Then he frowned because he had to return the tape on Monday. *What if Pat is still in the hospital by then? When will he be able to show it to his family?*

His worries were interrupted when his elbow hit Trey's head. "Ow!"

Trey didn't even notice the bump, probably because the boy bounced soccer balls off his head all the time. In a flash, Javier got an idea. "Hey, Eric, don't you film Trey's soccer games and make copies for all the parents? Could you make a copy of this tape for me?"

"Sure, no problem," Eric replied. He smiled. "How many do you need?"

"I want one!" said their mom, followed by a chorus around the table by every family member wanting to watch Javier on Guardian TV again. He didn't know whether to be embarrassed or flattered, but what really mattered was that Pat had a copy, and that *his* family made time to watch it.

"Firemen arrived on the scene of a house fire on Mistletoe Drive, not far from Woodlawn Lake. It was after ten p.m. when the Fire Department got the call to fight the two-alarm blaze." The young anchorman on the ten o'clock news described the events in a calm professional tone, but his words made Javier grip the remote control in his hand. He sat by his mom on the den sofa. His dad had just taken his seat in a matching overstuffed chair.

Visuals of Pat's grandmother's house crisscrossed with fire appeared on the television screen. Firemen sprayed the structure from two different directions, but the leaping flames, thick smoke, and messy drizzle looked just as dangerous on television as Javier remembered it.

The anchorman's voice continued to speak over the images: "The heavy drizzle did little to keep the fire from spreading through the old one-story house. The owner was identified as Adelita Mendiola, mother-in-law of prominent business owner, Benjamin Berlanga."

There was a quick edit to an on-camera interview with Pat's father. He was dressed in a tie and dress shirt. He stood under a dark umbrella. His thin face looked washed out in the harsh spotlight of the television camera. "We've been trying for years to move her home with us. She lived all alone. I've been so worried about her, and now this fire!" he said. "She's lucky to be alive." He nodded toward the camera. "I'm so grateful to our outstanding Fire Department, to those firemen who rescued her."

"What?!!" Javier yelled at the television. He sat up straight, planting his bare feet on the carpet. He stared at the television in disbelief. "There were no firemen! Pat and I rescued her . . . and she didn't live *alone*! What about Pat?!!"

The young anchorman was back on the screen to finish his report. "Fire Department officials are calling this home a total loss. Cause of the fire is still under investigation. In other news . . . "

"I can't believe that guy!" Javier clamped down on the remote control to mute the sound. "He totally ignored his own son! Pat's lying in the hospital, and he gives the firemen all the credit for the rescue? What a bastard! No wonder Pat hates living with him!" He hurled back like he might throw the remote.

His mom yanked the remote out of his hand. "Alright, Javier, calm down. I'll let the profanity go this time because you're still upset about last night, but I'm not going to let you break something." She placed the remote on the other side of her.

His hands tightened into fists. He did feel like breaking something or hitting someone. "I can't believe that man. What Pat did last night was amazing! First, he ran inside to save his grandmother. Then he carried me away from the burning house. Why didn't his father tell the TV news about his son? How could he ignore Pat that way?"

"How would his father know what Pat did, Javito?" his mom replied, gently stroking Javier's arm. "If you and Pat were already at the hospital and he didn't show up at the fire until later, how would he know?"

"Then he *needs* to know," Javier answered. He looked at his mom. "I want to talk to Mr. Berlanga, and he needs to watch that tape of Guardian TV too. The man's clueless, Mom. He knows *nothing* about his son."

"Even if he's wrong, Javier, I expect you to respect Mr. Berlanga," his father said. His voice was serious, and there was a disapproving tone to it. "Anyway, there's no talking to him tonight. You'll just have to wait until tomorrow. It will give you some time to cool down."

Javier breathed deeply, trying to find some patience within him, but it was like hoping to find fresh air in a smoky building. He stared down at his clenched hands and forced himself to open them up.

His mother had pressed the remote again. The news anchor's voice gave the details about graffiti sprayed on a city office building. Javier looked up. He stared at the television screen and suddenly noticed the letters printed under the anchorman's name.

Maybe I can do something tonight, Javier thought. He stood up, told his parents goodnight, and went upstairs to his room. Even before he turned on his computer, he was already searching his mind for the best words to type into the email.

Javier slowly peeked through the open door of the hospital room. He saw Pat sitting in an upright position in the hospital bed and a pile of empty juice and gelatin cups on a high table beside the handrails. He wore the same clear, thin tube with two prongs that went inside his nose like Javier had worn in the emergency room. He was wearing a blue hospital gown, but most of it was covered up by a white blanket. He stared at the TV.

Next to the window sat Mrs. Berlanga, reading a novel. She was dressed in dark pants and a black blouse. Feliz sat beside her, punching buttons on her phone. She wore a red dress and spiked heels—an outfit to wear to a party not to sit in a hospital.

"Aren't you going in?" his mom whispered. She had driven him to the hospital because she insisted he needed more recovery time before he could drive alone.

Javier nodded and then walked into the hospital room, his laptop under his arm. He smiled to see his friend awake and alert. "Hi, Pat. How's it going?"

Pat turned and gave Javier a grin. "Hey, Javier! You survived!" His voice still sounded hoarse and raspy from the smoke. "Last thing I remember, you got wiped out when I fell on you. I'm glad I didn't knock the stuffing out of you for good."

Javier laughed. "Well, I'm glad we didn't get barbecued that night."

"Oh, man, don't mention barbecue," Pat said and groaned. "Hospital food really sucks! I'd give my left arm to have a brisket sandwich right now."

"It's always a good sign when a boy gets his appetite back. Hello, Pat," Javier's mom said as she walked in behind her son. When Mrs. Berlanga rose, she hugged the woman like an old friend. "Hello, Erica. Get any sleep last night? How's your mom?"

"She's worn out. I don't know if I should be here with Pat or take care of her." Mrs. Berlanga's dark face wore a frown that made Javier feel sad.

Feliz's head had popped up from concentrating on her phone. She sighed and said, "Well, I'm out of here." She stood up and pulled her purse strap over her shoulder. "Sitting around watching Pat breathe is stupid. He's alive. I'm going home."

Mrs. Berlanga stared at her daughter. Her mouth had dropped open.

"Come on, Erica. You need a break." Javier's mother still had an arm around the woman's shoulders. "Let's go get a cup of coffee." She looked at her son. "Javier, you'll call my cell phone if you need us, right? We'll be back in a little while." And she led Mrs. Berlanga out of the room.

Feliz walked over and stood at the foot of the bed. She looked beautiful, but that was it. When she smiled, Javier felt suspicious right away. "Javier, I'm glad you're here," she told him. "I need more help with chemistry. I'll call you tonight, okay?"

"I can't help you, Feliz. Sorry. You need to find someone else." He didn't break eye contact with her as he said, "I'm having my own problems with chemistry. I even flunked my last test." He was relieved he could say that so easily now.

"Javier is a busy guy," Pat added. "Find your own friends to help you with homework. If he can spend extra time studying for a hard class, so can you."

An icy glare was her only response before she stomped out of the room, her heels clacking down the hall.

"Good, she's gone. What a pain!" Pat turned to Javier and said, "Okay, Jack, so why are you carrying your laptop? Don't tell me we're going to rewrite school announcements while I'm lying in the hospital with an oxygen tube up my nose."

"Not exactly." Javier grinned at his friend, relieved Pat's sense of humor was still intact. "I brought something to show you." First he put the computer on the bed and quickly cleared off the trash on the table so he could set up his laptop there. He turned it on and said, "My brother made you a copy of the school tape. I thought we could watch it together right now and have a few laughs."

Javier stood beside the bed to watch their first broadcast together. They both laughed at Pat's quick thinking when the flag image didn't change and Javier had gone into the second announcement not knowing what happened. Pat had saved them from looking like idiots, and he had been helping Javier out ever since.

They had just finished watching the first week of broadcasts when a husky Latino man wearing a dark suit came into the room. Javier recognized him immediately as the anchorman from Channel 12 news. Right behind him walked in a tall man who carried a heavy camera over one shoulder.

When Javier had sent the message to the station, he didn't expect the anchorman to really care or pay attention. It just made Javier feel better to tell someone what really happened that night at the fire. Now he felt a strange combination of anxiety and anticipation that simmered up and down his arms and legs.

"Which of you is Javier Ávila?" asked the anchorman. He smiled at them.

"Good morning, Guardians! This is Javier Ávila, and these are the morning announcements," came the voice from the laptop.

Javier quickly punched the *PAUSE* button. "Uh, I'm Javier. Hi!"

"I'm Edward Flores," the anchorman said, first shaking Javier's hand, then Pat's. "I guess you are the hero, Pat Berlanga."

"I'm not the hero, Mr. Flores." Pat shook his head in disagreement. "Javier is the one who got us out. He didn't let me give up."

"But Pat carried me away from the burning house," Javier quickly added.

"Obviously, you two are quite a *team* of heroes," the cameraman said.

"Oh, sorry! Excuse me! This is my friend Josh," said Mr. Flores, gesturing toward the cameraman. "I wondered if you both could tell us more about what happened on Friday night at the fire. Um . . . are your parents here anywhere? I really can't put you on camera without their permission."

"Our moms just went for coffee." Javier reached into his pocket for his phone. "I can call them to come back here."

"Would you mind? I want to use this story tonight on the five-thirty news."

Javier walked out of the room to make the call. "Mom, it's me. No, nothing's wrong, but there is a reporter who wants to interview Pat and me, but he needs you and Mrs. Berlanga to give permission. Okay, we'll wait for you. Bye."

Javier walked back into the room. He felt a sudden burning under his feet that spiked up his ankles. When he saw the anchorman and the cameraman on each side of the bed watching the program on the laptop. Pat watched with them, grinning proudly. When he caught Javier's surprised stare, Pat gave him a pair of thumbs-up.

"Hey you two aren't half bad," the cameraman said as Javier came up to stand beside him. "How long have you been at this?"

"About six weeks," Javier answered. "It's a new elective. Pat and I were the first team to do the announcements on school TV." He couldn't see too well from the distance and angle where he stood, but in his mind, he could imagine the facial expressions that matched the voices he heard. It was one of their better broadcasts.

They were all still watching the laptop together when their mothers walked back into the hospital room.

As the cameraman set up to film, Javier's mom took over the laptop. She sat down in one of the two chairs by the window. Mrs. Berlanga sat beside her, and they watched one of the broadcasts. It was the first time Javier had ever seen Pat's mom smile.

A few minutes later, Javier stood by the hospital bed and answered the questions put to him by the anchorman. He was surprised at how calm he felt talking to the camera, telling the truth about what happened the night of the fire. When he turned to Pat and let him take his turn to speak to the reporter, it felt natural to work as a team to tell a story just like they had learned to do together on Guardian TV.

Once the anchorman's interview, film clips of the fire as well as new images of the burned-down house appeared as the third story on the evening newscast, the

Ávila phone started ringing with calls from Javier's brothers, uncles, and aunts. Mr. Quintanilla also called about what Javier and Pat had done the night of the fire. It felt weird to talk to the Dean of Students at home, but Javier appreciated what he said.

"I'll talk to your teachers if you need more time to recover. Make-up work won't be a problem," Mr. Quintanilla told Javier.

"Thank you, but I don't plan to miss any school," Javier replied. He paused and then added, "But would you speak to Pat's teachers? He'll probably be absent this week."

"I just talked to Pat at the hospital," Mr. Q said. "We'll make arrangements for him to keep up with his classes, don't worry. Both of you have made us very proud."

About seven-thirty, the doorbell rang, and Javier was surprised by his best friends and their mothers. He had to endure kisses from Ignacio's mom and squeezing hugs from Andy's mom, but luckily, his mom took over, and all the ladies went off to the kitchen. Javier took the guys upstairs to his room.

"I can't believe all this drama happened and I had to learn all about it on TV," Andy said, flopping on Javier's unmade bed. "Why didn't you call me?"

"I did call you. I left you messages—at least three of them," Javier said with irritation. He sat down at his desk chair. "You never called me back!"

"Well, you didn't say in the message that you and Pat nearly burned up in a fire!" Andy replied. He grabbed a pen and a pencil off Javier's desk and started drumming on the pillow. "Here we are off at the band competition, and our best friends are dealing with smoke inhalation. You need to tell us what happened."

Javier was tired of talking about the fire, so instead he replied, "No, you tell me about the competition. How did the band perform?"

"We got a ONE!" Ignacio said in a happy tone. He had taken a seat in the canvas chair in the corner of the bedroom. It was painted with the team colors and logo of the Dallas Cowboys. "And the trumpet section kicked butt in the opening fanfare."

"And let's not forget the drumline got a trophy, thank you very much!" Andy replied. He pointed a pencil toward Javier. "My mom took video of our performance. Do you think you and Pat can work your magic to use the film with the announcement that we brought home trophies and scored a ONE in competition?"

"No, man, he and Pat should make one of those music videos instead," Ignacio said. "It would be so cool with band highlights. Not everything should be about football."

Javier smiled as his two friends started arguing about background music for a video. Everything felt pretty normal again, and he was grateful for that. He glanced on his desk and saw the corrected test sitting by his computer. He picked it up and stared one last time at the red grade.

Suddenly, he felt Andy's tapping pencil hitting the back of the paper. "Hey, I forgot all about that test," Andy said. "I better get my mom to sign my paper, too, just in case Mrs. Alejandro goes bulldog on us and expects everyone to do that." He sat up on the bed and said, "So, Jack, what happened with your parents? When they saw that F, did they freak out?"

"No." Javier looked at Andy. "After everything that happened on Friday night, failing a test wasn't that big of a deal to anybody. You know, for a guy who has a reputation as a smart guy, I was pretty stupid to think there was nothing else out there for me but a perfect GPA."

There was an awkward silence in the room. Javier rubbed his feet together.

"Okay, I get all that," Ignacio said from his seat across the room. "Especially since I don't have a perfect GPA, but, Jack, don't start flunking everything just to show us you're our friend, okay?"

Javier started laughing, as did Andy and Ignacio. At least, he'd always get an A + for finding good friends.

It felt weird to drive his truck to school Monday morning without Pat sitting in the seat beside him. Javier put on music for a while, but it annoyed him, and by the time he had left the neighborhood, he had switched it off and just accepted the silence. It gave him a chance to hear his own thoughts. For too long, he had turned down the volume inside his own head.

He wished he could just announce on Guardian TV, "Today Javier Ávila is giving up the phony reputation of 'smart guy.' Instead, he wants to keep a decent GPA, have fun with his friends, and get lucky with girls." *Yeah, right! If only my life could be that simple*, he thought.

Javier walked inside the media classroom fifteen minutes later, wondering if any of the guys had seen the news. His classmates were already busy, but he couldn't remember what job he needed to do. *Has it been only two days since getting the camera for Friday's game?* he wondered. *It feels like it's been much longer.*

Javier carried the case with the school camera and placed it on Mr. Seneca's desk. He held the tripod in one hand. "Good morning, Mr. Seneca."

Dylan yelled out from where he stood in the desk area. "Hey, hero! Do you have time to edit film so we can show highlights from the game?"

At that moment, every guy stopped working and started applauding. Even Mr. Seneca clapped his hands and said, "It's good to see you all in one piece, Javier."

"He's famous! He's famous!" cheered the three juniors.

Javier felt like he had swallowed a string of firecrackers.

The same noise happened three days later when Pat Berlanga walked into the media classroom. Every guy applauded, and Javier proudly joined in. Pat's face darkened with embarrassment, but he still gave a shy smile.

Mr. Seneca had been standing talking to the guys in the desk area, and he slowly walked over to Pat. The applause died down when Mr. Benjamin Berlanga walked through the door just a few steps behind his son. The man was dressed in a tailored business suit with a silver tie. He blinked a few times as he looked over Mr. Seneca's appearance.

Mr. Seneca had steadied himself so he could extend a hand to Pat, who smiled at his teacher and shook his hand. "You looked good on TV, Pat. You did us proud." Then he straightened up on his crutches and nodded at Mr. Berlanga. "We've haven't met. I'm Patricio's Media Broadcasting and World History teacher, Winston Seneca." He repositioned himself before he turned his attention to Mr. Berlanga. "Good morning, Sir."

"Good morning," Pat's father said. His dark eyebrows lifted up. "My son told me everybody's too busy and you wouldn't want visitors, but I wanted a look at the media classroom. I was *very* surprised when I saw the tape of Guardian TV."

"It's a new program with a great future," Mr. Seneca said, nodding in Pat's direction. Then he looked back at Pat's father, giving the man one of his intimidating stares. "Parent-teacher conferences are this week. I'll see you on Thursday night, right?"

Mr. Berlanga stepped back and tugged nervously on his tie. "Yes, well—"

"Good. Thursday night it is!" He slowly walked forward, forcing Pat's dad to move backwards, closer to the door. "You film a lot of TV commercials at your dealership, don't you? Our media students should watch how it's done. When's the next taping? I'll arrange a field trip to one of your dealerships. We can work out details at the parent-teacher conference Thursday night. I'll see you then. Good-bye."

Javier smiled, watching his teacher handle Mr. Berlanga. Pat wore a pleased grin as he walked to the computer desks where Javier sat.

"Good to have you back," Javier told his friend. "How are you feeling?"

Pat dropped his backpack to one side of the desk. "Still tired, but I just couldn't stay home another day." He sat down in the empty chair beside Javier. "I figured if I fell asleep in class, the teachers would think it's more of the same old thing for me, right?"

He had to laugh. "Right! So I guess your dad liked the tape, huh?"

"I barely say ten words to my father at a time," Pat answered. "Imagine his shock when I could speak in full paragraphs and say funny things that even made him laugh."

"My family got a big laugh out of us too," Javier said.

"So, do you think we should do stand-up comedy or become news anchors?"

"Luckily we don't have to make that decision right now." Javier stopped when he heard Mr. Seneca's creaking walk coming in their direction.

"Pat, find the digital file of the five girls running for Homecoming Queen on that computer where you're sitting," their teacher said. "You and Javier will feed it into the broadcast this morning. You need to listen to cues so you can match the picture when Dylan and Omar announce each girl's name. Don't mess this up, gentlemen!"

As their teacher walked away, Pat said, "Ha ha! No pressure!"

"No pressure at all," Javier replied, tapping his itchy foot.

FINALE

Pat: Good morning, Guardians! Welcome to the last day of school! Oh, yeah! This is Patricio Berlanga.

Javier: And this is Javier Ávila, and here are today's announcements!

The votes are in! Congratulations to the new leadership in the Golden Guardian Marching Band. It's no shock to anybody "in the know" that senior Robert Jones was selected as drum major. His assistant is a great surprise—drum roll, please! (Pause for finger drumming on the tables by everyone in the classroom.) The new assistant drum major is the one and only drummer boy, Andy Cardona. Congratulations and good luck!

Pat: Hey, there's more good news from the band. It appears new junior Ignacio Gómez had a successful audition last week and will play trumpet during the summer at Fiesta Noche del Río. Nobody plays a horn like my buddy Ignacio! Don't miss the show!

Javier: And a big salute to the graduating seniors in our media class who have big plans for next year. Dylan Romo and Omar Narsico are heading down Interstate Ten to play football for the UTSA Roadrunners! Ram Fierro is heading across town to play ball for the Cardinals of the University of the Incarnate Word.

Pat: Hey, guys, stay away from those college keg parties! Brother Calvin prayed really hard to get your SAT scores up to speed.

And speaking of Brother Calvin, he wants me to announce that any students who failed a class must register for summer school in his office TODAY!

Don't look for me standing in line behind Kenny García 'cause I *passed* Ms. Maloney's English class and all my other classes too. Not too shabby for the guy who used to sleep in class, right?

Javier: That's right! Now let's give a bigger shout-out to my friend Pat Berlanga. He was selected as one of the student summer interns at Channel 12 news, and the other two juniors in our class, Landry Zúñiga and Steve Sifuentes, got summer jobs working cameras at Sea World.

So when you see that big image of Shamu on the jumbo screen, that'll be one of our own Guardian students working the camera!

Pat: Let's not forget to give props to my buddy, Javier Ávila. His documentary film on the rebuilding of the Mendiola house earned him a spot at The Latino Filmmakers Workshop at the Guadalupe Cultural Arts Center this summer.

Javier will spend two months learning about screenplay writing, film editing, and film design. He will make a lot more movies that we can show next year on Guardian TV. Ha ha! No pressure!

Javier: Thanks a lot, friend! Hey, let's give credit where credit is due.

I would never have made that documentary if it wasn't for all of the Guardians who gave up their Saturdays to rebuild the house for Pat's grandmother. You students and teachers who carried away trash, painted walls, and did all the sweaty work on her lawn and planted new trees and bushes really inspired me. Special thanks go to Mr. Seneca and his wheelchair basketball team members who painted all the inside baseboards and new fence posts.

I heard a rumor that next year the Monticello neighborhood Parade of Homes wants to include Mrs. Mendiola's house on the tour. That's pretty impressive!

Pat: And that brings me to an announcement with a personal message. Don't forget that everybody who worked on the project is invited to the Open House next Saturday at my abuelita's house. Berlanga Motors is donating all the fajitas, sodas, and cake. Go, Dad! He was so surprised when the neighbors, the volunteer workers from Ávila construction, and our own Guardian families came together and rebuilt the house after the fire last September. On behalf of my grandmother, I tell you sincerely, *muchas muchas gracias.*

Javier: Now we come to the last announcement of the day. Next month two of our Guardians faculty members are getting married. We are not allowed to tell you who they are, as we were threatened with Fs on our report cards if we spilled the *frijoles*, but let's just say a happy congratulations and best wishes to two of our favorite teachers!

Pat: This is Patricio Berlanga.

Javier: And this is Javier Ávila, reminding all the Guardian students . . .

Pat: . . . if you look at your new schedule on Orientation Day . . .

Javier: . . . and you see the class called Media Broadcasting listed there . . .

Pat: . . . we have only one word for you . . .

Together: FANTASTIC!!

ACKNOWLEDGEMENTS

I deas for this novel developed slowly during the years my own children experienced high school. Originally, I wanted to write about my positive teaching experience at an all-boys high school in San Antonio. As a young English teacher, I helped coach the speech and debate teams at Holy Cross High School and saw public speaking give the Latino boys practical skills as well as great self-confidence. Going to speech tournaments and winning their events inspired the boys to choose college majors like journalism, public relations, and political science. More recently a Holy Cross education and experiences with speech activities helped my son Nick write and present his ideas at a contest in Washington DC that earned him a college scholarship. However, it was my daughter's remarkable experience in the first Media Broadcasting class at Providence High School that inspired me to set this novel about speaking to an audience and building self-confidence into a more contemporary context.

My brothers, my sister, and I are the products of single-gender Catholic secondary education, as are my husband and my children. This novel is one way to honor the familial spirit and deeper sense of community that comes from sitting in a classroom with students of your own gender. Honest, open class discussions, developing closer bonds with teachers, and discovering new talents in a smaller school atmosphere has helped many San Antonio students who are educated in Catholic elementary and high schools to become strong scholars and exceptional leaders.

This novel wouldn't have been finished if my daughter Suzanne didn't remind me constantly to "trust the process," the same advice I gave her when she struggled with a college essay. I am blessed by my writing friends, Carla, Kathy, Judy, Katy, and Lupe, valuable readers who offered honest criticism and encouragement. Friends like Mary Lynne, Kathleen, Melissa, Janie, and Marina let me vent when the writing stalled. Younger writers like Amanda King, Melissa Vela-Williamson, Suzanne Bertrand, and Nick Bertrand gave me ideas for revision that helped shape authentic characters. I also thank the student writers in my creative writing courses at St. Mary's University who suspected the anonymous fiction scenes in the class workshop belonged to their professor but were still brave enough to write down honest feedback.

Finally, I want to give a shout out to Therese Fleming, an exceptional middle school teacher and a wonderful friend. She kept asking me to write another novel to share with "her kids."

And as always, I am filled with deep love and gratitude when I think of all of my family, as well as the wonderful man who has been my husband, my best friend, and my source of laughter for thirty years. Nick calls me his star; he is my hero.

ABOUT THE AUTHOR

Diane Gonzales Bertrand began writing in fifth grade while she was a student at Little Flower School. She wrote plays and skits, poems to share with her family, and even composed her first novel inside a spiral note-book. She taught middle school and high school English for nine years before she stayed home with her young children and started graduate school at Our Lady of the Lake University in 1989, after which she began to publish her poetry and essays in literary magazines. She desires to see more Latino families and their experiences repre-sented in literature and writes the novels, picture books, and short story collections that she never found on book-shelves in the library when she was a child.

Diane was raised in an English-speaking home because bilingual books for children didn't exist. She is proud that many of her books can be enjoyed by readers of both English and Spanish, encouraging children to retain both languages. A list of her books can be found at www.artepublicopress.com.

Diane is Writer-in-Residence at St. Mary's University in San Antonio, Texas, where she teaches creative writing and English composition. She is married to Nick C. Bertrand, and they have two children, Nick and Suzanne, both recent college graduates. Diane is an author who visits schools and libraries across the country to share her books, to encourage more families to write their own stories, and to encourage everybody to turn off the television or computer and read a book instead.

Additional Piñata Books for Young Adults

Fitting In
Anilú Bernardo
2005, 208 pages, Trade Paperback
ISBN: 978-1-55885-437-6
$9.95, Ages 11 and up
Accelerated Reader Quiz #35022
Winner, 1997 Paterson Prize for Books for Young People and the 1997 Skipping Stones Honor Award

Available in Spanish as:
Quedando bien
Anilú Bernardo
Spanish translation by Rosario Sanmiguel
2006, 240 pages, Trade Paperback
ISBN: 978-1-55885-474-1, $9.95, Ages 11 and up

Trino's Choice
Diane Gonzales Bertrand
1999, 128 pages, Trade Paperback
ISBN: 978-1-55885-268-6
$9.95, Ages 11 and up
Accelerated Reader Quiz #35007
Named to the 2001-2002 Texas Lone Star Reading List; "Best Book of the Year," Young Adult category, ForeWord *Magazine; and Recipient, Austin Writers' League Teddy Award for Best Children's Book*

Available in Spanish as:
El dilema de Trino
Diane Gonzales Bertrand
Spanish translation by Julia Mercedes Castilla
2005, 144 pages, Trade Paperback
ISBN: 978-1-55885-458-1, $9.95, Ages 11 and up

Trino's Time
Diane Gonzales Bertrand
2001, 176 pages, Trade Paperback
ISBN: 978-1-55885-317-1
$9.95, Ages 11 and up
Accelerated Reader Quiz #54653
Named to The New York Public Library's Books for the Teen Age 2002

Available in Spanish as:
El momento de Trino
Diane Gonzales Bertrand
Spanish translation by Rosario Sanmiguel
2006, 192 pages, Trade Paperback
ISBN: 978-1-55885-473-4, $9.95, Ages 11 and up

The Ruiz Street Kids
Los muchachos de la calle Ruiz
Diane Gonzales Bertrand
Spanish translation by
Gabriela Baeza Ventura
2006, 224 pages, Trade Paperback
ISBN: 978-1-55885-321-8
$9.95, Ages 8-12, Accelerated Reader Quiz #113860
Recipient, 2007 Skipping Stones Honor Award; Winner, 2007 International Latino Book Award— Best Young Adult Fiction-Bilingual; and Finalist, 2007-2008 Tejas Star Book Award

Upside Down and Backwards
De cabeza y al revés
Diane Gonzales Bertrand
Spanish translation by Karina Hernández
Line drawings by Pauline Rodriguez Howard
2004, 64 pages, Trade Paperback
ISBN: 978-1-55885-408-6
$9.95, Ages 8-12
Special Recognition, 2005 Paterson Prize for Young People, and Finalist, 2005 Teddy Children's Book Award

Desert Passage
P. S. Carrillo
2008, 192 pages, Trade Paperback
ISBN: 978-1-55885-517-5
$10.95, Ages 11 and up
Accelerated Reader Quiz #127758

El año de nuestra revolución
Cuentos y poemas
Judith Ortiz Cofer
Spanish translation by Elena Olazagasti-Segovia
2006, 128 pages, Trade Paperback
ISBN: 978-1-55885-472-7
$9.95, Ages 11 and up

Riding Low on the Streets of Gold
Latino Literature for Young Adults
Edited by Judith Ortiz Cofer
2003, 192 pages, Trade Paperback
ISBN: 978-1-55885-380-5
$14.95, Ages 11 and up

Additional Piñata Books for Young Adults

Windows into My World
Latino Youth Write Their Lives
Edited by Sarah Cortez
Introduction by Virgil Suárez
2007, 272 pages, Trade Paperback
ISBN: 978-1-55885-482-6
$14.95, Ages 16 and up
Recipient, 2008 Skipping Stones Honor Award

Chicken Foot Farm
Anne Estevis
2008, 160 pages, Trade Paperback
ISBN: 978-1-55885-505-2
$10.95, Ages 11 and up
Accelerated Reader Quiz #123847
Finalist, Texas Institute of Letters 2008 Literary Awards

Mi sueño de América
My American Dream
Yuliana Gallegos
English translation by Georgina Baeza
2007, 64 pages, Trade Paperback
ISBN: 978-1-55885-485-7
$9.95, Ages 8-12
Accelerated Reader Quiz #120117
Winner, International Latino Book Award—Best Young Adult Nonfiction–Bilingual

Rattling Chains and Other Stories for Children
Ruido de cadenas y otros cuentos para niños
Nasario García
2009, 160 pages, Trade Paperback
ISBN: 978-1-55885-544-1
$9.95, Ages 8-12

Creepy Creatures and Other Cucuys
Xavier Garza
2004, 144 pages, Trade Paperback
SBN: 978-1-55885-410-9
$9.95, Ages 11 and up

A So-Called Vacation
Genaro González
2009, 192 pages, Trade Paperback
ISBN-13: 978-1-55885-545-8
$10.95, Ages 14 and up

The Throwaway Piece
Jo Ann Yolanda Hernández
2006, 192 pages, Trade Paperback
ISBN: 978-1-55885-353-9
$9.95, Ages 11 and up
Accelerated Reader Quiz #108531
Winner, 2007 Paterson Prize for Books for Young People, Finalist; ForeWord *Magazine's Best Book of the Year 2006; Named to The New York Public Library's* Books for the Teen Age *2007; and Winner, University of California, Irvine's Chicano / Latino Literary Prize*

The Truth about Las Mariposas
Ofelia Dumas Lachtman
2007, 144 pages, Trade Paperback
ISBN: 978-1-55885-494-9
$9.95, Ages 11 and up

Versos sencillos / Simple Verses
José Martí
English translation by Manuel A. Tellechea
1997, 128 pages, Trade Paperback
ISBN: 978-1-55885-204-4
$12.95, Ages 11 and up
Named to the 1999–2000 Houston Area Independent School Library Network Recommended Reading List

My Own True Name: New and Selected Poems for Young Adults, 1984–1999
Pat Mora
Drawings by Anthony Accardo
2000, 96 pages, Trade Paperback
ISBN: 978-1-55885-292-1
$11.95, Ages 11 and up
Accelerated Reader Quiz #47265

Brujas, lechuzas y espantos
Witches, Owls and Spooks
Alonso M. Perales
English translation by John Pluecker
2008, 96 pages, Trade Paperback
ISBN: 978-1-55885-512-0
$9.95, Ages 8-12

The Case of the Pen Gone Missing
El caso de la pluma perdida
A Mickey Rangel Mystery
Colección Mickey Rangel, detective privado
René Saldaña, Jr.
Spanish translation by Carolina Villarroel
2009, 96 pages, Trade Paperback
ISBN: 978-1-55885-555-7
$9.95, Ages 8-12

Teen Angel
A Roosevelt High School Series Book
Gloria Velásquez
2003, 160 pages, Trade Paperback
ISBN: 978-1-55885-391-1
$9.95, Ages 11 and up
Accelerated Reader Quiz #85593

Tyrone's Betrayal
A Roosevelt High School Series Book
Gloria Velásquez
2006, 144 pages, Trade Paperback
ISBN: 978-1-55885-465-9
$9.95, Ages 11 and up
Accelerated Reader Quiz #110766

The Almost Murder and Other Stories
Theresa Saldana
2008, 144 pages, Trade Paperback
ISBN: 978-1-55885-507-6
$10.95, Ages 11 and up

Alamo Wars
Ray Villareal
2008, 192 pages, Trade Paperback
ISBN: 978-1-55885-513-7
$10.95, Ages 11 and up
Accelerated Reader Quiz #123846

My Father, the Angel of Death
Ray Villareal
2006, 192 pages, Trade Paperback
ISBN: 978-1-55885-466-6
$9.95, Ages 11 and up
Accelerated Reader Quiz #110738

Named to The New York Public Library's Books for the Teen Age 2007, and Nominated, 2008-2009 Texas Library Association's Lone Star Reading List

Who's Buried in the Garden?
Ray Villareal
2009, 160 pages, Trade Paperback
ISBN: 978-1-55885-546-5
$10.95, Ages 11 and up

Walking Stars
Victor Villaseñor
2003, 208 pages, Trade Paperback
ISBN: 978-1-55885-394-2
$10.95, Ages 11 and up
Accelerated Reader Quiz #35002

Available in Spanish as:
Estrellas peregrinas
Cuentos de magia y poder
Victor Villaseñor
Spanish translation by Alfonso González
2005, 144 pages, Trade Paperback
ISBN: 978-1-55885-462-8
$9.95, Ages 11 and up

Scratch and the Pirates of Paradise Cove
Ricardo Means Ybarra
2008, 96 pages, Trade Paperback
ISBN: 978-1-55885-525-0
$9.95, Ages 8-12